Somewhere There's Music

Somewhere There's Music

A Novel

Sean Paul Bedell

CANADA

Copyright © 2022 by Sean Paul Bedell

All rights reserved. No part of this book may be used or reproduced in any manner whatsoever without the prior written permission of the publisher, except in the case of brief quotations embodied in reviews.

Publisher's note: This book is a work of fiction. Names, characters, places and incidents are either the product of the author's imagination or are used fictitiously, and any resemblance to actual persons living or dead is entirely coincidental.

The book contains scenes of violence and graphic descriptions. If you experience abuse or suffer a mental health crisis, please reach out to your local help line, or call 911.

Library and Archives Canada Cataloguing in Publication

Title: Somewhere there's music : a novel / Sean Paul Bedell.

Other titles: Somewhere there is music
Names: Bedell, Sean Paul, 1965- author.

Identifiers: Canadiana 20210369418 | ISBN 9781989689349 (softcover)

Classification: LCC PS8603.E32385 S66 2022 | DDC C813/.6—dc23

Printed and bound in Canada on 100% recycled paper.

Now Or Never Publishing
901, 163 Street
Surrey, British Columbia
Canada V4A 9T8

nonpublishing.com
Fighting Words.

We gratefully acknowledge the support of the Canada Council for the Arts and the British Columbia Arts Council for our publishing program.

For Lisa, with love and thanks. Ditto.

Chapter 1

The sirens through the night howled as a bad omen. They meant Joel's father had a rough night on back shift. Joel used to be able to sleep in on Saturdays. But too much coffee and too much stress stopped that. It didn't help that all night he heard those sirens, distant, but close enough to interrupt deep sleep. He got out of bed and stood by the window in his underwear. The pink hues of the early morning sun brushed the horizon somewhere far away in the mid-November sky. The silver maple tree in front of their house still had a few crimson and orange leaves hanging on.

Joel looked up, knowing he'd see David's bunk was made; it hadn't been slept in. Again, David had gone who knows where. He might come back by supper, hard to tell.

With no room to move, or think, both he and his brother David, crammed in this little room, in this little house, had outgrown the bunk beds, and the room, years ago. David claimed the top bunk since the beginning. He was older, he had said to Joel.

So many sirens, Joel lost track after being woken for the third time by their screaming. His father always said overnight Friday into Saturday morning was the worst. It could have been a bad car accident out on Route 6, could have been a house fire. Could have been shootings, stabbings, asthma attacks, heart attacks, anything, the usual. There would have been a time when he would have pulled the covers up around his head and gone back to sleep. Not now. His mother said that's what happens when you get older, you'd be wide awake when you should have slept in. Joel watched the snow start to fall. He had hours before he had to pick out some clothes, something clean, and get ready for work. The cold air blew in from around the windows that were soft and pulpy from age. On Saturdays and Sundays, he worked at a bookstore, Cumberland Books, from ten until four. If his father got home in time, he might be able to borrow the car to get to work. If not, he'd have to walk. And the snow was building, it'd be slippery, wet, and cold.

Looking out the window, he saw his father coming home. The car rounded the corner of Forest Road and turned onto Palmer Court. His father was driving too fast and the car fishtailed three times before it straightened out.

Their house stood at the end of Palmer, one half of a duplex. Joel and David's room was at the front of the house and from their window he could look all the way down the street. Their home together with their neighbour and landlord who lived in the attached unit, was surrounded by five other such duplex housing units. A dozen families were crammed together on a short street. If it were anywhere else in Amherst, Nova Scotia, it would have only three houses. Each with a front and a back yard. Not on Palmer Court though—families squeezed in, pressure from all sides. Tight enough to hear secrets that nobody needed to share.

His father was going too fast when he jerked the car into the driveway. One of the back springs was broken and it clunked hard when he turned in. He grazed the garbage cans at the end of the driveway. The light snowfall coated everything in a fresh blanket of white. The snow swirled on the ground.

Joel kept watching from his bedroom window. He could see his father reach into an opened case of beer on the passenger seat. Were two bottles already gone? He saw the snow-white sleeve of his father's paramedic uniform shirt move toward the case of beer. His hand gripped another bottle. He sat alone in the parked car for a long time.

Joel watched him, thinking. Then he saw his father's car door open. His father's uniform was crumpled, his shirt tail untucked. His stethoscope was looped around his neck. He stepped out and the earpiece of his stethoscope snagged in the seat belt. He yanked it off his neck and whipped it into the backseat. He looked at the front bumper and then kicked the garbage can he had struck with the car.

He walked up the front walkway drinking his beer. He peered into the mailbox and slammed the cover down. Joel knew his mother would have removed any overdue notices long before his father was expected home.

His father's rage swirled around him like the wind and snow swirled around the house. He shut the front door so hard that the house shook. His rage shuddered up through the floor vents. It reverberated through the chimney. The rage settled over the whole house like the snow was settling on the roof.

Outside, the wind pushed against the house, and snow was coming down heavier now. Gusts buffeted the house and the wind whistled as it blew across the gutter. The skies were dusky and the snow was turning to ice pellets that rattled on the windows. The wind was from the north, cold and raw, the kind of icy wind that stings your cheeks and toughens your spirit. Wind, the north wind.

The north wind does blow, Joel thought.

Downstairs, the shouting began.

Joel unscrewed the cap from his pill bottle. It was a new prescription. He hoped it would work. He didn't want any more episodes like the last time.

Joel searched his mind for a time when he remembered his father being happy.

The north wind does blow...

He thought back to when he was boy. Back many years ago, when things were warm and he felt safe and hugs were common. He couldn't remember how old he was... four? Five...? Many years ago, his father held him. Bounced him on his knee. The motion was kind and soothing. In this memory, his head bobbed up and down in delight.

The north wind does blow...

And he remembered his father blew hard on his little cheeks. While he blew, he shook his head back and forth to mimic the action of the wind. Joel remembered giggling with delight. Was he older... the memory of it was clear? He was six...? Or seven...?

And we shall have snow...

Again he remembered feeling his father's breath against his cheeks. Feeling safe in his father's arms. He knew that there was no snow, no blowing storm threatened him. Back then, it was kindness and love he had seen in his father's eyes. Unmistakable. It was there. It was real. It was for him.

And what will poor robin do then, poor thing...?

His father's voice was raspy but melodic. He could have been a blues man, his voice pleasant but tinged harsh with experience.

Now, Joel could hear the muffled shouts from downstairs. Snippets of phrases rose. "Past fucking due" and "cut off."

Years ago, Joel's father half-sang, half-spoke the words from an old nursery rhyme.

He'll sit in a barn and keep himself warm...

Then his father would look at him and duck his head under his arm. He'd bounce Joel even harder on his knee. He half-laughed, half-sang his way through the final line

...and hide his head under his wing, poor thing!

Joel remembered laughing. He would tuck his head under his arm, too. He remembered they laughed together. Then he remembered how his father would stop. He'd sit up straight and look at him with no expression on his face. Then he would suck in a huge breath of air. He'd puff up his cheeks and blow hard again at Joel's face. Then, in that same raspy blues voice, again:

The north wind does blow...!

The game went on and on. Joel held on to the memory like a child holds on tight to a kite. Especially when the high winds battered it before it crashed back to earth.

Downstairs now, glass shattered against the tiled kitchen floor. His mother sobbed.

This early game was the only time he could recall his father laughing, no matter how hard he to tried to remember. When he looked through photographs of family trips to the lake, he never saw his father joyful. In photos and in memories Joel remembered everyone else as happy. But not his father. He could only remember, at best, that his father hadn't always been angry. If it would have helped, Joel would have made something up. He would have created an event, a memory. He would have embellished some segment of his childhood. He would have dressed it up and made it wear happiness, in the same way his mother made him and David wear ties to church at Christmas. He would have dressed up a distant memory if there had been one to dress up. He would have made it like his father loved him always; that his mother and father loved each other. He would have made it so his family was stitched together like squares of a happy quilt. And together they were warm and cozy. But there was nothing he remembered. Nothing happy other than this song and the game and the puff of wind from his father's cheeks many years ago.

The north wind does blow...

The memories came to him like rags that flapped on a distant, abandoned clothesline in a brisk wind. Tattered parts of a dream after waking from a deep sleep. Fragments—like faded and torn black and white photographs—were incomplete, confusing. If Joel possessed the missing elements, or if he could remember, he couldn't be sure how to arrange them. He wasn't sure he'd have the order right. But Joel could not remember them. Not much else about his father through the years had ever been happy.

He remembered the emptiness and the shouting. The bottles; the fights. The broken glass. Rage and anger lived like rats in the walls of this house. Rage climbed up through vents and ducts. Anger scurried through walls and peeped out from dark corners of the basement. Gloominess shrouded the spirit of his home.

The north wind does blow...

But he remembered those words. This was the best memory that Joel had.

...and keep himself warm...

He clung to that memory, he embellished it and he remembered it in a way that made him feel warm and loved and real. A happy little boy with his daddy years ago.

From downstairs now, Joel could hear his father's muffled yelling. The angry slams of cupboard doors. Over money again. Or the drinking. Most times Joel's mother would not say anything. But sometimes the questions bubbled up and she would ask why. Why did he have to drink on the way home? That would always get a reaction. Or why drink at all? That one brought out the full force of his father's wrath. Joel saw the regret in his mother's eyes when she spoke those questions out loud.

Joel stayed in his bedroom. He wished he could pick up his guitar and strum away at it, maybe write a new song. But he knew if he did, the sound would set his father off. He stayed quiet and listened for a long time.

He wished David were back so he could reassure him. But he was not here. Sometime during the night he had slipped out into the darkness, like he did most nights. He would go to the hangout at the shed back by the river. He would meet up with a few friends. They'd shoot some pucks or toss around a ball. They'd have a few smokes and share whatever bottles they had. Then, sometime before dawn, David would creep back into the house the same way he left. Hop up on the porch rail, swing himself up and over on to the roof of the porch and in through the window. Joel would be lying awake in bed unable to sleep, but never a word to Joel either when he left or when he came back. The silence said this is a screwed-up family with a violent drunk in charge of the house. David's silence said it all.

The argument downstairs stopped. That last crash of glass from downstairs punctuated the fight. Put a period on it, Joel's father was done, he won. Or at least the action was suspended. A temporary reprieve that could be split open at any moment for any reason. Anyone within earshot knew his father could erupt again over anything, big or small. Then the violence would flow.

In the living room, below him, Joel heard his father put a Charlie Parker album on the record player. Charlie Parker was always a good sign. It signaled that his father was in the mood to listen to music and have a few drinks. The record was scratchy and hissed and then a few piano chords rolled out. Then came the lonely, sweet and sad sound of Charlie's saxophone as it rang out "Lover Man." An old jazz record always ratified a sort of ceasefire and it reassured Joel. Now, at least, for the rest of the day there might be peace.

The tension in Joel's body loosened, it was safe to go downstairs now.

"Hey," he said to his father and mother, as he walked into the living room and sat down. Joel was used to his father drinking, it was when he was drunk that Joel was uncertain, nervous. It was at that point that he wasn't sure what might come next. The cursing, the yelling, the throwing things. The temper that may swell into slaps, then punches. And always pain.

Joel's father was telling a story.

"After this call, we're on the way back to the base. Jenkins says he needs smokes. 'Okay,' I tell him. He pulls into the shopping centre on Albion. He says, *'You need anything?'* I say, 'I'm going to the liquor store and picking up a case of beer.' He says, *'No fucking way you're bringing beer in this bus.'*

"Jenkins, telling me the rules. I said to him, 'You worry about what you bring into this bus and I'll worry about what I bring in.' Like what the hell? There'll be nothing open when I get off in the morning."

Joel's mother was in her housecoat and had her hair tucked under a Boston Bruins cap. She sat in the armchair with her feet tucked underneath her as she listened.

"I said 'Fuck you, Jenkins, I'm getting a case of beer. I need a drink when I get home. It's the only way I can sleep coming off nights.'

"*'Yeah well if you do,'* he says, *'I'm calling the super.'*

"I say 'Go ahead. That jackass won't fuck with me. I know way too much.'

"*'Try me,'* Jenkins said, *'you don't intimidate me one goddamn bit.'*

"I glare at him the whole time. He calms down a bit. He goes, *'Look, Roger, it's been a brutal night. We don't need this shit between us. Let's get back to the base and ride this shift out until it's time to sign off and go home.'*

"But I don't let the little weasel off that easy. 'Look,' I say, 'sounds good, but I need a case of beer.' I tell him, 'It's my five o'clock.'

"*'Get it on your way home,'* he says, *'in your own vehicle.'*

"I say, 'Tell you what, I'll take off my uniform shirt, go in with my t-shirt. Get what I need, nobody knows.' Then, get this, he says, *'That's against the rules too.'*

"'For fuck sakes,' I say, 'you kids believe in rules too much. What you learn in school and what's written in the SOP's—let me tell you. They might be called standard operating procedures, but how we operate on the streets, is anything but standard.'

"Can you believe it? He gets his smokes and I get my beer. When we get back to the bus, I tell him go ahead have a smoke if he wants. 'I won't say a word about what goes on in the bus.'

"*'Nah,'* he goes, *'trying to quit.'* He doesn't trust me. The weasel.

"Then we're driving back to the base and he has the goddamned country music station on the radio. I've had enough, I can't handle it. I change the channel. Put on CBC Radio Two playing jazz. You know, something soothing. Not that twangy crap.

"*'Leave the radio alone,'* Jenkins says. I tell him, 'It's country—you know I can't stand country.'

"*'Country's what every person in Amherst listens to,'* he says. *'Country is the peoples' music.'*

"I say, 'It's not *this* people's music.' Roger jabbed his index finger at his chest to emphasize his point.

"*'It's been a long shift, a hard one,* he goes again, *let's leave it off.'*

"'Country? C'mon—jazz is the ultimate evolution of music,' I tell him. 'Someday you'll grow up and realize that.'

"Then he says, *'Shut the fuck up.'*

"'What are you, a wimp?' I say, 'This shift bothered you? The highway? That was nothing.' I say, 'I've seen worse. Two or three is worse, kids are all worse than that.' I tell him, 'Better get used to nights like this one, champ. Didn't they tell you about this shit in school? It ain't the movies.'" Joel's father leaned back and swigged a long drink of his beer.

Joel tried not to pay attention to his father's recounting. They were the same stories, but different players. Joel focused on the television. The sports highlight reel was playing but his father had muted the sound. Charlie Parker was blaring his soul away. Parker's sax provided a soundtrack to the sports highlights.

Everyone sat for a few minutes, not talking.

"It doesn't matter at all," his father said to his mother. She sipped at a glass of wine. Outside, the winds were subsiding now and the ice pellets had turned to a light drizzle of rain.

Joel's father had two full bottles of beer on the coffee table in front of him. "How long is life, and how good is it?" He spoke the words without directing the question at her. "How worthwhile is a life? Any life? It could be a long life or a short one, but how good is it? Months, years, days, weeks. Hours in some cases for newborns. Sick ones. It doesn't matter. It's all random. Random."

His father took another long drink.

Joel's mother didn't say anything and took another sip of her glass of wine. It was the cheap stuff. Red. She drank it because it gave Roger a headache. She bought it because she knew that his father would never touch it if he ran out of his beer or rum. She fidgeted with her housecoat. She wrapped it tighter around herself against the cold. "Joel," she said, "put some more wood in the stove, would you?"

Joel stoked the stove. The fire crackled and snapped as the birch log caught.

"And oh yeah, Jenkins came in on shift with this big fur hat," Joel's father said. "It was this big, grey puffy thing. Perched right on top of his head like a fucking giant grey squirrel. The tones went for a code one, a 62-year-old with chest pain. 'Come on,' I said, and I threw his fucking hat at him, biffed it right at his head. 'Grab your pet and let's go save some lives,' I said."

Roger finished that beer and opened the full one. His uniform shirt was off now and slung over the back of the couch. He removed his flashlight, Leatherman tool, and scissors from his pants so they wouldn't dig into his hip. He laid his work tools in a row, from thinnest to thickest, on the coffee table in front of him. His belt buckle was visible with its newly formed, homemade hole. His pants were cinched tight. His undershirt was soaked with sweat. Yellow stains ringed the armpits.

"Life's got no way of making the choice fair."

He tipped back the new beer and drank for a long time. "Now that's refreshing, don't you think, Gloria?"

Gloria nodded and took another sip of her wine. "You hungry, Rog? Can I make you a turkey sandwich or something? You're losing weight you know. Let me get you something to eat. There's leftovers."

"No, I don't want anything." He took another drink from his bottle. "Yep. See, it doesn't matter, I have figured it out. Evil or good, rich or poor, beautiful or ugly"—he took another long drink—"none of it matters. Black, white, red, yellow, none of it matters. When your number's up, it's up." He finished the beer. He stood up and pointed to Gloria's glass. "You need a fill up?"

"No, I'm good for now."

He went to the kitchen and called out, "Sure you don't need a refill?"

"No, I'll wait till later. I'm good."

The saxophone playing on the record was lonely, smooth and lonely. "That's what I need after a hard day. Bird blowing on his horn and a few nice cold ones," Joel's father said as he came back into the room with two more bottles. As the heat of the woodstove warmed them, droplets of condensation formed on the bottles. He took another drink. "From the start to the end you're a fucked-up piece of a puzzle," he said. "You don't know what this is all about. You don't know where you come from and you sure as shit don't know where you're going. No direct line from time you were born to the time you die. The one thing you can count on is your number's going to come up. And when it does"—he waved his hand in the air—"poof, you're gone. Done. Outta here."

Gloria got up and headed for the kitchen, "I'll make you a sandwich, Rog."

Joel felt his own stomach growl.

"You know, Joel," his father said, "you guys have no idea what grief is. Deep grief always lurks around the next turn." He was drunk now and his words showed how much alcohol he had consumed. "There comes a point when the whole picture starts to break up. It twists into little bits and pieces. Like a kaleidoscope, a child's toy. The parts lose their individuality and they become nothing. Nothing special, nothing unique." He looked at Joel and took another drink of beer. "You know what I mean, Joel? People's lives are like that." He pointed the beer bottle at him and asked again, "Do you know what I mean?"

Joel nodded. He learned that was the safest response.

"It's like a big number, like a million million billion. And if it's like years you're talking about, it's too big to even understand. If it's eternity you're talking about, it doesn't matter. None of it matters." He took another drink. "Like God is some big infinite idea. Like he's always there. Like he always will be. But put a number on it." He pointed his finger at Joel. "Give me a number of years that God will be alive, has been alive."

Joel said nothing.

"See? There is none, is there? You can't give me a number. See, God is not infinite." Roger sucked down the last of his bottle. "We are. Us little peons chip away down here to earn a goddamned living. We're the ones caught in an eternity of hell. God's got nothing to do with it. Then one day"—Roger tried to snap his fingers but couldn't—"one day, one minute, one second, you're gone." He tried to snap his fingers again but couldn't get them to make a sound. "Like that," he said. "Gone."

Charlie's saxophone wailed its melancholy melody. Roger closed his eyes and he started to snore. Joel got up, clicked off the television and left the room as the record played on.

Chapter 2

Upstairs again, Joel started to get ready for work. Saturdays this close to Christmas would be busy at the bookstore. Pritchard would hover out of his office and scoot up next to Joel while he was making a sale. "Recommend something else," Pritchard would hiss in Joel's ear. "Look," Pritchard would say, "you have a way with people. They like you." He would rub his hands together and grin, "you need to exploit that, my boy. Look at what they are buying and suggest one more title. Most of them will do it. Selling that one extra book drops right to the bottom line. It makes a world of difference."

Then Pritchard would skulk away to his office. He'd lock himself in there and watch the closed circuit monitors all afternoon. To Pritchard, the sound of the cash register was more festive than a chorus of angels singing "Joy to the World." He'd only come out if he thought one of his employees was slacking off. Or being too chatty with a potential customer, and not loading them up with purchases.

On Saturday afternoons Pritchard had Joel take care of the special accounts. Mrs. Payne was their best customer. Pritchard loved her. Well, not her exactly. But her propensity for buying books for the book club she hosted every two weeks. Joel liked taking a box of the latest bestseller up to Mrs. Payne in her big stone house on Victoria Street. It was good for him to get out from under Mr. Pritchard's gaze for an hour. And then by the time he got back to the store, he'd be working with Maria. Joel liked working beside her. He liked everything about it. Talking with her, looking at her, watching her stir her latte. His breathing froze when she licked the spoon.

Downstairs the ceasefire had held. Joel's father was snoring on the couch; he would have peace before he went to work. Joel had enough time to read two more chapters before he jumped in the shower. He flopped down on his bed and grabbed one of the fourteen books from the pile he had on the go. They were stacked on his nightstand and on the floor beside it. Brand new titles, but also Dante's *Inferno, Collected Poems* of T.S. Eliot and Shakespeare's *Hamlet.*

He flipped open the book to where he had left off. It was quiet downstairs. Only the soft sounds of Charlie Parker and Dizzy Gillespie sparring on the turntable. They were trading phrases like punches in "*Perdido.*" Trumpet versus saxophone. Joel understood why his father liked their music. Soothing yet energetic. He should tell him that, he thought. He should let him know that sometimes he liked that kind of music. He should tell him he understood it. The music was comforting yet pushed you to think of things in new ways.

After a rough start to the day, Joel felt as though his father's sleeping was a reprise. Temporary, he knew. But a reprise from the rage, the anger, the uncertainty. The more he drank, the longer he could go, even after working all night or doing a double shift. The booze fueled his father. Generated energy to harbour more anxiety, more hate. Everything was stable downstairs, for the moment. It was quiet except for his father's record and the snoring. His parents shifted out of the usual pattern. Today they were not on one of their prolonged screaming matches. This, Joel thought, was different. Different, and welcome.

Joel couldn't focus on the book he was reading. It was a new bestseller that he couldn't wait to read after he saw the review in the *New York Times*. He would read a sentence, but his mind drifted. He flipped the page in his book, but his mind vibrated with fear.

His father's episodes, as he referred to them, tired him out, drained him. The screaming, the broken bottles left Joel spent and empty. These images danced across the page instead of the words he wanted to read. He could not concentrate on the book.

He wanted to drift away to sleep, to dream, to wake up in a reality that was smooth and meaningful. Somewhere there was music that created a jubilant mood. He wanted to come to in a new world like a Charlie Parker song. A world enthusiastic and energetic. Somewhere fun and lively. Instead, he was stuck in this predictable drudgery. He wanted to be someplace where happiness danced into joy. Somewhere that he would not have to tiptoe around his father to keep things at a steady and even beat. Somewhere all on its own, where the rhythm was regular and consistent in the background. Enjoyable. Peaceful. A heartbeat for the house, for his family. Regular and paced. Like a drum beat that helps the troops march on parade. Not anything jarring or out of sync that would rally the troops to war. Joel's goal was the slow *tink-tink-tink* of a snare drum hanging in the back of the beat. That was the delicate dance he wanted to encourage. Anything beyond that and the battles would flare. The casualties would be stacked up like a row of empties. This delicate dance, the rhythm to the familiar song found itself inside Joel's head all the time now. Joel stood on guard, always.

The north wind does blow...

What changed? What changed in his father? His mother? What changed in him? He was a boy sitting on daddy's knee playing a silly child's game. Now he cowered in his room. Hopefully today would be peaceful. If anything set his father off it was possible his mother would end up with at least one new red mark. Or another chipped tooth. Like last time when he hit her and she tumbled into the kitchen counter. She had snapped an upside-down v-shaped chunk out of her front tooth. He prayed the calmness would last.

This flight of ideas in his brain, this rapidity of thoughts was a signal to him. He knew what they meant. He felt detached from reality as his mind flitted from thought to unrelated thought. His fiend, his villain was coming to visit. It liked to visit when his father had roiled in his rage. Joel's dragon was waking up, galumphing back into his life. Now? Yes, now. It had been this way since he was a kid. This was his aura. This beast, a seizure—an epileptic seizure—roared toward him. Joel braced himself. The seizure fumed toward him, snaking and whirling. A mad dragon breathing fire. Defenseless, he waited.

Joel felt its presence as real and concrete as the walls around him. The aura started out the same for both. Would it be petite mal? Grand mal? Once he realized he was experiencing his familiar aura, he always asked himself the same question. How bad would it be?

The fit came. Energy drained out of his body. It crept into his brain and scrambled his electrical circuits. It gripped his whole body like an unwanted hug from a stranger in a fur coat. Overwhelming doom loomed up and invaded his body. It mesmerized his mind into a serene calmness. In the small part of his brain where he controlled his thoughts, he remembered thinking, "I hate this." Then the seizure attacked him. The invasion spread from his mind into his body. His body twitched. He lost control. He felt the warm wetness between his legs when his bladder let go. He was looking down on himself. From high above he could see his face contorted as though in a grimace of pain, yet he felt nothing. His thoughts of being scared, of hating all of this, soon tumbled into relief.

'Abnormal electrical activity in the brain,' the doctors had always explained it.

Downstairs, in the background, Joel could hear that his father had woken up. He was yelling at his mother. He could hear his father rant. His voice was loud. It boomed through the vents, penetrated his room. Joel heard the argument, the fight, but felt removed from their world.

He could feel his face twisted in an automatic expression of gruelling pain. Yet Joel felt no pain. He felt loss of control—of his muscles, of his brain, of his body's functions. During this part of the seizure, Joel was granted a warped reward. He endured the physical grotesqueness. He had to live a life not knowing when a fit would strike. Nor how bad it would be. He never knew the potential for longterm damage. So, Joel reasoned he was awarded a small prize in exchange for the inconvenience, the uncertainty. The prize was always this: God or the universe or whatever greater power it was, allowed his mind to float up. It rose beyond this temporary torture that ravaged his body. His mind drifted above him, and it was like he was looking down upon himself, saw his own face locked in a scowl. He peered down at his own body as it twitched without purpose or rhythm, as the soft tapping of his heels and elbows on the wooden floor went unnoticed by his parents downstairs.

A body dancing under the spell of a brain playing a different tune. It was as though his eyes were blinded by a million flashes of light. He was lulled into serenity. Pulled in as though wooed by the sirens of the sea. They soothed him into a state of assurance, of certainty. It was like the universe imparted to him all its joyous secrets. There was a catch though. He could never verbalize these blissful secrets. He couldn't describe them. He only experienced these thoughts when his body endured the vigorous exorcism. His reward for having to deal with the physical seizure. It was a gift that insulted. His body twisted, but his mind was blessed with a safe and contented repose. When he looked down, as if he hovered above, he saw his earthly body twitch and squirm on the floor. Peace settled over him. He knew that everything would be okay. This was meant to be. That he would survive, not only this seizure, but everything. That the meaning of life came to him as one vibrant and clear image. An image that he could never sound out in words. But one that created, and then sustained clarity and of peace. The image he perceived was that life was pure and true, more than anything he had yet to experience. And then as he was thinking how all this was good. How everything would work out. His body started to relax. This euphoria drained away at the end of his seizure, like his energy drained away at the start of it.

Outside, the snow fluttered down.

He quivered one last time and noticed how cold his bedroom floor was. Now he was glad David wasn't here. He didn't like seizing in front of people. He could do without that humiliation.

The whole episode lasted forty-five seconds. To Joel, it was hours of being locked up as a prisoner in his own body. He was held captive and tortured by his own brain. It made him dance and shake to an inverted and odd song. Then, unlike how it had begun, it ended without announcement. His muscles slowed down their twitching, and after another few seconds stopped altogether. His eyes started to see objects in the room. The blinding flashes of light diminished. He could make out shapes and colours. He could focus. He saw the bunk beds. He could make out the stacked books next to his bed. He felt guilty that he had so many books on the go. I should focus more, he thought.

He could read the dark red lettering of David's *Foo Fighters* poster on the back of the door. He was coming back into himself. He was reentering his mind and body and spirit. His thoughts converted back to loneliness and fear. Those transitory thoughts of serenity vanished. He lay there, the twitching now over. The muscles of his face relaxed and returned to normal. He began to grow sleepy. The seizures ended with a silent thud in his head that blossomed into a severe headache in the middle of his brain. He knew, like all the other times before, the headache would creep across his whole head and would last for hours. The wetness on his floor and the headache forced him to stay awake, even though he was exhausted.

He thought of his doctor. How he slipped in that sliver of hope. "You may grow out of it, Joel. You *may*." But he was running out of time to grow out of anything. More and more the thought took hold of him that this was for life. He must either live with it, or he must die with it.

Downstairs the yelling had stopped again. The seizure was complete now. Joel knew that he had entered his post-ictal state. The deep peace dissipated, replaced by the booming headache. Reality was back. That meant he had to drag himself to work. Suck it up. Even with this billowing headache. The headache forced out all those assurances that everything would turn out all right. Everything was tinged in pain again. Joel shook his head trying, without success, to rid himself of the severe pain in his head. It persisted.

Joel was sluggish. His breathing became more regular, back to normal. In the living room downstairs, he could hear the jazz records playing again. Ella's voice skittered somewhere in blue skies. He focused on his clock radio; the red numbers straightened themselves out as he looked at them. He stretched his mind to clear it. What day? Time? Yes, Saturday, he had to be at work in twenty-five minutes. Jesus. He needed to focus on getting ready to get to work at the bookstore. He thought about calling Pritchard and telling him he couldn't come in. That would not go over well. Not this close to Christmas. Besides, he needed the money. Things were too tight around here not to work. Jesus. He'd be late. Pritchard would flip. What else was new? At least Maria would be the bright spot.

Feeling like he was at a party where he had had too much to drink, Joel rolled on to his hands and knees. His wet underwear stuck to him like a swimsuit after wading in a foul pond. He had a shower and got dressed in double time. He threw his dirty clothes in the laundry basket in the corner. He'd deal with those when he got home. The top bunk was still empty. David would never notice the laundry.

Downstairs, Joel went into the kitchen. He had his knapsack slung over his shoulder and went to the coffeemaker to fill up his travel mug. He poured the coffee and the last dregs from the pot dribbled out. Not even a quarter of a cup. "Shit," he said under his breath.

"Coffee gone?" his mother said. "I can make another pot."

"I've got to go, I'm late."

"Bye, honey. See you tonight. I'll keep your supper warm."

Joel poked his head in the living room. His father was flopped on the couch, snoring, a bottle of beer clutched in his hand. Joel debated waking him up, to ask for the car keys. "Worth it?" he asked himself.

The words of his neurologist's warning echoed in his head "...*one more time and we'll have to yank your license. Till we know it's under control. Six months at least.*" Worth it, to ask him for the car? To wake him up? A bad mood, at best. At worst, he could explode into rage and then—anything. "I'm late anyway," he thought, "let sleeping fathers lie." He headed out the door to work. Joel took a gulp of the old, burnt coffee and slid in the slush as he hurried down the steps.

In the driveway, Pierre, their next-door neighbour and landlord, chipped at the ice on his car windshield.

"*Bonjour*, Joel," he called out.

"Hey, Pierre."

"How are you, *mon ami*, my friend."

"Late for work."

"*Mon Dieu*, I'm going downtown soon as I clear this ice off. Come with me. We should be in Florida, no?"

"Thanks."

"Here." Pierre tossed the car keys to Joel. "You take the wheel, it's good to practice winter driving."

Joel turned the key, Pierre's car stammered twice before it caught. They headed down Palmer Court. "Too bad you're running late," Pierre laughed, "or I'd show you how to spin out doughnuts in the snow!"

Chapter 3

Joel's conversations with Maria were much more pleasant than thinking about Mr. Pritchard. He would order him around like a lackey, a robot; Pritchard would command him to see each customer as a twenty-dollar bill. Or better yet, he would say, as he straightened his bow tie and chortled, "See them as *two* twenty-dollar bills." Joel viewed the customers of Cumberland Books as people who liked to read, or at least wanted to learn. Perhaps some wanted to immerse themselves in a different world for a while. He saw the people buying books in the shop as more than a pay cheque. Joel saw them as human beings, each with their own stories.

At least taking a box of books up to Mrs. Payne's for her book club was a reprieve from Mr. Pritchard breathing down his neck. Mrs. Payne loved to talk. And she loved books. Joel liked that. And he liked working with Maria, when she wore a skirt. Like she did today. Black, tight, hot. Joel knew that after he would leave the store and head up to Mrs. Payne's, Pritchard would ogle Maria as she bent over to stock the shelves. The perv. He'll probably give himself a boner in the process.

"Mr. Pritchard gives me the creeps," Maria had whispered to Joel one time after she felt his look lingered on for a little too long.

Joel thought about asking Maria if she wanted to go to a movie. He thought she'd like the one about the kid that sees dead people now that it finally came to Amherst and was playing at the Paramount. He couldn't decide the best way to ask, and what he would do if she said no. Maybe he could just rent some movies from Hopper's Variety and bring her to his house to watch. No, he couldn't risk that.

Joel wrapped his scarf around his neck. He pulled on his gloves. He glanced at Maria, he'd be gone less than an hour, but he'd miss her. He could watch her all day long. And, at work at least, there was always something to talk about. So his big fear was never an issue, not at work anyway. He grabbed the box of best sellers for Mrs. Payne's book club. Didn't Pritchard love the old lady. *Bam!* Sell twenty copies like that. Hardcovers, too. "See ya later," he smiled at Maria as he pushed open the door with his back and headed out. She smiled back and gave a gentle little wave of her hand. Wow, yes, he would miss Maria.

On the sidewalk, the cold air grabbed him and his breathing tightened. It felt as cold as a stethoscope on a bare chest. He started towards Mrs. Payne's place a few blocks away from downtown.

Snow started to fall again in fluffy flakes that drifted down and landed on Joel's toque. As he walked, he saw Siggy Smith, pushing a rusted shopping cart ahead of him. Siggy was a giant of a man, well over six foot six, with a scraggy red beard. His meek and soft voice belied his size. He had been pushing a rusted shopping cart around Amherst as long as anyone could remember. The cart was laden with bottles and cans and stuffed with bags. Plastic shopping bags, black garbage bags, a dirty canvas bag. There was a large imitation brown leather suitcase on the bottom of the cart. If the cart were still being used at a grocery store, a big sack of flour would be there. The sleeve of a purple sweater poked out from the suitcase.

Most people in town ignored him. A lot of other people called him Sissy, not Siggy. If you spoke to him you never knew if you would get anger or pleasantries in return. Joel's father said he was harmless. He'd done calls on him when passers-by would see him passed out in the park from too much booze, so they would call 9-1-1, fearing the worst. Or he'd be slouched over in a bus shelter after he got his hands on a bottle of isopropyl alcohol, even though the drug store assured his family they wouldn't sell him any. Joel's father also said his real name was Sigmund. "He doesn't like Sissy," he told Joel. "They call him that because of his voice, and he hates it. He likes Siggy, though. That's what he calls himself."

The bottles clanked as the big man pushed his cart up the hill along the broken and bumpy sidewalk. As Joel approached, he could hear him muttering to himself. "They said it was supposed to be rain. This rain is snow, you know?"

"Sure is cold today, isn't it Siggy?" Joel said as he got closer to him.

"They said rain, but it's snow." Smith wrangled with the cart as he walked up the hill.

Joel walked past Smith and his cart. "Excuse me," he said as he squeezed by.

"Excuses don't excuse this freezing weather." He grunted as he forced a misbehaving shopping cart wheel over a deep gorge in the sidewalk.

Joel kept on walking up the hill, but looked over his shoulder, "See you later, Siggy." Joel could see Smith was struggling with the cart now.

Siggy stopped to take a deep breath. The cart slid back a foot. "No excuses for you, either," he said to the cart. He pushed it over the same deep gorge in the sidewalk, grunting the whole time. Siggy kicked at the cart, trying to coax it up the hill.

Joel carried on towards Mrs. Payne's. The box of hardcovers felt heavier and heavier as he trudged along. Siggy's conversation drifted into a soft muttering behind him as Joel continued. Joel was sure he heard him say "Oh, brother. Brothers are a bother, they'll make you shudder. Oh brother." Joel forged his way up the hill. At the summit stood Mrs. Payne's huge neoclassical home, four tall pillars gracing the front of the house. Its painted trim now faded, and in need of new shutters, the house at one time dominated Amherst.

Mrs. Payne was expecting him. The light dusting of snow had been swept off the steps. Joel creaked the iron gates open and mounted the steps to the door. He banged hard on the great brass knocker. Parker, Joel knew, would let him in.

"Good afternoon, Master Carruthers," Parker said as he swung the door open. He swept his arm in the familiar gesture telling Joel to come in.

"Hi, Mr. Parker."

"Mrs. Payne's waiting for you. Please, this way." He led him into the parlour. Heavy burgundy drapes were tied back, allowing sunlight to pour into the huge room. The fireplace crackled in the corner. The hint of wood smoke invited Joel. The warmth was welcome.

A teapot sat on the coffee table in front of Mrs. Payne. "Well, Mr. Carruthers, hello." She pointed to the huge oak sideboard. "You can set that carton of books up there, if you don't mind."

Joel slid the box up onto the surface. His arms ached when he put the box down.

"Come. Sit. Cup of tea?" She poured some of the steaming beverage into a bone china cup. He could smell the cardamom spice of the Earl Grey tea. "This will soothe you, young man." She slid the cup toward him. She had a bright afghan wrapped about her knees. "And warm you up. I can feel the cold radiating off you, and off of that box of books."

"Thanks, Mrs. Payne."

"That'll be all, thank you, Parker."

Parker bowed almost imperceptibility and closed the solid doors on his way out.

"And how's your family?" Payne sipped her tea. "Everyone is well?"

"Yes, ma'am. Everyone's fine."

She stared at him. "Fine, are they? You're sure? I talk to a lot of people in this town, Mr. Carruthers."

"Yes, ma'am. Getting ready for the holidays like everyone else."

"And the rat you're employed by? How is he? Scurrying about town after dark, I suppose? Feeding on the scraps and garbage?"

"Mr. Pritchard? Yes, he's fine too."

"I only deal with that rodent because he has a monopoly in this town." She sipped her tea, the cup dainty in her bony fingers. "And, of course, because he employs such fine young gentlemen."

Joel blushed. He withdrew an illustrated book on violins and cellos of the 18th century from the box he had carried in. He held it out to her. "I came across this in the order today and thought it would strike a chord with you."

"I don't recall ordering anything more than my regular book club items."

"Yes, I know, but last time I was here," he nodded to her two violins. Polished to a gleaming brilliance, they were balanced in their stands. Tuned up and ready to go, they waited next to the baby grand piano. A selection of bows were at the ready on a tall sofa table.

"I noticed your instruments the last time I was here." He passed the book to her. "There's no obligation, none. I thought you might be interested."

Mrs. Payne leafed through the pages. She admired the photos of one rare and precious instrument. She studied the dark vertical grain of the spruce soundboard which was contrasted against the lighter tones of the wood. "It's splendid."

"Look at the one in the center. See the picture there? I don't know, that struck me as cool."

She opened the book to the middle. She studied the photograph. She turned the book and cocked her head to get a better perspective. She traced her hand along the pages as if to feel the texture of the strings of the antique cello. A virtuoso in a flowing black dress was standing beside the instrument, ready to play. "Wouldn't you love to hear the tone out of that beauty?"

"Yeah, I know it intrigued me. I thought you might like to buy it."

"You are a salesman to the bone."

"I don't make any more if you take it or you don't. I thought you'd enjoy it. I thought it was your thing."

"Do you play, Mr. Carruthers?"

"Play, ma'am?"

"An instrument. The piano? Flute? Do you play?"

"I try to play—"

"I know! You're a guitar man aren't you. Of course you are!"

"I pick away at guitar, a bit. I wouldn't say I play."

"But you like it? You enjoy it? You find something—something what? Rejuvenating in it, don't you? Nourishing?"

"Most days I like it. It can be frustrating."

"Everything we like, and most of what we love, is frustrating, Mr. Carruthers." She put the book down on the coffee table and finished the last of her cup of tea. "I'll take it."

Chapter 4

Joel trudged through the snow and slush as he walked home. The late November dusk was deepening in darkness. His feet were wet and cold. The sidewalks had been cleared on the busier streets, but not his neighbourhood. Palmer Court wasn't even ploughed yet. The ache in his toes had gone from a dull, vague throbbing, to such numbness now he wasn't sure that they were even attached anymore.

Once inside the house, he took off his boots. His woollen socks were water-logged. Off they came too. His feet itched.

"Your supper's in the oven," his mother said when he walked into the living room. She was ironing Roger's uniforms. "Eat. Before it dries out. Nice roast beef."

The living room was tidy now. The broken bottles were gone. His mother would have whisked away all the evidence. Joel could hear the water running in the shower upstairs. "How were things here while I was at work?" He pointed to the ceiling. Above it he could hear his father singing a Sinatra song. He was wishing about being as rich as Rockefeller, on sunny streets.

"Don't be like that, Joel," his mother said, "you know he gets under stress. He doesn't mean it."

"Doesn't look that way to me."

"He doesn't mean any of it." She hung the shirt she finished ironing on a hanger. "Get your supper. I kept some gravy warm on the stove. And there's lots of mashed potatoes."

Joel went into the kitchen, took his plate from the oven and began to eat. "It's good. Thanks, Mom," he called out from the kitchen.

Roger came downstairs. His hair was wet. "My shirt?"

"Right here." Gloria passed him the crisp, pressed shirt.

"Anyone seen my scope?" Roger patted the pockets of the blue uniform cargo pants he had on. Nothing. He squeezed the striped pockets of his work jacket draped over the back of a chair. "My scope?" He pulled out the cushions of the sofa. "Anybody...?"

Joel poked his head around the kitchen door. "Try the backseat of the car," he said. That was a long time ago now. Early this morning, when he watched his father, drunk, stumble out of the car. He had hurled the stethoscope into the back seat, frustrated when it snagged on the seat belt. That seemed a universe away now. A different time, a distorted place.

"I tell you," Roger said, "Jenkins better behave himself tonight. I swear to Christ he looks for ways to grate on me."

"You're coming to your four off, it'll give you a chance to get some decent sleep, to rest up."

"I took an extra. The short shift tomorrow night. There won't be much rest."

"Oh Roger, why'd you do that?" Gloria's shoulders dropped. "You need to get a good stretch of time off. To rest, to wind down a bit."

"It's the short shift, I'll be off at two." The short shift went from six in the evening until two in the morning, eight hours instead of the usual twelve.

"I wish you hadn't taken it," Gloria said.

Joel handed his father his trauma shears and flashlight.

"You won't have any problem spending the money, though, will you?"

"It won't matter much if you get burnt out. It's not worth it, Rog, not in the long run."

"I'd be awake anyway. May as well make some money." Roger buttoned his shirt and tucked it into his pants. "I'll get some rest after the extra." He snapped out the longest knife blade from his Leatherman tool and tested its sharpness with his thumb. He nodded, satisfied and threaded the holster for his Leatherman onto his belt. He cinched the belt up tight and clasped the buckle's tongue into a new, rough hand-made hole. He sheathed the Leatherman in its holster and patted down the

Velcro clasp that held it snug. He pocketed his shears and Maglite flashlight and snapped them into place in his cargo pants pocket. He clipped his cell phone in its leather case onto his belt. He pulled his jacket on, the luminous PARAMEDIC blazoned on the back. "Good to go." He kissed Gloria on the cheek and headed out the door.

"See you in the morning," Gloria called out after him. "Ready for a piece of apple pie, Joel? Penelope came over when you were at the bookstore. She brought a pie she made." His mother cut him a big slice and placed it on a plate in front of him. "She said make sure you save a piece for Jo-Jo." Outside they could hear the car lurch out of the driveway. The bad spring clunked as Roger drove off.

"That's a bad cut over your eye," Joel said to his mother as he picked at the pie.

"Don't know how we can dirty so many dishes," she said as she busied herself at the sink. "Never can get ahead."

"Aunt Penelope must not have been happy about that cut."

"It's nothing. I had too much to drink, got tipsy. Me and Penelope got into the wine." She ran the water in the sink. "How was the store today? Busy, I bet, with the holidays coming."

"It looks like it needs stitches."

His mother started humming as she worked away at the sink.

He put down his fork and pushed away his plate without finishing the pie. "Seriously, you should have had stitches."

"Penelope is excited about the holidays. She's been sewing and knitting. You'll like what she's making for you, Joel. I had a peek today." She placed the mugs upside down on the dish strainer. "It's fine, it's nothing. You worry too much."

"Last time, you got me to run down to Zellers and get a tube of make up to cover it up. You wouldn't be seen outside for a week. This time it's worse."

"Don't look at me like that. Don't blow things out of proportion. We'll get through this." She picked up his dinner plate off the table. "Penelope would be hurt, not eating her pie."

"Penelope would be pissed if she knew you were lying."

"Call her yourself and ask her. I slipped and stumbled into the door frame. Tipsy from too much wine." His mother wiped the table with a dish cloth. "Call her yourself and see."

They heard a car pull up out front, then the muted thud as a car door slammed. A muffled 'see ya later' and the sound of footsteps coming up the front steps. The front door opened. Joel's brother walked in.

Joel exhaled a quiet sigh of relief. Right on cue, he thought.

"Hey," David said, as he kicked off his boots, and headed upstairs.

"David, Jennifer phoned," his mother yelled up the stairs, "make sure you call her back."

"Okay, thanks, Ma."

"And speaking of calling, you could phone your poor mother once in a while to let her know you're okay."

Joel flopped down on the couch, he felt like he might be able to relax. He felt that this Saturday evening was starting to feel normal. His father was at work. Beer bottles weren't being hurled against the floor. His mother was washing the dishes, humming a tune familiar to him as she worked. And David was home now. Upstairs, no doubt soon asleep, after being out with his friends all day and night.

"Put on my Joni Mitchell album, Jo-Jo," she called out to him. "Now that your father's out of the house I can get away with playing my 'sentimental crap.'"

They both laughed.

Joel put the album *Hits* on and moved the needle over to the track "Raised on Robbery." The unmistakable riff started, Joel turned it up loud and went into the kitchen.

"Okay," his mother said as she grabbed his hands with her own wet, soapy ones. "Let's dance!"

She twirled him around the kitchen floor, Joel tried to pull his hands away, but his mother hung on.

Joel stood tense and awkward while his mother shuffled her feet and threw back her head in laughter.

"I can't dance," Joel said. "You're a crazy lady."

"Well if you can't dance, then sing!"

He laughed. Joel had heard this album played so much that he knew all the words. He sang the "Boston B's" instead of the "Maple Leafs" when the song mentioned betting on hockey games.

His mother continued to dance, holding on to Joel's hands as tight as she could.

Joel realized she wasn't going to let him escape her clutches and he loosened up and moved his feet in time to the music. His posture was stiff and unnatural.

When the saxophone solo came on, Joel's mother twisted down as low as she could go, forcing Joel down too. Joel danced in a few jerky moves as his mother continued her spinning and romping. She twirled Joel around with one hand with perfect finesse as the song ended. She clapped.

Joel laughed. "You are out of it."

"Joni's great," his mother caught her breath. "I love that album. And just for the record, no one in this house is or was *ever* raised on robbery!"

The album continued with "Help Me." Joel picked up his guitar and started to play along when "Free Man in Paris" came on.

"Oh, that sounds good, Jo-Jo, you've got it," his mother called from the kitchen.

Joel kept playing along until the song ended. "Ever been to Paris?"

"No, but I'd love to. One of these days. It's so romantic."

The next song started, the piano chords playing a stylized "Jingle Bells."

"Oh, you should learn this song too, "River," it's beautiful. Not really a Christmas song, but Christmassy in its own way. I love it."

Joel strummed his guitar, providing a gentle rhythm under Joni's powerful voice as the song played.

"Skating away on a river," Joel put down his guitar when the song finished, "sounds enticing sometimes, doesn't it?"

Chapter 5

When Joel got home from school his father was sitting in the living room watching an episode of "Third Watch" that his mother had taped for him. The VCR was running but the sound on the television was low. A Charlie Parker album was on the turntable. Charlie's lonely saxophone bounced through "How High the Moon."

"You're home early," Joel's father said. He had his saxophone out of its case and was polishing it with a linen cloth.

"Yeah, I had a free block and my biology class was cancelled, so I came home."

"I get what he meant now," his father said.

Joel looked at him, puzzled. "What who meant?"

"Bird," his father said, "what Bird said when he talked about playing the sax. Bird. You know. Charlie Parker."

Joel nodded as though he understood. Never a risk in nodding agreement.

"Bird said that he could hear the music that he wanted to play, the way he wanted to play it." His father took a drink from his bottle. "He could hear in his head what he wanted to play, but he couldn't play it on his horn." He drank down the last of that bottle. "I get it now."

The record ended. The needle began a continuous loop, circling around the faded Verve label. "We should hear that again, Joel."

Joel got up and set the needle back to the first track.

"Could listen to him all day," his father said, his words slurred. He placed his saxophone to his lips and tried to play along. His fingers slipped off the keys. The alcohol affected his finger's movements as it affected his speech. He tried to play along with the Bird album but couldn't keep up. His fingers like big hunks of uncontrolled cork bouncing off the keys. When he managed to play a single note, it was neither in time nor in key. He talked while his teeth clenched the mouthpiece. "Jesus, Joel, see what he means? I know what he means." His father stared at the record revolving on the turntable. "I can hear the fucking music. But I can't play it." There were tears in his eyes. "I can't play it at all."

There was a knock at the front door. That gave Joel an excuse to get up. It was one thing to see your father drunk. It was something altogether more painful to see your father drunk and crying. Crying about not being able to play the saxophone.

His mother called from the kitchen, "Somebody get the door, I got my hands full of meatloaf."

Joel went to the door, glad to escape the living room and his father's melancholy mood. The late afternoon sun blazed through when he opened it. A man from Nova Scotia Power stood there. He handed Joel an envelope.

"Give this to your folks," he said. "They gotta pay this bill now, or we cut the electricity."

Joel walked into the kitchen and told his mother. Much safer.

"Mercy," Gloria said. She got up from making her meatloaf and washed her hands. She wiped them dry on her apron as she walked toward the door. "Joel, honey, run to my room and get my purse."

Gloria talked with the man in the uniform at the door. Joel came back with her purse.

Joel's father tried to stand up but stumbled back on to the couch. "Who's at the fucking door?"

"It's the power company," Joel's mother called out. Her voice as cheerful as she could make it. "I'm taking care of it, Rog." She was counting out money. "If I give you forty dollars, can the rest wait till Thursday?" she whispered. "Thursday's payday."

"I'll have to get approval from the office." He took the two twenties and went back out to his truck.

The man came back on the porch. "The account is past due. Two hundred dollars. We haven't received a payment in three months. We've phoned a ton of times. No answer. No response to our letters. We need at least half today." He looked down at his clipboard, "or it gets cut. I'm sorry, ma'am. It's head office."

"Mom, I got a few bucks. Twenty-five or thirty," Joel said and pushed the wadded bills into his mother's hand. She didn't say anything but nodded to him. He knew she couldn't speak, if she did, she'd start crying. She counted out the money.

"Here's eighty dollars all together. I'll get the rest for you on Thursday." She passed him the money. "I promise," she said, "Thursday."

"Mrs. Carruthers, I need another twenty dollars. It's head office, ma'am. The line truck is already on its way."

"Twenty? That can't wait till Thursday?"

"It's head office, ma'am, the disconnect order is already in."

"I'll write you a cheque, give me a second."

"Ma'am, it's head office. I'm sorry, cash or money order. No cheques."

"Wait a minute then, please," she turned toward the living room.

"I'll wait in my truck. You've got five minutes."

"Roger, you got any cash on you?" she asked. Asking her husband for twenty dollars seemed better than the alternative. She was more afraid of his reaction to no lights and no record player, and worse, no fridge to keep the beer cold.

Roger lurched to the door. "What the name of Christ is going on here?" What the..." He looked at the power company truck pulled up by the curb. "They threaten to cut the power again? Hey," he called out to the man in the truck and shook his fist at him. The movements were too unsteady and slow to be a threat. "You goddamned monopolistic bastards! You've got no right treating hard working, tax-paying citizens that way." The words were slurred and hard for Joel and his mother to understand.

"Rog, I need twenty dollars. Do you have a twenty? Cash?"

"I hate this." He fished in his pockets and drew out some crumpled bills. "This is it, this is all." She reached for the money and he snatched his hand away. "I hate living like this."

"Your cheque comes in this week, we'll be fine once that comes in."

"I'm saving up. I need a case of beer."

"They got the truck coming to cut the power if we don't pay them."

"Bastards." He plunked the money in her hand. "Pay the motherfuckers." He belched. "I'm going to build a windmill."

His father headed back to the living room. He turned the music louder. He wiped his fingerprints off his saxophone and put it in its case. He tottered.

"Need a hand, Dad?" Joel asked.

"I'm hocking Birdie Blue, Joel. I need the money. Besides," he said, "I can hear the music, but I can't play it. Bye-bye, Birdie Blue." His father picked up the saxophone case and headed outside. Joel followed him.

His father fumbled to put the key in the trunk of the car.

"Here," Joel said, taking the key from him and opening the trunk.

His father put his saxophone in, patted the case then slammed the trunk.

"Let me drive," Joel stood back a few paces behind him, on guard. "You're tired." He guided his father to the passenger seat.

"Head for that place on Church Street," his father said.

"You sure you want to do this? I got a cheque coming the day after tomorrow. I can let you use the money. I don't need it."

"That place on Church Street."

"I can pay the power bill. They won't cut it off."

"Church Street," Roger muttered, pointing his finger in a vague direction.

Joel backed out of the driveway and headed down Palmer Court. "Was it busy last night? I heard sirens all night long."

"Yeah, steady, lots of action up on Route 6."

"Anything serious?"

"You know what it's like."

"Bad?"

"You get used to it after a while." Joel's father stared out the windshield. "Young kids, they're the worst."

"Killed?"

"I'm sure you'll hear all about it soon enough."

"Anyone I know?"

"They were from Parrsboro, out driving around looking for kicks."

"How many?"

"You'll hear about it in the news soon enough. Don't ask me anything else about it."

The pair drove on in silence. Joel turned onto Eddy Street, heading towards the downtown area. Joel clicked on the radio, but kept it turned down low. Lou Bega's "Mambo Number 5" came through with exuberance.

"See," Joel's father said, "you kids know nothing. That song that's so in right now? It was a hit fifty years ago." His father turned up the radio at the trumpet break. "Love that horn." He turned to look at his son. "Had a call soon as we cleared from that one. A baby. Went into a febrile seizure. Couldn't bring him out of it. He went into status. We coded him to emerg. I tried every intervention in the book. He was in respiratory arrest by the time Jenkins pulled us in. I was bagging him. Couldn't get him back. Eight months old. I don't get it."

Joel nodded. He turned onto Church Street and found a parking spot in front of Big Bobby's Gem & Coin. Roger took the saxophone case out of the trunk, walked in stumbling, and plopped it on the counter. "What'll you give me for old Birdie Blue here?"

Bobby opened the case. He took out the sax and turned it over in his hands, his gaze travelled up and down the sleek brass instrument. He tested the key's action. They functioned, no sticking. Bobby ran his hand up and down, looking for dents and dings. He held it against his belly that wasn't quite covered by a stretched *Dark Side of the Moon* T-shirt. "She's seen her fair share of use and abuse."

"Who hasn't?" Roger laughed. "She's pure and sweet, the best tone you'll ever hear."

Big Bobby thrust the instrument toward Roger, "play it."

Roger shook his head and pushed the instrument back toward Bobby. "Nah, I can hear the music, but I can't play it."

"Two, if you don't play her, maybe more if you do. Need to know if it works."

Roger took the instrument from him and blew long and hard into it. His fingers slipped off the keys. He battled to keep his balance as he played. The notes of "All the Things You Are" were too slow and Joel struggled to recognize the song. The beer impaired his breathing as well as his fingers. But the saxophone's tone was sweet and pure. It was mellow.

"Okay, she works." Bobby took the saxophone back.

"*She* has a name. *She* is Birdie Blue." His eyes were moist.

"Birdie Blue?" He laughed, "okay Birdie Blue here is worth two-fifty. Deal?"

"Are you kidding me? Two grand."

"Look around, pal. You see the mills closing down? For sale signs on every street corner? You see any new factories starting up here? In this economy, that sax is—"

Roger glared at him. "Birdie—"

"Right. Your *Birdie Blue* is worth two hundred and fifty."

"I'm buying her back on payday."

"There'll be interest."

On the way home his father pointed to the liquor store. "Pull in. Need a pit stop." Roger came out a few minutes later carrying a case of beer in one hand and a paper bag in the other. "This'll hold us over for a while."

"Hey," Joel said, as they drove on. "Mom told me about the letter from the lieutenant governor. That's great, congratulations."

"I don't want it," his father said. "They can keep their *Star of Life* medal, give it to someone else."

"You deserve it. You saved those two kids. If it wasn't for you, they'd have died."

"I did what I'm paid to do. I'm not accepting a medal for that."

"The letter said you 'exercised heroic measures.' Sounds like you did more than what your job calls for."

"Son, listen, I can hear Marvin Gaye." He cocked a hand to his ear. "He's singing, 'believe none of what you hear.'"

Joel turned onto Forest. Fresh snow coated the street. "There's got to be something to it for the lieutenant governor to give you a medal. They don't hand those out to everybody."

"They can give it to somebody who can or did make a difference. If you think I had control over saving those two boys, you're wrong. The lieutenant governor is wrong. I had no more control over saving those boys than I did losing that baby last night. By rights, they should take away the medal, because I lost three people last night. Two at the car crash and that little baby."

Joel pulled down Palmer Court and eased the car into the driveway. Roger finished the bottle he was drinking and they went inside.

As he kicked off his boots, Joel looked at his mother and shook his head. His father staggered past heading to the kitchen with his purchases. "Need a drink, Glor?" He plunked the liquor down on the kitchen counter. "I got reinforcements."

"You didn't have to do that. You didn't need to pawn your saxophone."

He reached into his pocket and pulled out the money he had left and shoved it into Gloria's face. "Pay the goddamned power bill and shut up about it." He let the bills cascade to the floor. "I could hear the music, but I couldn't play it."

Joel went up to his room, collapsed on the bed and stared at the ceiling. Below he could hear the Parker album being played again. The saxophone was haunting. He could hear his father yelling at the turntable. His voice shook. "You could play it, Bird. Jesus, you *could* reach it."

Chapter 6

As he left school, Joel could feel his muscles tense up the closer he got to home. His father worked night shift tonight. Joel hated the overlap of a few hours between the time he got home and when his father would leave for work.

"Joel! Get in here," his father called from the kitchen.

Joel threw his knapsack and jacket on the floor and went to the kitchen. "Hey," he said.

His father pointed to the overflowing garbage can beside the counter. "Get that shit cleaned up and out of here." He popped open a beer and chugged the whole thing down and grabbed another. He walked past Joel's mother. She was standing at the ironing board.

Whack! He smashed his fist down hard on the ironing board. "Don't you look at me like that."

Joel's mother winced.

His father headed to the living room. He popped the cap off the second beer bottle and fiddled with the VCR. "Don't stand there open-mouthed and fucking gawking at me. Make yourself useful. I need that shirt." He pressed play and the opening credits of "ER" came on the screen.

"If you can't make yourself useful," he hollered, "why don't you get your scrawny ass out of this house. Once and for all."

Joel looked at his mother as he was tying up the garbage bag. Her eyes were focused on her chore. She pressed the shirt collar with extra steam. Joel shook his head towards the living room. He wanted to stand up to his father. He wanted to challenge him. *What the fuck is your problem?* or *Why don't you leave her the Christ alone?* Instead, he cinched up the bag, carried it outside and stuffed it in the garbage can.

"I swear to Christ," Joel's father clenched his fist and shook it in the air, "I'm going to pop that fucker in the mouth if he starts any of his shit tonight." He paced waiting for Gloria to finish ironing his uniform shirt.

"If who starts what?" Joel's mother didn't look up as she worked away at the ironing board.

"Jenkins. Who else? That fucker wrote me up again last night."

"For what?"

"Fucking morphine."

"What do you mean, morphine?"

"The lovely and talented Mr. Jenkins wanted to report a broken vial of morphine."

"Aren't you supposed to do that anyway?" Gloria pressed the button for steam, "Report it?" She slid the iron down the crease of the shirt sleeve.

"He thinks I'm using. Fucker. Because of my hands." Joel's father stuck his hands out, palms down, in front of his mother's face, and held them there. "That weasel thinks I'm using. He thinks my hands shake."

Joel detected a slight tremble, but he never said a word.

"Steady as a rock," his father said.

Joel couldn't wait till his father left for work. As soon as he did, the relief was real for all of them. Joel noticed how his father was always so careful before work. He'd drink, but he wasn't slurring his words or staggering to his car. He must have been buzzed, he thought, but not outright drunk. Why not be like that when he wasn't going to work?

Joel remembered how a few months ago his mother would cry when his father talked to her like that. But she had grown used to it now. Or she didn't want to be seen to buckle in front of his father. He had no mercy for being soft. Now, Joel just watched this new detachment she employed to take the abuse from his father. The same way he watched the physical scars heal over, time and time again.

By now he was used to it, too. Joel had watched his mother grow resistant. Like nothing hurt her anymore. Joel figured his mother's healing was timed right now. Her body knew when the next beating was going to come. It was like her body knew how much it could take. How much she could hide from the outside world. Not from Joel or David, but from her friends. Those she bumped into at the library, or church, even acquaintances she might encounter at the grocery store. She would want to be healed before the next punch landed. Joel compared it to a billboard. How they tore down the previous ad before a new one went up. He figured that his mother wanted to advertise her resilience, her ability to bounce back. To whom? His father? Aunt Penny? Herself? Joel noticed she would style her hair in a different way if she needed to disguise a bump on her forehead. Or how she would change the shade of her lipstick or get a deeper shade of makeup for her cheeks, depending where the cut or mark was on her face. Joel noticed her scarf collection grew weekly. A colour or design to go with every outfit now. She liked to mask herself appropriately, even to greet a bill collector at the door. His mother went to absurd lengths to keep the truth from her sister. Joel knew she disguised things whenever she was around people. But most of all, her sister Penelope.

"I'm worried about you, Mom," Joel said after his father had left.

"Don't worry about me, Jo-Jo. I'm fine."

"That's got to hurt. And even if it doesn't hurt—"

"The pain isn't tender anymore, Jo-Jo." She had her back to him and was working away at the kitchen table. "There's no pain when you realize that he's not angry at you."

"But Mom." Joel drew a deep breath. Conversations like this had become useless. They always ended up in an argument. Not at all the outcome he intended. Joel never wanted a confrontation with his mother.

"I've learned ways to survive it."

"Shouldn't the best way to survive it be by not having to suffer through it in the first place?"

"You don't understand. You see what you want to see."

"I see reality."

"If you take things from his perspective, if you consider where he is coming from, it becomes easy. You understand it's your duty—"

"Jesus, 'duty'? You're talking like we're in a mediaeval serfdom. Like it's the Middle Ages."

"You give in and give up. That's how you survive it." She turned from the towels she was folding and faced Joel. "Stop your cursing. You know I don't tolerate cursing."

"Sorry. But come on, 'duty'?"

"What I've learned over the last little while, the tactics I've relied on, are to give in and give up."

Joel shook his head. He reached for an apple from the basket on the counter.

"You need to remember that it'll blow over. Give in to what is happening. Give up trying to fight back—"

"And accept it?"

"No. To know that it'll pass. And to remember it's not directed at me. I give in to this man, my husband who, after every time, tells me that he is sorry and that he loves me. Deeply." She placed the last of the towels on top of a neat stack and started with a pile of face cloths. "If you knew, Jo-Jo, how sorry he is, how remorseful—that's the part you never see. David doesn't either."

Joel bit into the apple. "You should give up accepting that he beats you up. Call the cops or something. Then he'd stop."

"He doesn't mean it, he never does. It's the stress, it's the job. You don't know everything that he's dealing with."

"It's the liquor, Mom, can't you see that?"

"That's another symptom. There's a few problems. They're getting better."

"He gets drunk. And takes out his frustrations on you."

"You have to trust me. It'll get better. It is getting better. Every day."

"I don't think your philosophy is working for you." Joel crunched another bite of the apple; Joel was starting to understand his family was nowhere near normal. "You want to give in? You should give in to what David thinks. He can't stand it."

"What you two never see is that things are getting better. We are moving towards happiness. Someday, somewhere we'll be at happily-ever after."

"Mom! This isn't a fucking fairy tale." Joel hurled the apple core into the sink.

"No cursing, Joel. I'm warning you."

"You're talking fairy godmothers and princes on white horses. I'm telling you it's getting worse and worse. Why won't you see that?"

"Because it's getting better, that's why. You're looking at the wrong things."

"Yep, you are." Joel looked at her. Her hair had lost its shine and looked coarse and brittle. His mother's eyes were tired and sunken, which was significantly different from early photographs. And even a change from the way she looked a few short months ago.

Joel's mother passed the basket of laundry to him. "Now do your poor old mama a favour and take these upstairs and put them away in the linen closet." Joel took the basket.

"Yep," he said, "something's got to give, Mom, this is going from bad to shit—I mean worse. From bad to worse."

"Have faith. Listen to me, it will get better. He'll be okay. And then we all will be too."

"Aunt Penny buy your theory of give in, give up?"

"Don't you mention a goddamned word of this conversation to her."

"Cursing, are we?" Joel laughed. "No double standard here is there?"

"And bring down the dirty clothes after you put those towels away my darling little Jo-Jo."

"Sure, Mom." He gave her a kiss on the cheek. She looked at him. Her eyes had a look of exasperation. They looked like she wanted to surrender and that she would take whatever punishment came her way without resistance. Their starkness showed a despair deeper than defeat. Joel took the basket of linen and headed upstairs. He had seen that stark, hollow look before in his mother's eyes. He'd seen it in his father's eyes, too.

It was right after a big house fire. Joel remembered when his father had come home that morning. It must have been over a year ago. The explosion had rocked the night. Everyone in the town heard it. Sirens screamed all night. Joel and David called their friends to find out what was going on. The fire cast a rosy pink hue in the sky above the whole west side of Amherst. The smoke billowed up from the raging inferno. The house had blown up. A gas leak was what everyone said, as rumours sprang up. Two dead at the scene. They worked them but it was no use. They transported two more to the hospital. One died enroute, one made it there still breathing, but badly injured. Joel and David knew the kids in the family. Everyone in town knew someone in that family. That's how small-town Amherst worked.

Joel could still see how his father had dragged himself up the steps that morning. The smell of charred wood hung off him. The rich chemical aroma of burnt plastic wafted off his uniform—the distinct residue of a house fire.

Joel and his brother were eager for information. They waited at the front door for their father to get home from work. Rumours abounded and needed to be put to rest. They needed to know the truth. They were worried about their friends, their school mates.

Their father had trudged in, his shoulders stooped. No smile, no greeting, no hello. Joel remembered he looked tired, deflated. He had the air of defeat around him.

Joel's father sat down at the foot of the stairs. To Joel, he moved in slow motion, untying the laces of his boots. His shirt was splotched with soot.

"Did everyone get out?" Joel had asked his father.

"Who was it?" David asked. "Was it really the Graysons' place?"

He looked at Joel and David. "You know"—his eyes seemed vacant, like he was staring at a spot a thousand miles out on the horizon—"I'm not allowed to give out personal information about what happens on calls."

"Yeah, but we heard it was Scott's family. His cousins."

"Some made it, some didn't." Joel's father peeled off his boots. Joel saw his eyes hollow, distant. "I tried, boys, I tried the best I could."

Joel went upstairs. David was stretched out, lying down on his bunk, the bottom one. His lanky legs were cramped in the too-small bunk and his feet stuck out the end. Joel could smell alcohol, rum he thought, as it wafted up every time David exhaled. A magazine, opened to the centerfold, was laying on David's chest. David closed the magazine when his brother walked in. Things were settled when his father was at work, and Joel, his mother and his brother approached being normal. The tension that coiled up tighter and tighter when his father was home, relaxed as soon as he headed out the door.

"You had another one," David said. His eyes were still closed. He flopped his arm out and pointed in the direction of the laundry basket heaped with the dirty clothes that Joel had thrown in the corner after his seizure. The laundry had the subtle odour of fermented piss.

"No," Joel said. "You been out at the shack? Or just driving around?"

"The bastard triggered it, didn't he? Came home drunk again, smashed some bottles, punched Mom in the face?" David rolled off the bed. "I've about had it with his bullshit." He stood up to his full height and lit a cigarette. "He's gone overboard one too many times." David rummaged in his jacket that was draped over the desk chair. He took out a bottle, a pint of rum. "Swig?" he asked Joel.

Joel shook his head and laughed. "You took a bottle of his? Better not let him find out."

"I'm getting out of here," David said. He took a long drink from the bottle, grimaced, and then shook his head. He took a drag of the cigarette.

"Mom will shit if she knows you're smoking. Especially in the house."

"I'm taking off. I can't stay here anymore. I'm done." David opened the window, pulled the curtain to one side and exhaled. He held his cigarette out the window.

"This will blow over. You know it always does."

David watched the smoke vanish as it curled up and drifted out into the cold air. "I'm not sticking around to find out. You'll need to take care of things."

"Me? It's not that simple."

"You need to."

"What about you? I know that's what you want to do Dave," Joel straightened up the books on his desk. "But you know it's not practical. Seriously, where would you go? What would you do?"

"You're right. It may not be practical. But it's what I have to do. I can't stay here another minute." David drew on his cigarette and blew the smoke up toward the moon. "That bastard infuriates me. He's a fucking bully."

"It'll get better. You know that. It comes in waves." Joel picked up the laundry basket with his dirty clothes. "I'd best throw these in the wash."

"Was it a bad one?"

"Nah, a focal."

"And you pissed yourself? You don't piss yourself with a focal."

"It was a focal. Jesus, I went to work right after. Pierre even let me drive his car. I'm fine."

David sucked on his cigarette again. He stuck his head out the window and exhaled. "Boston," he said.

"You're going to Boston?"

"Nothing around here. It's the easiest."

"What about the plan to live with Aunt Penny?"

"Truro doesn't have anything either. It's as dead there as it is here."

"Yeah, but it'd be a place to stay."

"And do what?"

"Ever wonder why he goes off? Like has it always been this way forever?" Joel took the rum bottle from David. He twisted the cap on tight. "I'm putting this back. Dad will freak if he finds out you took it."

"He doesn't go off on you. You're his favourite."

"And Mom? What about her?"

"She should leave too."

"Jesus. Where would that leave me?"

"She could take you with her."

"Hilarious."

"He should smarten the fuck up and act his age."

"Think he's an alcoholic?"

"You are the original bubble boy," David laughed and sucked the last from his smoke and threw it outside.

"Better pick that butt up off the driveway." Joel shook his head. "Mom will know it was you."

"Jo-Jo, I'm leaving."

"When?"

"I'm done."

Chapter 7

Joel heard music in the middle of the night. It was unmistakably Charlie Parker's stuttered short bright bursts of saxophone followed by long sighs of silence. He thought his father must have fallen asleep, more likely passed out, and left the music playing. He looked at his watch. It showed ten minutes past four. He went down to the living room to turn off the music.

His father was sitting cross-legged on the couch. He clutched a steaming mug of coffee in his hands. A grey flannel blanket was draped over his shoulders. He was naked underneath. An anatomy textbook was open beside him.

"Jeez, Dad, I thought you'd be asleep." Joel looked past him to the record player.

His father stared straight ahead, unblinking. "Tried. Couldn't."

"Won't the coffee keep you up?" Joel motioned to the mug in his hand, surprised that he didn't have a beer, or worse yet rum.

"Nah. There's no point in sleeping now. Enjoy the music. Bird could hit it, couldn't he." Charlie Parker bopped and dipped through "Bird Gets the Worm."

"Listen to that tone. So pure. Hey, help yourself," his father held up the mug, "there's a full pot in the kitchen, better to not waste it."

Joel shrugged, "I guess." He came back with his own mug, he had added lots of milk and sugar.

"Look out in the sky, Joel," his father gazed out the window. "In the middle of the night," his father continued, "when it's the quiet hours and your shift is done—what time is it now? Three-thirty? Four?"

"Yep," Joel nodded, "after four."

"This is the quietest time of the night. The party goers and the rabble rousers are passed out sound asleep somewhere. The early morning crowd hasn't stirred yet. This is the in-between time." His father nodded toward the window. "When the sky is steel blue and all the shadows on the streets are quiet. Everything is grey. Car lights move across the bridge in the distance." His father stared straight ahead. After a minute he said, "Turn out the light, Joel."

Charlie danced through "Constellation." Joel clicked the switch off. The soft luminous glow from the dials on the turntable was the only light in the room. Outside the stars fanned out in the sky.

"You're on guard for the whole city, sitting, quiet, in wait, in an ambulance." Joel's father nodded toward the music. "You've got the glow of the dash lights, the radio's on low. Provided, of course, you can convince the moronic idiot you work with to play decent music. That's when you're ready to respond to any emergency—man-made or natural. Your thoughts turn and return again to the meaning, the deeper meaning of all this. This bullshit."

Joel took a sip of his coffee. Parker quieted down, slow and smooth he swept into "Parker's Mood."

"You wonder where you line up on the scale of importance. Your mind races, it's quiet and the lights are soft. The music is soothing. But panic crawls on your skin like an unwelcome guest and your head twirls. Everything whirls around. You have thoughts that flick in and out. It's quiet and your heart rate bounds into triple digits. You start to think in this quiet steel-cold darkness." Joel's father stared out the window. Without breaking his gaze, he raised his mug to his lips. Joel noticed the blanket shift, revealing that a few of the curly hairs on his father's chest were grey.

"You ask yourself, am I nuts? What if I snap? Your arteries banging in rhythm against your temples. You hear it and feel it. In the dark hours, you slide your hand up"—he slid his left hand up—"you palpate the rhythm, the rate, right here"—he rubbed his temple—"tachycardic." He dropped his hand and took a sip of coffee. "You think what if I save a life tonight? What if I lose one? Do I control what type of call I am going to get dispatched to? Who I'll treat? Can I determine how effective that treatment will be? Who am I to call the shots? I'm nobody."

Joel sipped his coffee, grimaced at its bitterness.

"Isn't it a random rolling of the dice? A tumbling series of ifs... that's what determines who lives or dies. *If* a driver crashes his vehicle into a guard rail, and *if* someone else sees the crash, and *if* they can get to a phone and call it in, and *if* my unit is available and *if* we're the closest to the scene and *if* I'm not lined up in a coffee shop, and *if* my truck is awaiting, like it should, with engine running. I'm sitting there with the diesel throbbing just waiting for the tones to send me in my sleek white greyhound of mercy to save the fucking day." Roger paused to listen as Charlie played. His head bopped gently along. He never said anything for a long time. He took a drink of his coffee. Then he started again.

"*If* I can get to the scene of the crash without taking a wrong turn, and *if* I can grab my kits, and *if* I don't slip going down the bank of the ditch and *if* I can get inside the mangled car, and *if* I can reach the driver and *if* I can start a line, run some oxygen and *if* I can stop the bleeding..." His father stared out the window again, his face registered no emotion. "*If* I can somehow wrangle him out of the vehicle, the mangled, upside down vehicle, and *if* I can get him up the bank, and *if* I can rapidly assess him there in the quasi-comfort of the back of my bus, and *if* I don't miss life-threatening things—a flail chest, cardiac tamponade—and *if* we can drive to the hospital and arrive in one piece..." He sipped his coffee. "If, if, if, after fucking if." He looked at over at Joel.

"I'm listening," Joel said.

"Thought you might have fallen asleep."

Joel shrugged and shook his head.

"When the *ifs* tumble together and line up in a neat little row, then the waiting, the stand-by, the engine running and the equipment and medications and the skill that stood by waiting for this opportunity to make a real difference will have been worth it. But when shit goes sideways who knows what the outcome would have been. Even when the ifs line up like those stars"—he waved his hand toward the window, and shook his head—"no guarantee."

Joel peered at his father sitting cross-legged on the couch. The blanket had slipped down. Joel observed his immense biceps and the triangular shape of his fit pectorals. His eyes traced his father's tattoo of the caduceus symbol on his chest. The image of the serpent that uncoils itself into the shape of an electrocardiogram wave that then morphed into a stylized heart. The tattoo heart directly over where his father's own heart would be. Even with the well-toned muscles, and the tattoos, Joel thought that his father looked small and forlorn. Charlie breezed away. They were both quiet and listened to the music.

"You don't know, though," Joel said, "if—"

"When all the permutations are calculated, when all the science is tallied, it comes down to pure faith. Or fate. No one, not the medic, not the doctor, not the family, not the priest can sway the outcome. None of us can pry any human being from the jaws of death when they clamp down."

Despite his father's bulging biceps, Joel thought he looked weak. The saxophone tattoo on his right arm, looked comic and sad. Three quarter notes floated out from the horn. Joel looked up and down his father's body and saw sweat glisten in the low light. He swallowed the last of his coffee. Charlie Parker swooned into "I Didn't Know What Time It Was."

"I better get some sleep," Joel said.

"Thing is, death will come. Early or late. Sometimes with fury and gore and guts; sometimes in silent tranquility. We fight it. But death owns endurance, its stamina wins. Death always wins, eventually. Death never tires or weakens. This mystery hanging above should govern us." Joel's father's eyes were fixed on the spinning turntable. "We're smacked around by the breath of life the same way we smack at mosquitoes around a campfire. When we realize that we are nothing, we can become something. Peace arrives when we surrender. That's when we can gain some power. When we know we're nothing but a piece of shit. That's when we flow into our..." His father stared at the turntable and held his coffee cup to his lips but didn't drink. "Flow into what? Our true destiny." His hands trembled.

"Good night, Dad." Joel headed for the stairs. "I've got to get up for school in the morning."

Chapter 8

The bell rang to signal the end of class. Joel headed out, his head ducked down.

"Joel, I want to speak to you for a moment," Miss Corbin said.

He felt his face get hot. He stood at his teacher's desk. He knew this was about his paper. He didn't pass one in.

"It's not like you to miss deadlines," Miss Corbin said.

"I know, I'm sorry. Things have been a little nuts lately." He slung the strap of his book bag over a shoulder. "I'll have it for you tomorrow."

"You're on track for an A in history. Don't blow that, Joel. Universities do take notice of your marks."

"I promise—tomorrow." He turned toward the door.

"Joel," Miss Corbin said, her voice hushed, "if there's anything major going on you can always talk with Mr. Barnstead."

"Okay," he said and kept walking out of the classroom. Talking to the guidance counsellor was the last thing he wanted to do. "Tomorrow," he said without looking back.

When Joel got home, he headed into the kitchen. His parents were sitting at the table.

"I've got to get a new partner. I can't handle Jenkins anymore," his father said, flipping through the newspaper.

"Another coffee, Rog?" Joel's mother said.

"You'll never guess what he was beaking off about last night."

"You think any more about taking a few days off? Getting away on that shopping trip to the city we've been talking about?"

"He was complaining about how he couldn't sleep because he took an extra shift. One. One extra. I laughed at him. These kids, are they all like that nowadays?"

"I tried to talk to David about a job," his mother said. "You know when we were all a little more calmed down. All of us."

"And what did Mr. I'm-Entitled-to-Everything-for-Free have to say?"

"He agreed to go down and fill out an application."

"Isn't that a surprise. I thought he'd want to lug loads of bricks around for the rest of his life."

"He thinks it's useless because he doesn't have a trade." Joel's mother took a drink of coffee.

"And who, did you remind him, has told him he needs a trade? How many times have I told him that? Every time he was lazing in bed when I got home from work. After I've been schlepping around patients all night, breaking my back."

Joel put some bread in the toaster. "I took as many nights as I could at the bookstore this week and next. It's getting busy, Pritchard needs as much help as he can get."

"I get that David doesn't want to keep going to school. Once he graduated high school he's finished with classes," Joel's father said. "Fine. I get it. But I know I have always worked as much as I could. I would even do gigs on weekends to make a few extra bucks."

"Didn't you tell me that was for fun?" Joel was poised by the toaster.

"Nothing wrong with having fun while you're earning some cash too. But this lagging around, he's been out of school since June. Six months of nothing. Fits and starts. Where'd I go wrong?"

"If you keep talking to him like that, he'll leave," his mother said.

"And?"

"He takes everything to heart, may not show it, but he cares—"

"About himself, above anybody."

"Rog, you remember what it's like to be seventeen, nearly eighteen?"

"Yeah, that's why he needs a job, or he needs to pick up a trade. Jesus, don't you see?"

"I don't want him heading to Boston or out west on spec. You keep talking to him like this and that's where he'll end up."

"And you think that's a problem? Sometimes the birdie got to learn to fly on his own."

"Give him some time."

The toaster popped. "Anybody want some toast?" Joel asked.

"You're going to spoil your supper," his mother said.

"Listen," his father said, beating his fist on the table, "you're the reason he's loafing around." He raised his voice. "You're too fucking soft."

"Here," Joel said. He reached in between his parents with a plate of toast and jam. "Have a piece."

"Same thing with Jenkins. Last night he starts dissing being a medic. The kid's been on the streets for a few months. Doesn't even know what the job is, and already he's restless."

"It's not for everyone, Roger, look at Simpson. You remember?"

"Simpson was a fucking wuss. Let things get to him. Thought too much." Roger shook his head. "Could never just let shit go."

CHAPTER 9

The next morning, Joel was quiet as he was getting ready to leave the house and head for school. The last thing he wanted to do was wake his parents.

David was awake and urged him to cut class. "C'mon Jo-Jo, skip first period. Have a nip before you have to face old Miss Corbin."

"No, I can't," Joel said.

"History's bad enough without that old bag. A little spike in your coffee is what you need to get you through that torture. Meet us out at the shack."

The shack was an abandoned shed the boys used as a hideaway, located far enough away in the wooded area behind Palmer Court that they were effectively alone in the dark when they were there. The darkness did make it tricky to navigate the path back home, taking care not to trip on boulders or tree roots that grew progressively more difficult to traverse the more they'd had to drink. Beyond the shack, another hundred metres or so, the path opened up into a barren clearing, the site of the now abandoned and derelict railway car foundry from the late 1800s. A stream meandered past the old foundry toward the current industrial park and crossed the railway tracks and the Trans Canada Highway before emptying into Cumberland Basin.

The shack served many purposes over the years. The shack was a place to go when their parents were mad at them, or when they were mad at their parents. The shack was a spot to get away to when they needed to get away from girls, and when they needed a place to go with girls. The shack was a place to drink without having to worry about getting caught.

They had fashioned it out of wooden pallets scooped from the soda bottling plant. The roof and walls were a patchwork of old, faded plywood signs advertising a real estate development that had gone bust years ago. Over the years, they dragged down odd pieces of furniture—a couch, a torn armchair, an office chair with no wheels plucked from the curb on garbage day, a wobbly card table—all of which sat lopsided on the dirt floor.

Joel remembered overhearing David on the telephone one time convincing his girlfriend to come out with him to the shack.

"Jennifer, it's nice and quiet," David had said.

Then the next time Joel headed back to the shack, he heard the sofa creak and groan in the cabin as he walked up the path. He stopped and listened. The battery powered radio was playing Sarah McLachlan singing how love was better than ice cream, better than chocolate.

When Joel was close enough to the shack he leaned in and looked through the crack in the door. His breathing increased. Jennifer was sitting on top of David. Her long hair covered his eyes. Her breasts bounced with the movement from her hips. Up and down.

Joel couldn't see his brother's face. But he had heard him. "Jen, you're awesome."

The bouncing grew in rhythm and intensity.

"God," his brother had whispered.

Joel was aroused. He should leave them in peace. But his body, his legs, wouldn't budge. Even now, as he remembered, he felt his face get hot. He couldn't look away. Her breasts were full, her nipples erect. Her buttocks smooth and pale slammed against his brother's crotch. He should go, he thought, but he stood there fascinated with her movements, her nakedness. He couldn't look away. His heart rate sped up. Blood pounded in his veins. He slid his hand down his pants and watched her move atop his brother.

David headed downstairs and left through the front door this time.

Hanging out with his brother, Scott and Zack was a better proposition for Joel than history or math. He was accepted by them and felt comfortable. He justified it to himself: "I'm learning how real life works."

So Joel followed his brother to the shack. When he got there, his brother was already sipping from a bottle. David would spend every day he could splitting a bottle with Zack and Scott. "One month and I'm a free man," David told them. "Nobody can stop me. I'll never have to step foot in this shitville of a town again."

In one month, David turned eighteen.

"It's not my birthday," he grinned, "it's my escape day."

He had begun to plan his escape the day his father chipped his mother's tooth. Nothing was the same after that.

"Jo-Jo, my plan just tumbled together naturally. It's like pieces of a jigsaw puzzle clicked into place. The day I turn eighteen," he said, "the day I'm legal, I'm outta here. I'll take every penny I've scraped together—it'll be a couple of hundred bucks—and I'm hitting the road. I'll get as far as Boston. Couch surf with some buddies until I get a job and get my own place. I'll be out of this nowhere town once and for all." He looked at Joel and nodded his head. "I promise you, I'll make a go of it. Once I'm out of here, I'll get a job, a real job, work like a sonofabitch. Life will be great. Eventually I'll head for New York City, or even California. I'll be that much further from this backwater scum pond. One month," he said between sips on the bottle, "and I'm flying out of here. This little shitville will never see me again."

"You're a big talker," Scott said.

"We all think like that," Zack said, "but none of us will ever do it."

Joel took a sip from the bottle and grimaced.

"Your little brother doesn't have your cast iron guts, Davey," Scott said.

"I'm going," David said, "I won't look back."

"You'll get homesick before you even hit Moncton," Zack said. Everybody laughed except David.

"You'll be second-guessing yourself soon as you hit the highway," Scott said, still laughing, "crying for your momma so bad you won't even be able to see the road."

"There's nothing here for me, I'm telling you, once I leave"—David took another sip from the bottle—"that's it."

"Why wait? Why don't you leave now?" Zack asked.

"I'm not running away like little kids do. I'm not going off to sulk for a while and then come back," David said.

Joel got up. "I'd better get going. I have some school shit to deal with."

David drained the last liquid from the bottle. "I'm leaving," he said. "When I go, no one or nothing is going to be able to force me to come back here."

Chapter 10

His mother sat on the couch. She folded the Harlequin Romance she was reading across her lap. "We'll be okay, I hate it when you talk like that, Rog."

Joel was spread out on the floor in front of the wood stove. His eyes were closed, but he wasn't asleep. He was tired from working at the bookstore. Saturdays were getting busier and busier. His father would be heading into work soon. Joel prayed that things would stay calm until his father was gone.

"It's the truth," his father said.

"Why don't we go visit your mother, she'd like that."

"She doesn't know anyone anymore. There's no point."

"She always knows you, Rog, she knows you're her son. She may not remember anything much anymore. But she knows who you are."

"Too long of a drive; this time of year is not good for a road trip." Joel's father took a drink. "You're right, though, she's no spring chicken. A change of scenery might do us some good. Maybe if a stretch of clear weather lines up with my days off."

"She's all we have left on your side. Except for Heather, of course." Heather was Roger's younger half-sister. Roger's father died when he was five and his mother remarried a few years after that. Heather came along when Roger was ten years old. Heather had flitted in and out of their lives at her convenience. Last they heard she was holed up at some commune in upstate New York, farming two acres of land with a disbarred lawyer and a crop of failed hippies. Joel remembered the Christmas card they sent to her last year came back, with 'UNKNOWN' scrawled across the address. Nearly a year later they hadn't heard from her.

"I'm not wasting a stamp on Heather this year," Joel's father grumbled.

"Your mother would love it if we went up."

"Forget it, can't afford to miss any shifts." He took a drink. "We can't afford it. Besides, she'd think I'd just be bucking to be kept in the will."

"Ha! She hasn't got a penny to her name anymore. The home has taken everything." Roger's mother had moved into a nursing home shortly after she became a widow for the second time.

Joel's mother swished her coffee cup and peered down at its deep blackness. "You could go. I can pick up some work at the hotel again. Christmas parties, New Year's coming up. They can always use the help."

"Gloria, it would be like visiting myself. She doesn't have a sweet clue."

"I think you need some time away from work."

"I'm waiting to hear about the flight medic job. I'm not going anywhere till that comes in. They should be letting people know soon. I'm in line for it. Seven bucks extra an hour will come in handy."

"The helicopter would be so cool," Joel said. "Flight paramedics go to the most wild calls, don't they?"

"The helicopter is dangerous," his mother frowned. "Look what happened in Kansas last month."

"That pilot was at fault. He should have known there were wires there. He shouldn't have tried to land."

"Why not the mill?"

"What about the fucking mill?" Joel's father smacked his fist into his open palm. "I am never going back there. What you don't get, what nobody gets, is that this is a calling. It's not a job. It's not for the money—it's a calling. Who else gets to say they save lives every single day? My boring job becomes a matter of life and death for the people I touch, the people I take care of. I remember when I decided that I had to become a medic. I just left a gig at a club in downtown Halifax. A drunk driver careered up on the sidewalk. He struck this young, happy couple. They were just out having a good time, dancing and having fun. The ambulance came and the medics rushed to help. The young lady was hurt the worst. And her boyfriend was panicked. The medics, all while they were treating the girlfriend, talked to him and reassured him that things were under control. That they were helping her. The boyfriend was so relieved. He was so grateful. All I could think was this lovely young couple had their whole lives ahead of them. The medics preserved that for them. They saved her. That's when I knew I wanted to be a medic. That's when I got my calling. And you want me to go back to a grunt job at the mill?"

"They are hiring. The retrofit is finished. It's good steady work, Roger, good hours, regular hours, good money."

"Yeah, seems to me I got my calling to be a medic right 'round the same time I met you and your new little baby." Roger swallowed a mouthful. "You go work at the mill then. I'm not taking any backward steps."

"For a few months, till winter's over. Take a leave of absence. It would be good to get on a regular routine. Regular hours. Regular sleep. Get rested and healthy again."

"Tell David to go work there. Or him." He pointed to Joel.

"I have a job," Joel said. "Plus I go to school. Jeez."

"Hey, David!" His father called upstairs, "Your mother and I think you should apply at the mill." He went to the foot of the stairs and hollered up, "They're hiring again." He sat back down. "He thinks I'm joking, but it would do him good."

"Okay, if not to your mother's then," Joel's mother said, "Maybe we can get away somewhere. Go to the cabin, you know, kick back at the lake." Gloria was referring to a camp at Loon Lake that had been in Roger's family for years. The last time they were there it was showing its age and the amount of attention they gave it lately. A leak developed in the roof and there was evidence of mice all over the place.

"You hate that place."

"You like going there. You always did, at least. It would be nice to get away, just the two of us."

"Nowhere till I hear about the flight medic job. That might be a good place to celebrate."

"You and me, Rog, the two of us. You remember? The fireplace? The rug? Just you and me, Rog. It would be good. Remember the chardonnay?"

"David!" Joel's father hollered again. "Now! I need to leave soon."

Joel lay on the floor and closed his eyes again, trying not to draw attention to himself. He shuddered and drew in his breath when his father went to the foot of the stairs.

"David, get down here." No response. His father kicked the bottom stair with his steel-toed boot. "Move it. I need to leave."

"Leave then," David yelled down from upstairs.

"Your mother and I want to talk to you."

"About what."

"Come down here."

"Dave," his mother called. "Come on down would you, honey? Your father's going on shift and we want to talk to you before he leaves."

David shuffled down to the middle of the staircase and let out an unimpressed sigh. "What?"

His father took a step toward the stairs, "I want to know about you, what you've been up to, what you're planning."

"Planning to leave this nowheres-ville shithole."

"David," his mother shook her head.

"Talk civil," his father said, "your mother is standing right there."

"Right." David said. "I'll be vacating this pleasure palace at my earliest opportunity."

"They'll be hiring at the mill soon. The retrofit is done. Why don't you try and get on there?"

"I think I'd rather pick up garbage."

"You think you can afford to be selective? You need to either get a job or get out."

"Rog, he needs some time," Gloria said.

"Time? How fucking much more time does he need? He's already loafed around here for months."

"Not months. I've been laid off for three weeks." David turned and headed back up the stairs.

"And before that they cut your hours way back. Did they know you were afraid of hard work?"

"The job was winding down. Whatever. I have plans."

"Does it involve earning money? Or is this grand plan of yours to keep sponging off me?"

"Plans," David grunted.

"I don't know where you got that mouth. I can't stand your disrespect. I want the details on your so-called plans by the time I go off shift tomorrow night."

"You'll be sober enough to come home?"

"David!" his mother was terse. "Stop."

Joel switched on the record player, some music would distract them, cool things down. Sarah Vaughan started to jump for joy.

"Listen, bub," his father's face reddened. "Instead of judging other people, look in the mirror. I got a job, I earn my keep." He gritted his teeth. "And I pay for yours."

David stomped up the last few stairs. "Don't worry about me," he yelled down.

"Gloria, your son has a foul mouth. And an attitude." Roger finished buttoning his shirt. "Where in the Christ does he get off talking to us like that?"

Joel turned up the volume on the stereo, hoping his father would be soothed by Miss Vaughan.

"That boy needs some old-fashioned hard labour to burn up that hateful energy. He's dangerous."

"He doesn't want to work at the mill, Rog. He's not interested."

"It's work. That's why they call it work. You don't have to like it, you just have to do it. You know, work, money, pay your bills. That's the way it goes."

"He wants to get a trade, you know he wants to go to college."

"If that's what he wants, why isn't he there?"

"Come on, Rog, you know why."

"Money?"

"Roger, stop."

"Vicious circle then, isn't it?" He left the living room and headed for the kitchen.

Joel hoped that putting Sarah on the record player would calmly whisk his father away with her to Key Largo.

"Did you pack the lunch I made for you?" Gloria asked. "It's in the fridge. Let me get it for you."

"Thanks, Glor. At least somebody takes some responsibility around here. Look at him," his father said as he walked by the living room where Joel was reading a book he had brought home from the bookstore—*The History of Jazz*. "At least he respects his elders."

"It says in here that when Charlie Parker died," Joel said, looking up from the book, "the doctor thought he was in his sixties."

"Yep. He ran his body ragged. He put it through the grinder."

"But he was only thirty-four years old when he died." Joel closed the book.

"Well he sure made those thirty-four years count," his father nodded.

Gloria passed him the lunch in a brown paper bag. "Here you are." She sighed. "You remember what it was like when you were David's age, Roger. It's even worse for kids today."

"Momma is making excuses for the momma's boy."

"It wasn't always easy for you. It took you a while to figure out what you wanted to do."

"He can't run around town doing whatever he pleases forever, sooner or later he needs to start earning some dollars. That is being an adult."

"You worry too much, Rog." Gloria leaned in to give him a hug and kissed him on the cheek. "Have a good shift. I'll work on him when you're gone."

"Ha, you know what Saturday nights are like. Wrestling with drunks." Roger slipped on his jacket and headed out the door.

"See you tomorrow night, Dad," Joel pointed to the record player. "You're right, by the way, this music is pretty good."

"Good?" his father said, heading out the door. "It's the best."

Chapter 11

When Joel got home from work on Sunday evening, he went up to his room. His mother was watching television and his father wasn't home from work yet. That would leave a couple of hours of peace. Joel thought he might be able to get some reading in and get caught up on some schoolwork. He started reading but dozed off.

He was awakened by his father's ranting. He got out of bed and started to head downstairs, stopping short at the bathroom.

His father stood in the bathroom doorway. He was breathing heavily and his face was red. Joel looked past him into the tiny bathroom. His mother was leaning over the toilet. Joel heard the gush of vomit going into the toilet bowl.

His father leaned in and struck her. *Slap.* The sound sickened Joel. Joel felt his own torment every time his father punched his mother. His torment had to be on par with the seething physical pain she must feel from the strike itself.

His father's watch caught her forehead when he backhanded her again. The watch had a large glow-in-the-dark dial. It's second hand moved with a definitive *tick.* It was perfect for measuring seconds when he was taking a patient's pulse or counting one of his patient's respirations. Here, the watch dug into his father's skin. A trickle of blood traced down his wrist.

Joel wanted to scream *Stop!* but he couldn't. He clenched his fists. He wanted to smash his father in his twisted angry face. He wanted to yell *Leave her alone!* at the top of his lungs. He didn't say a word to his father. Here was a man who helped other people when they were sick or hurt. A man who helped others in their time of greatest need. Here his father was, though, inflicting pain on this woman. On his own wife. Instead of screaming or striking out at his father, he reached out toward his mother.

"Here, Mom, let me help you," he said, and took a step into the bathroom.

"Mind your own business," his father said, blocking the doorway.

The bathroom was tiny. Too small for one person. Impossible for two. His mother slumped over the toilet to throw up again. She didn't say a word. Nothing. For the first time in months, Joel saw tears in his mother's eyes. This was the worst in a series of bad episodes. They were frequent, now. Blood oozed over her eyebrow.

Joel's mother spit into the toilet. She tried to clear her throat. "Please, Roger, please stop," she gasped though tears. "Please. Leave me alone." She sat cross-legged on the bathroom floor, her face crammed against the smooth, cold side of the vanity. The bathroom smelled like stale urine. In the distance, Ella Fitzgerald was asking "How High the Moon." As though she were assuring her audience that somewhere there's music. Joel could see his mother's eyes were closed and her head bobbed along with the tune. As if answering Fitzgerald's question, outside the small window, a full and bright moon hung high up in the sky on this clear December night.

His father steadied himself against the bathroom door frame. He drank deeply from his beer bottle. His face was distorted, he was unrecognizable as his normal self when he was this drunk. "Fuck you," he slurred to Gloria and spat on the floor.

"Dad, let me—"

"Stay out of this, you little shit," he said to Joel.

"Come on, her head's bleeding. Let me just—"

He shook his fist at Joel, "Do not make me." His voice was as cold and distant as the moon that dangled in the sky. He finished the beer and threw the bottle at Gloria's head. Gloria flinched at the crash of the glass. She did not open her eyes. They were swollen now and Joel wanted to run and grab some ice for her, but he didn't dare move. He didn't want to leave her alone with his father. The bottle bounced off her hands as they protected her face. It smashed to the floor. Blood oozed from her index finger knuckle where the bottle had struck.

Roger walked over to where she was sitting on the floor, leaning against cool porcelain of the toilet. He whacked her across the face again. Her head snapped back.

"Jeez, Dad." Joel tried to push his way into the bathroom.

His father turned around and pushed him hard on the chest. "Butt out." He turned back into the bathroom, "I got to piss," he said, "move it."

His mother moaned. She was sprawled over the toilet, hanging on to the cold, white porcelain.

"Move!"

His mother sobbed. She tried to move. She slumped down onto the cold, hard tile floor again. Joel couldn't tell if she was paralyzed in pain or in fear. Or both.

"Get the fuck out of my way, bitch!" His father's chest heaved with each breath. "You are the one," he slowed his speech. He exaggerated each syllable. "You're. The. One. With. God. Damned. Issues." He punched the wall to emphasize each word. The sheetrock cracked, then crumbled into a fist-sized hole. He stepped toward the toilet. She slouched against the porcelain. Roger took another step closer to the toilet. Gloria did not look up.

"Let me help her up, and then you can go," Joel whispered. His father turned around, his fist raised. Joel ducked.

And what will poor robin do then.

He raised his arm to cover his head.

"I told you to mind your own fucking business," his father barked. "She can get up on her own." He turned back to Gloria. "Can't she? I need to piss. Move." He stared at Gloria, and he unzipped his fly. "Move. Now."

His mother pulled herself up and sat crosslegged on the floor. Her head leaned against the wall. Her breathing sounded more like a faint yelp. It reminded Joel of a wounded animal. She struggled to get up.

"Let me help." Joel tried again to get past his father. Roger didn't budge.

"Get lost." His father reached down to his fly. "She's fine. She can get up on her own." He stepped closer to the toilet.

"If she wants to." He started to go, spraying in and around the toilet. Then he swayed his hips, spraying on Gloria. "I said move."

Gloria sobbed.

"Dad, stop. Leave her alone," Joel whispered.

Joel looked at his mother. He could see her physical body as it was crumpled on the bathroom floor, but he knew her mind and soul were elsewhere. Her thoughts were distant and far, farther than the soft yellow moon so high in the sky. He was sure he could see her head nod in a gentle rhythm, like she was listening to a beat, to a faraway tune. A smile crept onto her lips. The look in her eyes was vacant. Lonely.

His father finished his business and zipped up his pants. He turned and pushed past Joel. "I told her to move."

Joel bent down to help his mother up. Now the look in her eyes said she was in a place where things were settled and free. To Joel, she looked like she was somewhere there was music playing. She was in a place where only she could hear it. He tried to listen, too, but he couldn't hear it.

Joel heard his father's footsteps going down the stairs. Then the fridge door opened and he heard his father pop open another beer.

Gloria hummed along to some melody in her head. Her fingers moved, imperceptibly, as though she were playing an invisible harp. Joel thought she looked like she was slipping away, out of it, sinking into some place private and safe.

"Mom," he pulled on her arm, "let me help you up." Her fingers continued to pluck and strum the invisible instrument beside her.

Joel bent down closer to his mother and put his arm around her neck.

"Easy," he said, "I got you," Joel helped his mother to her feet. Should I call an ambulance, Joel thought. Or the cops? Oh, if I do, we'll all pay for that.

Downstairs, he heard his father change records on the turntable. A hiss, then scratches, and then Charlie Parker started playing "Lover Man." Soon the springs on the couch creaked, the unmistakable signal that his father had flopped down upon it. A tense, tentative calm settled on the household.

Chapter 12

David walked into the house and kicked off his boots. They were muddy. He smelled like campfire smoke. Joel knew that he must have been back at the shack. Joel could smell that he'd been drinking, too. His mother stood at the counter slicing some roast beef. She had taken a shower and was now dressed in a pink terry housecoat and her pink fleece slippers. Joel passed her some ice cubes wrapped up in a dish cloth. "Put this over your eye. For the swelling."

She didn't turn around. "Hi, honey," she said to David.

"Something the matter?" David walked over to his mother put his arms around her and hugged her. "Oh jeez, how bad did he get you this time?" He looked at her face and saw her eye. He towered over her and took off her Boston Bruins cap. He looked at her. She did not look up. "This can't go on anymore, Mom." He squeezed her tight and kissed her on the back of her head. "This has got to end right now or you'll end up dead."

"Oh David, let it go. This will blow over."

"Mom," David said, "he beat you."

Joel looked at David and shook his head. He mouthed the word 'no,' but David either didn't see or didn't agree.

"David, you know he's been going through a tough time. A bad spell."

"He beat the crap out of you."

"A few bad shifts, then he can't get a good sleep during the day, it all adds up. He doesn't mean it. Not any of it. Don't worry, honey. Please."

"This has to end," David raised his voice.

"Come on, David," Joel said, "back off her a bit, would you."

David thumped his fist on the counter. "You have to tell him to stop!"

"Tell him to stop?" His mother turned around and faced him. "Tell *him* to *stop*?" Her face grew angry, making Joel uncomfortable. "You don't think I haven't asked him to stop before?" Seriously? You're treading water in the deep end of the pool. You think you know everything. You're a teenager, a kid—"

"I'm eighteen in a few weeks."

"You're a baby." She brushed his cheek. "You don't know anything. Listen to me, David, we all go through that stage. Where we think we know everything. Everything looks like it has a simple answer. Well, life's not like that." She patted her forehead with the ice Joel had given her. She winced in pain. "Life's not that simple." She dabbed her eye with the ice. "Not something you can fix because you want to." The cloth was dripping as the ice melted. Streaks of water trickled down into her eye.

"Tell him to stop...?" she gave a soft laugh.

"Tell him you'll leave if he doesn't stop," David said.

"Right. And go where?"

"Anywhere—Penelope's, Halifax, a shelter. Anywhere safe."

Joel plugged in the kettle. "Cup of tea, Mom?"

"It's not that easy. Nothing is that simple. How would I live? What about you boys. School? Work?"

"None of that will matter if you're dead," Joel said.

"I'm not going to die, Jo-Jo." She forced a smile. "You don't understand. He doesn't mean anything by it."

Joel passed her a tissue and she dabbed at her eyes. For some reason, Joel took the tears as a good sign. She threw the tissue in the garbage and finished spreading mustard on the sandwiches. "Roger, your father, loves me. He loves you both too." She cut the sandwich in half. She put it on a plate and shoved it into David's hand. "Eat, you look skinny."

"He doesn't show it." David took a bite of the sandwich, "I'll be out on my own soon enough. Brainiac over there can go to college and live the dorm life. You could go live with Aunt Penny."

"Your father loves me."

"He beat the crap out of you. *Again*. That's not love in my books."

Joel went to the fridge and poured two glasses of milk.

"Look in the fucking mirror," David said, "I can't stand this anymore. Either you tell him you're leaving or I'll take care of it."

"David Edward Carruthers, you are not going to do a damn thing. You are going to eat your sandwich and forget all about this. We'll go on together to live our normal, civilized life. The life a of a hard-working, decent family. We're going to have a nice turkey dinner when you father starts his days off. We'll make a goddamn snowman in the front yard if the mood strikes us." She wrapped up the rest of the roast beef. "And you aren't going to do a thing except stop cursing."

She put the plate of meat in the fridge. She walked over to David and put her hand on his shoulder. "Promise me, honey, that you'll let this go."

Joel set one of the glasses of milk in front of David. "Come on, Davy, don't be so hard on her."

"It's not getting any better, it's getting worse. He hits you more often. He hits harder. He hits with more force all the time. The tooth? Remember? Now this? Is that what you call getting better?"

"You need to worry about your own situation. About getting a steady job, about spending some quality time with Jennifer, about your own life. Let this go. Stay out of this. I'll be okay."

"But it's not you alone. It's all of us, together. Look at him, too"—David jerked his thumb in Joel's direction—"Mr. Bookworm there and his seizures. They don't come out of the blue. He had another one the other day. Didn't tell you, though, did he?"

"Jo-Jo," his mother said, "is that true?"

Joel shot a look at David. "It was nothing, it lasted a few seconds. It was a focal."

"Oh, baby," his mother said. She wrapped him in her arms in a tight hug. "Oh, sweetie. We need to make a doctor's appointment right away."

Joel wriggled out of his mother's hug.

"That medication isn't working," his mother said, tears welling in her eyes. "We have to tell your father."

"Medication won't fix it," David said.

Gloria shook her head. "There's so much you don't understand."

"About Dad? That he beats you? That he's out of control? What the Christ is there to understand beyond that?"

"I'm telling you he loves his family more than anything. There's things you don't know, that you'll never know. Roger loves me, loves *us*, loves this family."

"I can tell."

Joel drank his milk and scowled at David.

"It's not him, David. That's not the person I fell in love with." Her voice cracked with emotion. "Your father is sweet, caring. This is temporary, I know it—"

"It's been going on for months. And getting worse like every day now."

"He's working through some things you don't understand. He has built a good solid life for his family."

"A good solid hell," David snorted.

Joel finished his milk. "Come on, we don't need you two going at it on top of everything else." He put his glass in the sink. "Please."

"He always settles down by the next morning. All those extra shifts. He regrets it when he realizes." Their mother looked upwards, as if grasping for the word. She looked at Joel, then David. "Tortured," she said, "your dad is tortured."

"Stop defending him and stand up for yourself," David raised his voice. "This has not been a wonderful life. That drunk has beat the crap out of you so much lately."

"David," Joel said, "this isn't going anywhere."

"Tortured is definitely the right word," David said.

Gloria ran the water at the kitchen sink and squeezed some dish soap into the water. She starting humming.

"Oh, for Christ sakes I can't believe this. This is hopeless." David turned and walked out of the kitchen. He shook his head. "Totally hopeless." He stomped up the stairs.

Chapter 13

Joel's father reclined on the couch, clutching a beer. The television was on the sports channel. The ever-present jazz record spun on the phonograph.

Joel was lying on the floor in front of the wood stove, flipping through a book. The sportscaster's voice was animated and raised in inflection, ascribing excitement to a mundane game.

"Bruins made a trade for some new kid from Saskatchewan," Joel's father said, speaking over the sportscaster and over the jazz solo from the record that was playing. "A real hot shot, apparently."

"Yeah?" David said. He stood in the doorway and nearly filled the whole door frame.

"Your mom was looking for you earlier, needs you to run an errand."

"Why'd you do that to her." David's hands were clenched at his sides. He slurred his words.

His father took a drink of his beer. "Things between a husband and wife are nobody's business but their own."

"Answer my question."

"You need to know your proper place, you little puke. Show respect to your elders."

"My proper place," David said, his face growing redder, "is to look out for my mother. If anyone in my family gets hurt, I'll take care of things."

"Don't threaten me."

"Not a threat. Fair warning. Stop hurting Mom."

"You know half the story."

"I know what I see and what I hear. You see her face?" A trumpet trilled from the record. The sportscaster screamed "Scores!" and a long celebratory foghorn blared from the television.

"David, go shoot some pucks in the driveway. See if you can aim good enough to hit a trash can. Burn off your hateful energy." Roger drank his beer. "Do it before I need to teach you a lesson."

"I'm ready for you, old man. Don't hurt her anymore."

Joel closed his book and stood up next to David. "Let it go," he whispered, "come on." Joel tried to edge him out of the room.

His father got up from the couch and drank down the last of the beer. He looked at David; David was a full two inches taller than his father. David was more muscular from years of working out and playing hockey. David was in control of his own body. By comparison Roger looked sick and shrivelled.

"You mind your place, hotshot. You might be king shit out on the ice, you might be able to throw your weight around out there, but this is my fucking castle, my fucking roof. I pay for this." He waved his arms around, indicating the whole house. "Mine!" His father drained the last mouthful from the beer bottle and smashed it down against the coffee table. Glass flew everywhere. "I'll do as I goddamn well please. You"—he took a step closer to David and jabbed a finger in his chest—"you do not tell me what to do."

David looked at him, his eyes were cool and fixed. "You hurt her again and I'll teach you a lesson."

Joel murmured in David's ear, "Come on, Dave, man, back off."

"I told you, that's no way to talk to your elders. No way to talk to your father."

"And I told you, hurt my mother again and I hurt you. Simple."

His father snarled his lip and mocked David with a forced laugh. "You think you might be able to take me, but you can't."

David shrugged. "Then I'll go down trying." Joel could see David's chest heave with every breath.

"Dave, let's go," Joel said, and nudged him toward the stairs. "Stay cool, man. You'll regret this down the road."

"You're a disrespectful bag of shit," his father yelled after him.

"Learned it from you!"

"Little weasel! I do and say as I please in my house."

Joel saw the veins on his father's neck bulge out. He edged David over to the stairs.

"Get the fuck out!" his father screamed. "Bastard!"

Joel pushed David towards the stairs. "Dave, you've got more self-control than him, I know you do."

CHAPTER 14

Joel sat at the kitchen table, eating a bowl of cereal, his face buried in a book. And he would love it, if only he could focus on it.

Roger downed his seventh beer since arriving home from work. "You know what," he said to Gloria as he walked into the kitchen, steadying himself against the counter. He reached into the cupboard above the fridge and pulled out the bottle of rum. He kept it up there for special occasions. "Your little bastard's right, you know," he slurred his words, "he has a valid point and he might not be right in everything he does and says, but on this one he has got a good point." He poured the rum into the tumbler and drank it down. "He is right that I should not continue. He is right that I should not go on this way." He poured himself another shot and drank that down and then chased it with his beer. "The boy has a fucking point." Spit flew as he talked and he wiped his mouth with the back of his hand. "Some of the things I've done in my life are not correct and not moral or upstanding; I'm not proud of everything I've done. But I believe that I have a right to be angry. He's right that I should not continue to do the things that I have done." He drank another shot of rum.

"The world," he screamed, "is shit." He threw the beer bottle to the floor and reached for another one. "Shit!" He screamed again. "It is not worth anything; it doesn't matter in the least." He reached for the bottle to pour another shot and stumbled and fumbled with it. "I don't know why?" He had tears rising in his eyes. "I don't get the purpose of this fucked-up existence on this fucked-up planet with a fucked-up job and a fucked-up family. I don't fucking get it." Tears rolled down his cheeks. "Gloria," he talked slow to enunciate his words, "I'll never understand any of this.

There's no point in going on. Nothing means anything." His eyes were hollow. He had trouble keeping his balance. "You tell me what the purpose of all this is." He flailed his arms, then put one arm out to steady himself against the kitchen table. He stared at the geese-shaped salt and pepper shakers in the middle of the table.

Joel thought he should move the shakers, for fear his father would sweep them off the table. Joel knew his mother cherished them; they used to be his grandmother's.

His father swayed against the table, like he was trying to focus. "You go ahead and define for me the goddamned purpose." He drank down the last of the rum. He hurled the bottle on the floor.

"Your little bastard son is right. I have never done anything worthwhile in my life. That's because I've been so goddamned busy working my ass off to keep a fucking roof over everybody's head that I don't have time to do anything else. I'll never fucking be able to work my way out of this."

"My life is worthless. It doesn't matter to a goddamned soul here if I am alive or dead. Life is a big piece of shit from the time you wake up in the morning until the time you go to bed. From the day you were born until the day your sorry ass leaves this godforsaken fucking planet. Nothing means anything. It is a useless fucking fool's pursuit for everyone. The ultimate dream? My ass. This is the biggest crock of shit ever. You mean to tell me that some goddamned fucking eternal being, some lowlife fucking scum that calls himself God, wants this shit? We're nothing but a Jesus freak of fucking nature. A goddamned accident when a bunch of fucking stars lined up the right way." He raised his hands in the air and waved them as though he was a magician. "And *ka-boom!* Next thing you know, you have people. Well I can tell you this is nothing but a cosmic coincidence of crap."

Joel stopped turning the pages in his book. He wasn't absorbing anything anyway. He no longer crunched his cereal. He hoped not to draw attention to himself.

His father continued, "It's cause and effect. The cause is that life is a piece of meaninglessness, grueling fate. The effect is that it should mean something. We think we're important. Well, we're not. What we are is fucked up the ass. Period. We're given the shaft and yet we go on smiling in our ludicrous little ways thinking that this is wonderful." He paused and drank from his glass. "Well it's not wonderful, it never has been and never will be. The idiots are the ones who stick around and try in vain to make it wonderful. I'm done trying. I give up. I have given it my best shot. I can't do this anymore. I need to beat the shit out of something." His hands were clenched and he kicked the box of empties beside the back door. The glass broke and rattled around inside the box. His mouth distorted into a snarl. "I need to pulverize something." His face was bright red. The veins on his forehead engorged.

"Jesus Christ." He slammed his fist down hard on the table. Joel flinched.

"Come on, Rog. Let's go to bed and get a good night's sleep," his mother said. "Come on, honey, I'll help you relax." She touched him on the arm. "Bed, Rog. I'll be waiting for you." She put her arms around his neck and kissed him on the cheek, then moved to the lips. She walked out of the kitchen and headed upstairs. "Come to bed, Rog. We'll find a way to fix all this." She went into the bedroom.

He kicked the beer carton again and the glass rattled around in it once more. Tears dribbled down his cheeks. "A fucking waste of time," he said out loud. He opened the fridge and took out another beer. He opened the cupboard above the fridge and poked around inside of it. "I know I had another bottle of rum up here." He went to the living room and turned on the record player. Charlie Parker was on the turntable. That sad and sweet sound drifted up and Roger started to sob.

Joel could hear his father talking to the turntable.

"You know, Charlie, you know what it's like, don't you? You remember. You remember that you ached when you said you could hear the music but never play it? I know what you mean, Charlie. I don't deserve to be here, I can hear the music in my head, Charlie, but I can't play it."

Joel headed upstairs. He crept by the living room, he didn't want to incite his father. His father spoke to Charlie Parker on the record player as though he were sitting beside him in the living room.

His father's words were slurred, but Joel could make out what he was saying. "I need to go somewhere there's music playing everywhere. Somewhere everyone can hear it. And where everyone can play it. Where they can reach it." His father looked at the record player. The record played and Charlie continued blowing his horn. "Right, Charlie?"

Chapter 15

Joel went up to his room. "Hey, man" he said to his brother, "that was tense."

"That fucking asshole irks me." David slammed the door of his dresser. "He irks me so fucking bad." He yanked the bottom drawer out. He dumped its contents on the floor. He pawed at the pile of sweaters. "Yes," he said as he pulled out a thin metal flask. "I knew I stashed this in here somewhere." He shook the bottle and it swished. He unscrewed the cap and downed the contents.

"Slow down," Joel said.

"I'm just getting started." He stuck an unlit cigarette in his mouth.

"Don't, Davey," Joel said, shaking his head, "please don't. That will just get him riled up even more."

David patted his pockets. He unzipped the pocket of his knapsack and peered inside. "You got a light?"

Joel shook his head. "Please don't."

"I've had enough of his shit." He riffled through the pockets of his jacket slung over the chair, pulled out a book of matches, and moved over to the window. "He thinks he's so tough." He threw open the window with such force that the pane of glass cracked down the middle. The glass stayed inside its frame.

"Jeez, Dave, come on." Joel went over and traced his hand along the glass. The vertical crack separated the window pane into two nearly perfect halves.

David struck a match and held it to his cigarette. "He's not going to stop. He gets worse and worse."

"It comes and goes." Joel grabbed a notebook from the desk and fanned the smoke toward the window.

David took a long drag and threw the cigarette out the window. "I've got to put an end to this right now." He ran out of the bedroom and thudded down the stairs.

Joel cautiously closed the window, and followed after him, shutting the bedroom door.

"You hurt her." David stood tall in the doorway and glared at his father. "You hurt Mom, you deal with me. This is a new day, I'm no little boy. I'm not a scared rabbit. Your days of beating people around are done."

"Your days in this house are done." His father picked up an empty beer bottle from the coffee table. He hurled it at David's head. David ducked. It struck the door frame and smashed. Joel covered his eyes.

"Get out!"

"You get out. You see what you did to her face?" David was flushed. His voice trembled. "You cut her one too many times."

"Mind your own business."

"My mother is my business."

"Don't get between a man and his wife."

"Don't hit her again."

His father snorted a laugh. "Or what?"

"Try me."

"You're all talk, big boy." His father picked up the remote control. He shook it toward David.

"Throw that at me and I'll shove it down your throat."

"You need to learn your place." He got up from the couch. He took a step toward David.

David moved out of the doorway and into the room.

Joel pushed his way in past David. "Come on," he said to his father, "let's watch the game. Need another beer, Dad?" Joel pulled at his father's arm to guide him back to the couch. His father wrenched his arm away.

"Ungrateful weasel." Joel could smell the alcohol that drenched his father's breath. "David, I'm warning you. Mind your own business. Get out."

"Think you can order me around?" David's chest heaved. "Fuck you."

His father pushed past Joel and lurched toward David. "Piece of shit."

David punched his father hard in the jaw. His father stumbled backwards.

"You little fucker." Roger stuck out his arms, waving them in the air to keep his balance. He braced himself along the wall to keep from falling.

There was a bang from the other side of the wall. Pierre's muffled voice shouted through the thin Gyproc. "Keep it down!" Pierre thudded the wall again. "*Crisse!*" he said, his French-Canadian accent strong. "Stop making so much noise. *Crisse!*"

His father staggered toward David and swung his fist. David blocked the punch with his left hand and drove his right fist at his father's face. It struck his chin. His father groaned. He tottered back and crashed against the wall. The force knocked David's high school graduation picture down and onto the floor. The glass smashed. His father tried to balance himself. He tried to catch himself from falling. He reached out against the wall; framed school portraits of David and Joel tumbled to the floor. Glass shattered everywhere. Roger tried to balance himself. His arms flailed. He knocked more pictures down trying to keep himself upright. Everywhere pictures tumbled to the floor. Broken glass crashed. The shards tinkled like a piano's highest C note when they landed on the floor. Photos of Roger and Gloria, taken years ago, at the lake. A picture of Joel, the day he won an award at school, now obscured by a starburst of broken glass.

His father caught his balance. He lurched toward David. David hit him again. His father went down. He struck the floor. His eyes rolled back into his head.

From next door, thumps on the wall again. "*Crisse!*" Pierre shouted. "Settle down over there! *Crisse! Tabernacle!*"

David was breathing heavily and wiped the sweat off his forehead. Joel could see his hands trembled. Joel stepped between him and his father lying on the floor. His father opened his eyes and moaned.

"Don't hit her again." David thundered out the front door. "I fucking mean it!"

Their mother came into the living room. She was holding a Danielle Steel book. "What's going on in here? Sounds like a war." Joel could see her eyes flash with worry, like she was thinking *here we go again*.

Joel crouched down beside his father. "Come on, let me help you."

He pulled at his arm to get him on his feet.

"Leave me alone."

He struggled to get up on his own, batting Joel away. He lurched and twisted each time he tried. He grabbed at the shelf and knocked over the statuette of Jesus with the exposed red heart. The statue's outstretched arms snapped off. "Your little bastard son hit me," he said to Gloria. He pointed to his jaw. "He hit me."

"Let me look." She dropped the book she had clutched like a shield. She took a step toward Roger, hoping his energy of anger was spent and there would be no slaps or punches. Roger's chin was scraped, blood oozed from it. "You got a big lump here," she said, feeling the back of his head, "do you want some ice?"

"The little fucker hit me, Glor. He's got no respect."

"Why don't you lie down, Rog. I thought you guys were watching the hockey game. And then all this?"

"Joel, buddy, grab me a cold one, would you?"

Joel headed for the kitchen.

"Better make it two," his father called out after him.

When Joel returned, his father was sitting on the couch, his eyes closed. The book his mother had dropped leaned against the door frame. A few minutes ago, David had leaned there. Joel placed the two bottles on the coffee table. He wanted to grab one and drink it down himself.

His mother was cleaning up the broken frames and pictures. She tucked the two broken arms of the Jesus figurine into her housecoat pocket. She cut her finger with a shard of glass. It was bleeding.

His father grabbed a beer. He twisted off the cap and guzzled it back without stopping. He put the bottle down on the coffee table and reached for his second.

"I brought you some ice, too." Joel held out ice wrapped in a dish towel.

"You should take it easy if you get bonked on the head." Gloria placed the few unbroken photographs back on the shelf. "You of all people should know that. Let me get you some coffee, or better yet some tea instead."

"Yep, tea, that's what I need," Roger said. "Tea. What I need is a handful of sleeping pills." He sucked down the second beer. "Or a thirty-eight to end this."

"Rog, stop." Tears welled in Gloria's eyes as she picked away at the broken shards on the floor. "Don't talk like that, please, it's not right. And not in front of him." She cocked her head toward Joel. "It scares me."

"Your precious little boy slugged me. That's not right, Glor. That's what is not right."

"Things came to a head, that's all. It's over now." She stood up and licked her finger where it was bleeding. "He's got a temper, you know that, he takes everything to heart. He doesn't—"

"Oh, he meant it. He meant every part of it."

Tears streamed down her face. "Do you?"

"Jesus, we've been through this a thousand times. I don't mean it. I never *mean* it. It's the job, it's the—things get to me, that's all. I never—"

"Well, David never—"

"I'm telling you, he meant it. He would have been satisfied if I'd keeled over on the spot." He rubbed his jaw again.

Joel held out the dish cloth. "Here, some ice."

His father took the ice and put it on the back of his head. He winced, and leaned over and looked at his jaw's reflection in the window. "He can't stay here anymore. There's no way." he said.

"He's staying here, Roger. You are not kicking him onto the street because of this."

"He needs to leave. Now." He looked across to Joel. "Grab me another beer, would you, Jo-Jo?" He held the beer bottle upside down and shook it, proving it was empty. "On second thought," his father shook his head, "bring me my rum."

Joel headed to the kitchen.

"And a glass with some ice in it." Roger threw the dishtowel down. "That's the only ice that'll cure me."

Joel heard his mother start up the vacuum cleaner.

"If you don't like it, you can go with him." His dad's voice was raised, loud and deliberate over the sound of the vacuum. "Both of you can get out." Roger's voice was as automatic and detached as a radio announcer introducing a long-forgotten single at three o'clock in the morning.

Chapter 16

As Joel wound his way through the path toward the shack, he looked up at the moon. It was big and white as it lit the way. As he approached, he could hear the voices of his brother and his friends. Joel thought the moon looked so close tonight. The words of one of the songs his father always played echoed in his mind. *How high the moon?*

Ahead, the rich scent of wood fire filled the air. The smoke curled out of from the rusted piece of pipe they had shoved through the roof of the shack to fashion a chimney for the equally flimsy stove they had made out of two fifty-gallon drums. Joel heard Scott and Zack giggle at a crude joke his brother must have made.

Joel entered the shack. "Hey."

David stood in front of the stove and peered into the fire. To Joel, he looked pale and had a vacant look that worried him.

"Hey Jo," Scott said.

"Swig?" Zack said, holding out his bottle.

Joel shook his head. "No thanks." He turned so only Scott and Zack could see him. He pointed to his brother and mouthed the question, *He okay?*

Scott shrugged.

Zack rolled his eyes. "No clue."

Joel nodded, but didn't say anything.

David moved from the front of the stove and held out his hand to Zack.

"Have a swig," Zack said. He passed him the bottle. "Rough day isn't it?" he asked David.

"It's fucked up," David said. He took a long drink. "He's an asshole to my mother."

"Yeah," Zack said, looking down at the dirt floor. "I know." Zack took the bottle back from him.

David lit a cigarette and took a drag. "Mom's pissing me off too. She needs to stand up to him. She was on the phone to her sister when I left. She'll need to get used to me not being around." He flopped onto the old couch. He held out his hand to take the bottle again. His knuckles were still red and raw. "The old man needed to be taught a lesson." He took another sip. "I'm hitting the road."

None of them said anything for a long time. After a few more pulls on the bottle, Zack said to David, "Where you going to go?"

"Away from here," David said, "and not coming back."

"It'll blow over. Stop saying that." Joel picked at wax droplets running down the side of a beer bottle candle. "You've got to stay."

"Who knows," David answered, "it doesn't matter. Nothing matters. I need to get out of here."

"I don't get it," Scott said, taking the bottle from Zack.

"You don't get it?" The liquor was taking hold of David. He raised his voice. "None of you get it." He drained the last of the bottle. "I fucking failed her. I should have stopped him." His voice trembled. "Man, this is so fucked." His eyes stayed clear, fixed on the dull orange flames licking out from the steel drum of the wood stove. He drilled the empty bottle into the fire. "Boston. At least at first."

"Jesus, David," Scott said, "I don't know all the ins and outs, but this is your old man's deal. And your mom's."

David reached for another smoke. Zack and Scott looked at each other. Scott said, "I don't get why you think you have to leave. Especially with no plans."

"I have a fucking plan. Boston is my plan." He flicked his spent match into the fire. "Look at me! What the fuck do you think I am turning into? Fucking look at me! I drink too much. I beat the shit out of someone in my family!" David's voice quavered. He grabbed Joel by the jacket and shook him. Their faces were less than an inch apart. David's mouth twisted into a sneer. "Who in the fuck does that remind you of?" He pushed Joel down onto the couch and stumbled out into the night.

Chapter 17

Joel was sound asleep when he was awakened by his bedroom window opening. David crawled in. Joel could smell the alcohol wafting from his brother.

David rummaged in the closet and pulled out an old canvas knapsack. "I'm leaving," he said, his speech slurred.

"I'm telling you this will blow over. It always does."

"Not this time. I already called Scott. He's coming to pick me up." He grabbed some socks, underwear and a few T-shirts from his dresser and stuffed them in the knapsack. He yanked some shirts off their hangers and shoved them in, then he swept some items off the top of his dresser into the knapsack as well. He tucked in a Polaroid photo of his mother, with a much younger, fresher face, holding him when he was a baby. He slid in a key chain, the pair of silver cufflinks his grandfather had given him when he knew he was dying. He stopped at a Bobby Orr hockey card shrouded in a plastic case. He looked at it and paused a moment. "Here," he said, "have this. Keep care of it. It will go up and up."

"I don't want your stuff. Why don't you go to Scott's and hang out there till things cool down?"

David picked up a glass ornament, a gift from Jennifer. It was a clown holding a bunch of lollipops like they were balloons. He put it back down and pulled out a red lollipop and unwrapped it. "Tell Jen I'll be fine. I'll call her as soon as I can."

Joel felt himself turn red as he remembered seeing her naked and on top of his brother. He swallowed. "Sure."

"Take care of her for me." David looked at his brother. "From a distance, though, don't be a perv."

David shoved a couple of pairs of jeans into the bag. He punched the clothes down so he could close the zipper. "I hit the fucker. Right on the jaw. Rattled him, too."

"He'll sleep off the booze and forget all about this by the time he comes around. You don't need to take off." Joel threw the hockey card back on his dresser.

"All this does," David zipped up the pockets of the bag, "is speed things up. I can't stay in this place any longer." He looked in the closet, grabbed a sweater. He picked up some books, hefted the weight of them and put them back down. He searched the rest of his drawers but didn't take anything out. "That's everything I need." He drew the last remaining zipper and went to the window. "You saw the bastard. He didn't even do anything. He's a fucking coward."

"He was piss drunk. He couldn't even stand up."

"No hitting back. Just lay there like a crumpled piece of shit. No screaming, no hitting back. A coward."

"Are you afraid he will come after you?"

"Let him. He's a fucking coward. He lay there in a sorry heap."

"You don't have to go." Joel moved over and stood in front of the window. "You never left any of the other times."

"Jo-Jo, if I stay here, one of us is going to end up dead. Either I'll kill him or he'll kill me."

"What if he stops?"

"Jesus, now you sound like her. Move it."

"It could happen. Maybe tonight will bring everything out? We can deal with it?"

"Like that will happen." He nudged Joel away from the window. "How many times have we heard that promise?" David slid the window open, and the bitter cold air blew into the room. Joel felt a part of himself, a part of his life, being sucked out into the night.

"A hundred," he said. "But what if this time he makes it? What if it stops?"

"The drinking or the hitting?"

"I don't know, but this isn't the way to do it, Dave, we need you. Me and Mom, we need you here."

"There's no other way. If I stay here, he'll take it out on Mom, or you. He's a bully and a coward. He won't come after me again." David slung the knapsack over his shoulder. "Promise me, Jo-Jo, *promise me* you'll look after Mom. He's got to stop."

"How in the Christ do you expect me to do that?"

"Club him over the head if you have to. Whatever it takes. You'd get off, it'd be self-defence," David laughed.

"Yeah, sure. Self-defence. Like I can take him."

"Call the cops. That's what needs to happen from now on."

"Then you promise me you'll stay away only until things settle back down."

"I can't. Boston's calling." David zipped up his jacket and put his hand on his brother's shoulder. "I have to do this."

"Let me know you're okay. I'll let you know when it's okay to come back," Joel said.

"Jo-Jo, I told you—"

"Let me know."

David slid out the bedroom window. The gentle breeze teased the tips of the maple's branches. He hopped out onto the porch roof, jumped down onto the front lawn. Peering down, Joel could see the headlights of a car approaching. Scott had good timing. The snow fell in soft white flakes. David climbed into Scott's car and disappeared into the white bleakness of the night.

Chapter 18

Joel woke up. Maybe David had a change of heart and decided to come back sometime through the night. He jumped out of bed. He looked at David's bunk. No, this wasn't a bad dream. David was gone. But he would be back, wouldn't he? Yes, of course David would be back soon. Where else could he go. He had to come home.

Joel went downstairs. He put on a pot of coffee, knowing he had to be leave for work in about an hour. While he moved about the kitchen, he could hear the phonograph turning in the living room. He could hear what he thought was the repetitive hissing of the album long after it had stopped playing its music. He knew his father must have fallen asleep on the couch.

He hesitated. Should he risk going in and disturbing his father? Everyone knew that on the best of mornings his mood could be unpredictable after a bout of such heavy drinking. What would his mood be after the drinking and the fight with David?

Joel walked to the living room. Something was not right. The room was cool and dark; the sun hadn't hit it. The window was open and cold air blew in. It gave the room a feeling of detachment that Joel could almost touch. The first thing he noticed was his father's Leatherman lying on the floor. Joel knew something was wrong. He once referred to his father's Leatherman as a Swiss Army Knife. His father had blown up at him. He had screamed *"It's a goddamned PST. This"*—he'd waved the knife blade at him—*"is a Personal Survival Tool or a Leatherman."* His dad had wrenched out the pliers and all the other attachments with deliberate disdain. *"Don't insult it again. Call it by its proper name. It's a Leatherman or a PST. It's a medic's best friend. It could save your life!"* Now, to see the Leatherman's blade open and the tool lying on the floor unattended made Joel nauseous. His father would never treat his equipment like that. His father's gear lying carelessly on the floor was every kind of wrong.

Then he saw his father sitting on the couch in a position that looked uncomfortable, unnatural. He looked stiff, as though he were posing for a photograph. He was sitting up, but tilted to his right, and his chin was pressed down on his chest. His arms dangled beside each leg. Joel's father looked like a big, life-sized stuffed teddy bear sitting cockeyed on the couch.

Then Joel saw the blood. First on the floor, then on the Leatherman's knife blade. Joel realized the Leatherman must have tumbled out of his father's hand. The knife struck the floor and lay where it was now. That's when Joel knew. Joel's chest constricted. He stopped breathing. He felt a dribble of urine run down his leg.

Joel knew from the puddle of blood at his father's feet. And then from his father's face. His eyes were wide open. They stared without expression toward the record player. His face was a bloodless grey. Joel knew his father was dead.

Joel jumped. "Jesus!" His whole body trembled. "*Jesus!*" He clenched his teeth. Tears rolled down his cheeks. He clutched his hair with his hands. He was crying. Panicked thoughts flooded his mind.

He backed away from his father. He needed to scream. He tried, but no words came out. He wanted to scream, *Wake the fuck up!* Instead, his mouth moved but no sound came out.

He backed out of the room. He tried to say something. "Mom," he whispered, "help." He turned and ran upstairs to his parent's bedroom door. Panting, Joel pounded with both fists on the door. "Mom, help!"

His voice shook. "Mom," he tried again. It came out louder this time. "Mom!" he said, pounding on the door. "It's Dad."

His mother's door flew open. "Joel? What's going on?"

"Something's wrong."

"What? What's the matter?"

"It's Dad." Joel panted to catch his breath. "He's on the couch. Slumped over. There's blood everywhere."

His mother pushed past him and ran down the hall. Her nightgown fluttered as she ran down the stairs. Joel followed her, his face ashen.

She barreled into the living room, stopped short and looked at her husband. She wailed.

Joel stood behind her, trembling. "His knife," he said, "he's not moving..."

Joel watched as his mother shook her husband's shoulder.

"Roger?" She dropped to her knees. "*Roger!*"

She collapsed into a sobbing heap on the floor.

Chapter 19

After the priest left, Joel's mother and aunt sat at the kitchen table. Joel went to the phone, picked up the receiver, and listened for the dial tone. "It's not hooked up yet," he said.

"God damnit, didn't they say it would be hooked back up?"

"I'll take care of it, Gloria," Penelope said. "I'll put the kettle on. Jo-Jo, I need you to go get those suit pants and put them on so I can hem them for you. I don't want you tripping down the aisle." Penelope had told Joel that she could take in his father's suit so he could wear it to the funeral. "We don't need any more calamities."

Joel came back down, the legs of the black suit pants dragging on the floor.

Penelope pulled out a chair from the kitchen table. "Okay, hop up." She scrunched up the waistband on his hips and nodded, "We'll need an inch or so taken in there." She pinned the hems up. "Okay, they're marked. Get them off and I'll start sewing."

He came back a minute later wearing his jeans again, his father's suit pants hanging on his arm.

Penelope poured the tea. "There are some things you'll need to decide," she said to Gloria, "hymns, scripture readings, you know."

"We can't do this till David gets back."

"You need to make plans. You need to get this done, hon. It's already been five days."

"Rog always said "Amazing Grace" was a great tear-jerker for a funeral. He always joked that he wanted them bawling their eyes out."

"Typical. Mr. Sensitive," Penelope said.

"And "The Lord is My Shepherd". He loved that psalm. Other than that, I don't care. But I'm waiting till David is here."

"Here's your tea." Penelope put the cup down in front of her sister. "Is there anybody else you can think of that we should call and let know?"

"The phone is still disconnected."

"Your neighbour has been so kind to help."

"I can't think straight at all, Pen." Gloria sipped at her tea. "I think everyone's been called. But it's a blur. It's like I'm on autopilot. I can't think. I just want David home."

"The notice was in the paper today," Joel said. "Anybody else that doesn't know will see it there." He was thinking of David.

"The whole town knows. Not like they couldn't with the sirens and lights and all the cops that were here."

"They thought it was you. You know, after how many times before?"

"Pen, don't. Please." Gloria sipped her tea. "He's gone, Pen." Her eyes filled with tears. "He's gone."

"You knew it was a matter of time. I can't shed too many tears. I'm sorry for you, Gloria, hon, I am. For you too, Jo-Jo. And God knows, for David. But it was only a matter a time before he'd have killed you, Gloria."

"Pen, please!" Gloria slammed her teacup down.

Joel jumped at the force.

"You don't know Roger like I know Roger. He doesn't mean it. None of it." She dabbed at her eyes. "Meant, I guess I should say. I can't get used to it."

"I know what he has done to you, and to the boys. If you ask me, if David hadn't run off, it would be his funeral we'd be planning and not Roger's."

Joel flipped through the prayer book the priest had given them to find some appropriate readings for the service.

"Stop," Gloria sighed. "You don't know that." She yanked another tissue from the box on the table. "You don't know what he was like. You dwell on the bad and the pain."

"I'm going by what you said, hon, everything you've told me. He would have broken David's neck if he was here. David was smart to take off like that. Christ knows what would have happened. He's unpredictable. He *was* unpredictable," Penelope cleared her throat. "With a streak of mean. I'm sorry for you, sugar, but not for him. I'd be a hypocrite if I said anything else."

"What about this passage?" Joel asked. "'Though I have fallen,'" he read, "'I will arise. Though I sit in darkness, the Lord is my light.'" He looked at his mother, his eyes welling with tears.

His mother nodded. "I like that, honey. It's fitting." She turned back to Penelope. "It's not easy. We had our ups and downs. Who doesn't?"

Penelope looked away from her and drank down her tea.

"Are you forgetting he took me and David in?" Joel's mother made a fist and tapped her heart, a gesture Joel knew from church. "With open arms?" His mother's voice cracked. "A week-old baby and no place to go? He gave us a chance when we had nothing."

"Gloria, that was eighteen goddamned years ago. Over the years he showed his true colours. He changed a lot since then."

"Who hasn't? Life changes you."

Joel felt the fabric of his father's suit pants. It felt shiny to him, shiny and sad.

"You know that as much as anybody," his mother said to Penelope.

Penelope picked up the suit pants that Joel had draped over the chair. "You should try and get some rest. It's going to be a hectic few days. I'll fix the trousers."

"I don't think I can rest anymore. I need to get moving, to do something, to stay active." Gloria looked around the room; she got up and walked down the hallway and peered into the living room. She looked at the couch and at the phonograph. She stayed in the hallway. The room showed no sign of what had happened in there. The police had suggested a company that specialized in cleaning up that type of mess. Thanks to Penelope she could afford the clean-up.

Penelope hummed "Amazing Grace" as she prepared her needle and thread. Joel was looking for more readings for the funeral.

"It's empty," his mother said. "Cold and empty. It's not home anymore. It's like you're in a familiar place, like you've been here before, but somehow you don't belong. That's what it's like."

"Too bad we couldn't play a rip-roaring Charlie Parker saxophone tune at the service," Joel said. "Dad would like that."

"Come have some pie, Gloria. Its ready." Penelope sliced a piece and placed it on the table. Gloria came back to the kitchen and sat at the table. She stared at the golden-brown crust and broke off a few flakes with her fork, but didn't eat any. "Where do you think he is?" she said out loud.

"Jesus, hon, burning in hell where he belongs."

"No," Gloria said. "David. Where do you think he is?"

"He'll be okay wherever he is."

"I wish he was here right now." Tears thickened his mother's voice.

Joel looked up from his book. "David will be back." He closed the book; the words were meaningless to him now, black marks on a white page. "As soon as he hears something through the grapevine, he'll be back."

Penelope massaged her sister's shoulders. "He'll be here, sis, soon as he finds out. He'll call. He'll come. I know you're worried. It will work out. It always does."

"No, it doesn't. It doesn't always work out. Not for me anyway." His mother snatched another tissue and blew her nose. "My son is gone and I'm planning a funeral for my husband." She balled the tissue in her hands. Her lips started to quiver. "Everything's a mess. How could he do this to me, Pen?"

"You don't want to know what I think about Roger or how he could do things to you."

"I know what you think of Roger. But you've got to remember, I prayed every night after Kevin was killed." Gloria looked up at her sister. "I prayed for God to please send me someone to help me through this. I would hold that little baby. I would rock David in my arms and pray for help." Joel's mother balled up the tissue in her hand. "I promised Jesus I'd dedicate my life to the man he saw fit to send to me."

"It's not going to be easy. You can get through this. I know you can. You can and you will. Look what you've been through already. You've always made it."

"This is different, Pen. You know it is. This time it's different."

"You have me and Jo-Jo."

"And David," Joel said. "He'll be here."

"I need him, Joel. You two are all I have now."

Chapter 20

Joel wore his father's navy-blue suit. Aunt Penny had done a perfect job hemming the trousers, but the sleeves of the jacket hung down and partly covered Joel's hands. He was constantly pushing them up at the elbows.

Joel's mother wore a red dress and a black overcoat. Tied around her neck was a black scarf with red roses on it. "Roger always liked me to wear this red dress," she had whispered to Penelope. "Do you think it's disrespectful?" She smiled, "Because he always said it made him horny when I wore it."

"You look fabulous, sugar."

"Amazing Grace" strained on the church's organ and sounded painful and hollow.

Joel had one thought occupy his mind. Did David know?

St. Francis Assisi Church was cavernous. Even though the seats were filled, it seemed empty, like something was lacking.

Joel and his mother followed the coffin as the undertaker pushed it down the long aisle. The pallbearers walked behind it, identical in their dress uniforms. Joel remembered seeing his father wear the same uniform to funerals and ceremonies over the years. Aunt Penelope linked her arm in Gloria's as they walked together to the front of the church. Joel walked alone behind them. He thought his brother should be walking beside him. David's absence magnified the sombre bleakness.

It was quiet except for the occasional creaking of the floorboards as people shuffled from one foot to the other as their small procession passed. As the pallbearers moved down the aisle, their polished black boots struck the floor in unison, like a slow and steady heartbeat.

His father is gone. David is gone. One could come back and hadn't. One could not come back, yet was in front of him in a gleaming wooden box. Joel had been at this church many times. He remembered church as boring and he would get fidgety. When they were younger, he and David would entertain themselves and occasionally burst into a case of the giggles. But now, this was the first time he remembered church being sad. And never before had he sat in the frontmost pew.

The service neared its conclusion. His father's casket was wheeled from the front slowly to the back of the church. Discreetly guided by the funeral director, the family, so small now with David absent, filed behind the casket. He could see his mother's head bent forward; Penelope draped her arm around her for support and comfort. Joel looked straight ahead at the necks of his mother and aunt. He chose not to consider any of the faces that peered out from the edges of the pews. He avoided travelling eyes that searched to make contact with his.

The priest chanted more prayers at the back of the church. He waved a censer full of burning incense over the coffin. Designed to rise like prayers, Joel thought, like his father's soul should be. His mother and aunt filed along behind the box that contained all that was his father. Outside, the pallbearers slid their colleague's remains into the hearse. The burial, the undertaker told them, would take place in the spring once the ground had thawed.

Joel stood beside his mother and aunt. They stared after the coffin. The finality of that action settled on Joel like the penetrating cold of this winter's day. His mother's rose patterned scarf billowed around her neck as they stood on the steps of the church. Penelope was at her sister's side and their breath was visible in the cold air. Joel's mother clutched the bouquet of red roses that had adorned the top of the coffin.

Overhead, the sleek LifeFlight helicopter thudded low and loud and came into view through the clouds. The helicopter circled over the church, its huge fuselage a vibrant red and white, and tipped its nose low in a sombre salute to a fallen colleague. Its big rotors thwacked the air *whump-whump-whump*. The rotors drowned out all other sounds. The air smelled of jet fuel. Joel felt the vibrations beat in his chest like a pressure on his heart.

The presence of the helicopter invoked power. Joel recalled how his father always said its arrival triggered an adrenaline rush. The helicopter created urgency. Joel's father, and all the other paramedics, referred to it as 'The Bird.'

It was a hot call. We needed to bring in The Bird.

Joel smiled at that. His father would appreciate the irony. The only sound that could be more bittersweet would be if that big bird blared out a Charlie "Bird" Parker solo as it hovered over the church. Joel looked up. His mind was already crammed with questions, but there was room for yet one more. What if his father had gotten the flight medic job? The tears that tickled down his cheeks surprised him. He thought he was all cried out days ago.

His mother clutched his hand tighter. Her shoulders heaved as she sobbed.

Chapter 21

In the basement of the church after the funeral service, Joel, his mother and Aunt Penny shook hands or hugged the mourners who lined up to greet them.

Jennifer, David's girlfriend, came up first.

"Do you have any idea at all where he might be?" She was crying. Her eyes, usually a dazzling blue, seemed dark and distant to Joel. Beyond sad, she looked pale and frightened. Her hands were shaking. "I need him." She hugged Joel and whispered in his ear, "It's urgent, Joel. I need to talk to him. Help me, please."

"He'll be back," Joel whispered, his voice breaking.

Mrs. Payne came up and Joel introduced her to his mother and aunt. "Mom, Aunt Penny, this is Mrs. Payne. She's not only our best customer at the store, she's also my favourite."

"I'm so sorry for your loss." She gave Gloria a hug. "This is a fine, fine boy you have here." She rubbed Joel's arm and clutched his hand. "Now remember, young man, if you need anything, and I mean anything at all, you come see me." She turned and moved away, allowing the other mourners to greet the family. "Anything, Joel." She clutched her linen handkerchief, her initials monogrammed on it in a flourish of burgundy.

Mr. Pritchard came up next in line. His white bow tie peppered with big orange and black polka dots seemed out of place. Joel thought that it belonged with a clown's costume at a Halloween party more than at a funeral.

"Mrs. Carruthers," he shook Gloria's hand. "I'm sorry. At least he's..." his voice trailed off. "Take as much time as you need, Joel. I understand this is difficult." He shook Joel's hand. "We'll be fine at the shop without you. But, if you're able, if you could be back by Saturday, that would be good. If you're up to it. I'll understand, of course, but all those Christmas shoppers," he chuckled, "they don't stop for anything." Pritchard shuffled away, his eyes focused on his feet.

Penelope turned her car onto Palmer Court. "Do you think he's come home yet?" Gloria asked.

"I asked Scott and Zack to let me know as soon as they know something," Joel said. "No one's heard a thing."

"The funny thing is," his mother said, "that if Roger were here, he'd know exactly what to do."

Once inside, Joel put a pot of tea in the middle of the table. The house felt hollow, strange with emptiness. Gloria and Penelope sipped at their steaming tea. Its tangy scent of peppermint filled the air.

Joel noticed the ticking of the second hand of the clock above the stove. Out on Forest Road a lonely siren wailed down the street. A dried brown leaf skittered across the kitchen window and hooked onto the screen. The leaf fluttered with every breeze. Then, with one big gust, the leaf fluttered and broke free from the screen. It tumbled away through the air.

The north wind.

The clock grew louder. Neither his mother nor his aunt said anything. They sat at the table, each lost in her own thoughts. Joel felt that the space between the clicks of the second hand grew longer and longer.

Joel heard a vehicle pull into the driveway. He hoped it was David as he went to the door. Behind him, his mother sipped her tea, seemingly oblivious to the ambulance's diesel engine throbbing outside.

Joel opened the door to find a man in a paramedic uniform, head bowed. It was Jenkins.

"Hey, Joel."

"Come in," Joel said, and lead him into the kitchen.

"Afternoon, Mrs. Carruthers," Jenkins nodded to Joel's mother. "Afternoon, ma'am," he said to Penelope.

Gloria took another sip of her tea. "Anthony," she said, "come, sit down."

"Tea?" Penelope said.

"I can't stay long." He leaned against the counter. "I didn't get a chance to talk to you at the funeral. I wanted to—"

Joel could see tears well up in his eyes. Joel poured a cup of tea and passed it to Jenkins anyway. He held it with both hands. His hands trembled. He took a mouthful of the tea. "I wanted to say how sorry I am. It's awful."

He paused, gathering himself.

"Sorry we had to leave before the service was over," he continued. "We had to get back on duty. A lot of medics and units were there. We were on duty. They were stacking calls. There was barely any coverage in three counties. All of us were fighting to be able to attend. But we drew the short straw and had to respond to a call."

He took another swallow of the tea.

"Roger was a great healer. Such a good medic to work with. He was my mentor. My first regular partner. He taught me so much."

"Thank you," Joel's mother dabbed at her eyes.

Penelope nodded.

"Working with him, we got close, me and Roger. I can't believe it." Jenkins chugged back the rest of the tea in his cup. "I'm so, so sorry..."

"We're all still in shock, honey," Penelope said.

"Yeah, I know, but for me, I should've known. I should've seen it coming. I'm a medic for Christ sakes."

Chapter 22

"Hey guys," Joel called as he walked into the shack. "Take a look at this!" He held up the end of a yellow extension cord. "I plugged the other end into the outdoor outlet on Mr. Robinson's garage. David gave me the idea a while ago."

"Cool," Scott said. "We're getting civilized."

Scott and Zack went outside and peered down the path that lead out to the road. Joel followed them out. "See," he pointed to the yellow cord snaking down the path, "we've got power!"

"I'm assuming Mr. Robinson is unaware of his generous donation of electricity?" Scott said.

"He is totally unaware," Joel laughed. "I had to use two cords. But I duct taped them where they join together." He grinned and held out a box of Christmas lights and a radio. "I also grabbed these from home. Let's go get a tree!"

A short time later they dragged in a spruce tree and propped it up in the corner. Joel wrapped the Christmas lights around it. "This place is jollier already." He plugged in the string of lights.

"Very Christmassy!" Zack said. He pulled out a bottle of Southern Comfort. "To our small but merry looking Christmas tree!" He twisted off the cap and took a long drink. "Here, boys," he said as he passed the bottle to Joel.

Joel took a drink from the bottle. He shut his eyes and shook his head. "Wow, that's got a kick."

Zack drank as well. "Makes me feel like we should sing some carols."

They all laughed. They passed around the bottle until it was empty.

Scott sparked up a joint and they all took turns smoking it.

"I'll turn on the radio. Get some tunes going." Joel plugged in the radio and tuned into Moncton's Magic 104.

Scott fished around in his knapsack and brought out a bottle of Dr. McGillicuddy's Fireball Cinnamon Whisky. "Here boys." He held it up to the Christmas tree. The lights reflected in the bottle. "Some more Christmas cheer!" He took a long drink and they shared that bottle too.

They laughed again. The radio blared out Tom Petty. He was telling them they didn't know how it feels.

They finished the second bottle. The lights on their Christmas tree started to flicker. The radio cut in and out.

"Maybe the connection's loose." Joel reached over to fiddle with the plug. "Holy shit! That's hot." He dropped the cord.

The lights flicked a final time and went out, immersing the shack in darkness. The radio gave a squeal of static then went silent.

"Must have come loose where the two cords were joined."

"Or somebody unplugged it from that garage," Scott said, standing up.

"Let's go check," Zack said. They went outside and started down the path that lead back towards Palmer Court.

"Oh fuck," Joel said. In the distance they could see orange flames flicking up over the trees. A puff of thick black smoke curled up from the garage at the end of their path. Joel yanked the extension cord as hard as he could. He reeled it up as much of it as he could on his arm. "Let's get out of here!"

All three grabbed their coats and bags from the shack. They took off, running in the opposite direction from the garage on fire. Joel dragged the extension cord behind him as he beat it through the woods. The place where Joel had joined the two cords together and wrapped with duct tape was a blackened, molten mess of copper and yellow plastic. Joel yanked the remnants of the extension cord and wound it up over his shoulder.

They ran as far as the stream. Joel balled up the extension cord as much as he could and heaved it into the bushes. They agreed to split up and go their separate ways to get home. In the distance they heard the fire engines heading toward the garage.

Joel decided to walk along the stream toward the old foundry. He figured he would take the long way home. Scott and Zack each went up towards the highway and would circle back.

Joel was getting cold. He buttoned his jacket and pulled his toque down over his ears. He started to feel the alcohol take hold. He felt like throwing up but resisted the urge. A walk around the trail had always been an adventure in solitude for Joel and he enjoyed it. It re-energized him. The fresh air would do him good.

He walked past the ruins of the foundry; its tumbled down walls were covered with frost. He slowed his walking. He wanted to catch his breath. He sat down on the rock wall. He heard a gentle sound in the woods behind him. Was it *hoo-hoo?* An owl? Or was it *Jo-Jo?* Was someone calling him? Joel stood up, wobbled and tried to stay as still as he could.

He heard it again. *Jo-Jo.*

The hair on his neck bristled. Goosebumps broke out on his arms. He swallowed hard. The Southern Comfort and Dr. McGillicuddy's surged in his throat. The moon ducked behind a cloud and cast the whole scene into a dim, dusky shadow. Joel felt like he was on the sound stage from a 1950s black and white horror movie.

Jo-Jo. Jo-Jo.

Joel's heartbeat pounded in his ears. He felt like passing out. He became conscious that he was holding his breath. *Jo-Jo.* He froze on the spot. Was there a shadow moving behind some crumbling boulders? A shimmering figure moved toward him. Joel's hands trembled. "This is not real," he said to himself. He took the mini cigar he had stolen from his father's bureau and plugged it into his mouth. His lips quivered. He struggled to light a match his hands shook so bad.

Jo-Jo, the voice whispered, *listen to me.*

Jesus, Joel thought. The match lit. He drew a deep breath of the rich, rum-tinged tobacco. He squeezed his eyes shut. "You're not real." He opened his eyes and turned his head to where the voice had come from. The moon emerged from behind the clouds. The shadow shimmered. Bushes rustled. Joel thought he could see a figure. Was it a ghost? No, ghosts aren't real. What then? Was it his father?

Jo-Jo!

"Dad?" Joel said out loud. He staggered closer toward the shadow. He slurred his words. "You're freaking me out."

He looked at a boulder on the ground. He was sure he could see two sunken spots that were the eye sockets on a skull. It was a boulder though, right? Yes it was a boulder. A god-damned talking boulder. "I'm drunk, I'm high. You're not real."

I need you.

"You're not real. I'm hallucinating." A wind blew through the trees. The bushes swooshed in the breeze. "Maybe I passed out? Maybe I'm dreaming?" He drew in a breath from the mini cigar. He coughed. "Nope, I'm awake for sure." He coughed again.

In the distance he could hear a dog bark followed by another more distant dog's lonely reply.

Tell your mother I'm sorry.

"What the serious fuck? Tell her yourself." Joel's words were incoherent. He stood wavering in front of an old building and its crumbled section of wall. The ground was covered in snow and the old stones were weathered. Maple tree saplings and young evergreens grew here and there along the former wall.

Tell her I love her.

"I'm supposed to tell my mother I was strolling around the old railway car factory in the middle of the night after burning down a garage, corked out of my mind?" Joel had trouble keeping his balance while he was addressing the pile of rubble. "And by the way, I bumped into the ghost of dear old dad and, oh yeah, he's fucking sorry? How fast you think they'll lock me up in the loony bin after I blurt that out?"

The moon disappeared behind some clouds. The shadows on the rocks deepened. Joel sat down on the wall again. "Everything's a shit storm. David's gone. Aunt Penny's heading out to the West Coast. And I'm talking to a pile of fucking boulders in the middle of the night."

I'm sorry.

"Fuck you." Joel drew deep on the cigar. The wind rustled behind him. Joel held out his hand. "Stop. Don't get any closer." He closed his eyes. "I'm trying to get over you, to get through all this, and presto you just show up?"

Tell her I'm sorry.

"Tell her yourself! Leave me out of your shit. Why are you always dragging me in between you two?"

Joel's ears were frozen. He pulled his toque down tighter on his head. His fingers grew numb. Snow whisked across the broken stone wall as the winds picked up. Joel slowly got to his feet.

"Where is David!" Joel threw the lit cigar at the pile of boulders. He kicked out, his boot sliced through the shimmering shadows and struck the rock hard. Joel winced in pain.

"Don't leave me again, you bastard," Joel screamed. The vision faded before his eyes. He could feel himself crying, the tears streaming down his cheeks.

"Don't leave me here by myself." Joel was crying now. "Don't leave me here to become a fucking nutcase." He searched the crumbling walls. His eyes moved fast left to right. Joel was now sure there was nothing. In the distance the dogs brayed at the moon.

The owl cooed a soft *hoo-hoo*.

"Where is David!" Joel screamed into the darkness.

Hoo-hoo.

"I need him." Joel kicked at the stones in the wall. "David!" He kicked at the wall again, then sank to the ground. "David! I need you!"

Chapter 23

"I will be here for you, you know that. I mean I have to go back to Truro to pack up," Penny said as she dragged her suitcase toward the front door. "I can take more time off in a couple of weeks. I'll be back soon. But I'll be here for you, whenever you need me, whatever you need me for, at least for the next week or so." She peeked out the front window to see if Frederick had pulled up yet.

"You know I promised Frederick I'd be there for him too. We've sunk everything into this opportunity. We sold the house, land, everything. We're risking it all for this new venture. San Francisco is the future. It's going to be fantastic."

"Cool," Joel said, filling a glass of water at the kitchen sink. His hands were shaky. He didn't feel well. This hangover was brutal. "There's amazing things happening in Silicon Valley. Remember your broke nephew when you strike it rich."

"I'll be back for Easter. I'll check in on you guys. You'll make it through okay. I'm sure of it." She gave Joel a hug. "We're the all-time egg finding champs. We'll work our magic again at Easter. I promise."

"Hey, see if you can get Lawrence Ferlinghetti's autograph for me." Joel swallowed some headache pills.

"What?"

"Lawrence Ferlinghetti. The poet? He started City Lights Bookstore?"

"Oh. Okay, Jo-Jo."

"City Lights. It's only one of the most famous bookstores in the world. All the cool hippies hung out there. You must know it, Aunt Penny, you of all people." He went upstairs, and returned a moment later with a copy of *A Coney Island of the*

Mind. "See if you can get this guy to sign this for me, will you? There's magic in that bookstore."

"Which bookstore?"

"City Lights? It's a San Francisco landmark? Jeesh, and I'm the one who knows nothing."

Aunt Penny shook her head. "Nope, sorry."

"Penny, you don't need to worry about us," Joel's mother said. "We'll be fine."

Fine? They couldn't even pay the phone bill or electricity bill when his father was working; where were they going to be in a month's time. Out in the street because they couldn't make rent most likely.

"I'll be able to work more, too, mom," Joel said. "We'll be okay."

"I paid your phone bill for you, Gloria. Your phone is working now."

And what about the rent? Did they think Pierre would wait forever?

"Pen, you didn't have to do that, you didn't need to bail me out." Gloria's words were slow and deliberate, as though she needed extra time to gather her thoughts.

"I did it for David. He'll call soon, I know it."

Joel's mother stood behind the chair at David's usual place at the kitchen table. She hesitated a moment and rubbed her hand on the chair back. Then she took a deep breath and pushed the chair back in and sat down at her own spot, the end opposite of where Roger would have sat.

"Can't you just see David stuffing a handful of Jujubes in his mouth right now," Gloria said. "Always munching on those. Lucky, he didn't give himself diabetes."

"He's a chipmunk with those things," Joel laughed. "If—and that's a big if—he'd ever offer you some from his little brown paper bag, never take any of the black ones." Joel felt his voice crack with emotion. "He'd squeeze your hand till you dropped it."

"Take orange or yellow," his mother laughed too. "'Leave me the black ones. They're the real licorice.'"

They all smiled.

"I might go back to the Mansion Inn. They're always busy over Christmas. They'll bring me in for a few shifts." Joel's mother looked around the room. I'll be up and running in no time." She looked around the room again. "I'll make it," she said. "Joel and David and I will make it." Her words were garbled.

"You feeling okay, hon?" Penelope asked.

The phone rang.

"Please, God," his mother raised her eyes to the ceiling and whispered a prayer, "let it be David." Her face contorted into a lopsided frown.

Penelope got up to answer it. Gloria raised the cup up to her lips but didn't take a drink.

"No, she's not," Penny said as she turned her back to Gloria and talked into the telephone.

She sat back down, across from Gloria. Gloria was staring straight ahead, her eyes locked on nothing specific. She didn't blink.

"Nova Scotia Power," Penny said. "I told them you'd call them back."

Gloria dropped her teacup. It struck the floor and shattered.

"Oops," Penelope said, bending over to pick up the pieces, "let me get that."

Gloria didn't respond.

"It's no biggie. I'll make you another cup."

Gloria was motionless.

"That cup didn't have sentimental value, did it?" Penelope picked up the most intact piece and started putting the smaller fragments inside it.

Gloria never answered.

"It wasn't sentimental, was it, Gloria?" Penelope looked up at her sister. "Gloria?"

Gloria's eyes rolled back in her head. She slumped down in her chair. She slid onto the floor.

"Joel!" his aunt screamed, "call 9-1-1!"

His mother slid further down onto the floor. Penelope scooped her up in her arms. "Call an ambulance!"

Chapter 24

The doctor stood at the foot of Joel's mother's hospital bed. He read her chart. Joel noticed the deep frown on his face.

"Your mother," the doctor glanced at Joel before turning to Penelope, "your sister, has had a stroke." He flipped the pages in the chart and looked up. "It's too early to tell what her prognosis is. But the next few days will be crucial."

"Will she come out of it? Like will she be able to talk again?" Joel's voice shook. He wasn't sure if he wanted the answer.

"She's got a long road of recovery ahead of her. We've given her some medication to help break up, and prevent, blood clots. Her brain's been injured; it's early yet to know how much she'll recover. But she has things going for her. She's relatively young, and fairly healthy. All that helps. She may need to make some lifestyle changes. Alcohol, smoking, the usual. It's going to take some time."

Joel looked at his mother in the hospital bed. The array of tubes and hoses and IV's was overwhelming. His father would have been able to explain what all this meant to him, no problem.

"How long do you think, before she'll talk? Can she understand us?"

"Yes, she can hear and very likely understand. Her brain's been assaulted. It needs time to heal."

"See Jo-Jo, no swearing then, your mother will know." Aunt Penny forced a smile.

"What about you?" the doctor asked. "Your aunt has told me some of what you've been through. I've arranged for someone to come talk to you. And you will need to see your neurologist. I can help arrange that too." He patted Joel on the shoulder. "We need to take care of you as well."

Chapter 25

Joel paced outside his mother's room. A woman carrying a leather portfolio walked up to him.

"Hello," she said, extending her hand. "I'm Cynthia Fowler. I'm with the department of community services."

"Hey. Dr. Bradbury said you'd be coming to talk to me."

She led Joel into a consultation room and closed the door. "We can talk in here."

They sat down. She flipped open her file and checked the notes, then closed the folder. "Things have been quite rough for you lately. Want to tell me what's been going on?"

Joel mentioned his father's funeral and how his mother had just slumped down to the floor while they were talking.

"And your brother?"

"He'll be back soon," Joel nodded.

"Have you heard from him?"

"Not recently."

"Here's the concern, Joel. I checked with your school. You've missed a lot of time. Your grades have been slipping. Your illness isn't under control."

"I can pick up my grades."

"This isn't just about grades. Your father has passed away. Your mother's in hospital. She is incapacitated and not able to take care—"

"The doctor said she will get better."

"Yes, her prognosis is cautiously optimistic. But a lot can happen; it's early yet. And a full recovery is going to take some time."

"She's getting better."

Fowler turned over a page in the file folder. "Your aunt is heading to San Francisco. Your grandmother has dementia and is in a long-term care facility in New Brunswick."

"My aunt isn't leaving until tomorrow."

"You have no other close relatives, and your brother has left home. And nobody knows where he is."

"My brother is in Boston."

"When we look at it all, Joel, we're going to have to set you up in care."

"In care? You mean a foster home?"

"Yes, we need to ensure—"

"You can't." Joel stood up.

"Joel, it will only be temporarily—"

"My brother's coming back."

"Maybe he is, Joel. But he didn't come back when your father passed away. He's not here now, and we know he told his friends he's going to Boston to get a job. We have to conclude that's what he's done. He's an adult, and in the eyes of the law, you are not."

"I can take care of myself."

"Not according to the law."

"Aunt Penny can look after me." He sneered, "She can be my babysitter."

"She's flying to San Francisco."

"I'll get her to stay with me until David gets back. And when David comes back, that means everything is fine? He's an adult, legally, right? I won't need to go anywhere?"

"Yes. If David comes back, that may work. But in the meantime, I'm going to start working on finding a suitable place for you once your aunt leaves. I'll check up on you the day after tomorrow."

Joel swept the file folder off the table. "David will be back!" Papers fluttered to the floor. "I'm not going to a fucking foster home. I'm not an orphan off the goddamn street."

Chapter 26

Frederick beeped the horn twice when he pulled into the driveway. Joel carried out Aunt Penny's suitcase.

"Give me a hug, Jo-Jo."

"Have a safe trip," Joel said. "I'll keep you posted on Mom."

"I hate to leave you, honeybunch. I just have to. Things will work out. Soon as I get Frederick set up I'll be back, sweetheart." She hugged him again.

"For Easter?"

"No, sweetie pie, before that. In a week or two. The second I can, I'll be back."

Joel waved as they pulled away. He returned inside the house and closed the door. It was so quiet he could hear the fridge running and the clock ticking. That was it. There was no other sound. The house was quiet and empty. For the first time in his life, Joel was completely alone in the house. Everyone else was gone.

He took the phone off the hook. "Let's see that social worker call me now."

Chapter 27

Every time Joel tried to think about something else, no matter what he thought about, his brain was bombarded by painful questions he couldn't answer. His mind flashed back to seeing his father's body—the blood, his father's eyes, that Leatherman tool, haphazard on the floor. What unknown reasons drove his father? The memory was so sharp that he knew it would haunt him forever.

His father's final act was a tragic statement for a man whose years of experience and training had helped people in distress. He had cared for the sick and injured. Then he turned his skills perversely inward. He knew where the veins were and how to rapidly lose a fatal amount of blood. Yet days, even hours earlier, he had used that skill to help people in need. Did he ever show compassion?

His father never spoke about the pain he must have felt. There had been nothing except the booze-fuelled blue streaks of yammering. Did those rants only buff around the edges of hurt? Did he keep all the pain inside until it killed him? Did he want to inflict pain upon those left behind? Did his father want them to suffer even after he was dead?

Joel's mind raced. He couldn't sleep. The house was dark. His father's deed, his final act of violence, was all Joel could think about. It must have been a sickness. His father would never have done that if he hadn't been sick, would he? Joel's illness was recessive and hidden. He knew it was poised to burst out anytime. It wasn't like a broken arm or a gaping wound or a festering skin rash. It wasn't something that you could fix with a cast or some stitches or a prescription from the drug store. Maybe this disease of his father's worked the same way. It was latent, repressed and ultimately became fatal. His sickness must have burrowed down to the roots of his ligaments, inflamed his sinews, hid in his bones until it roared to life one day. Until it rattled like a bleached and bony skeleton emerging from a pitch-black closet. The silent pain and turmoil screamed louder every day. The urges to hurt bubbled up to the surface and wriggled down his arms and found their way outside his body through his fists. The fists that he used to smash the face of his wife and the fists he used to bash his son's nose. The same fists, the same big, warm hands he used to help and heal others. Those same fists that gripped the weapon he used to slit his own jugular. Those fists that banged on no door for help. Fists, instead, that collapsed, relaxed and harmless at his side as he died.

The alarm clock's ticking was loud; in the empty still house it sounded like the crisp *rat-tat-tat* of a snare drum. Joel could not sleep. He got up.

The cold breeze whistled up the staircase as he bounded downstairs. Wind poured through the broken window in the front door. He should fix that, he thought. He pulled on his boots, laced them up, and picked up his jacket which lay crumpled on the floor.

He walked out to the dark street and pointed himself downtown toward the coffee shop. Moonlight shone dull through a low layer of clouds. Rain was coming, or maybe it would turn to snow.

Joel hoped the coffee shop would be a warm oasis from this blasting cold. The wind had picked up now and it pushed against his back, propelling him forward. The cold bit into him. Joel couldn't remember the last time he had been comfortable and warm.

He got to the coffee shop and settled into a booth with his beverage. He looked around to see what other refugees were taking shelter at this hour. A couple of taxi drivers, three college students who had enjoyed one too many, and a young woman in black fishnet stockings and red high-heel shoes.

The mug warmed his hands and the heat slid down his throat. His mind drifted. Did he just sigh out loud? He looked around the shop. Had he cried out? No, it was okay. Nobody was looking at him. All the various conversations continued. The hooker fished around in her tiny black handbag. The students slurred their words and talked too loudly.

"Sure is coming down out there," the cabbie closest to him said.

Joel looked out the window. The winds whipped the rain and it bounced hard against the glass.

"Sure is." Joel stared into his coffee cup.

A truck pulled up to the newspaper box on the street corner. The driver dropped a bundle of the morning edition papers into the box. Joel stepped out into the driving rain, fumbled in his pocket for a few coins. He dropped them in the box and took out a newspaper. He hurried back into the coffee shop. Thank goodness refills were free.

Joel spread the paper out on the table and started reading an article. A person who had gone to the woods to get a Christmas tree never came home. They found his body frozen beneath a fir tree he was about to chop down. He had died from either a heart attack or from the cold, they couldn't tell.

Joel couldn't go on like this, pinching pennies, wandering around coffee shops in the middle of the night in the freezing rain. The time had come to act. Joel didn't know what he was spending his time doing anymore; hours rolled into days with nothing accomplished. He was no closer to finding David. How long before the social worker caught on to the phone being off the hook and tracked him down in person. Who was he kidding? David was not coming home. The only way David was going to come home was if he went and found him and brought him back himself. Joel Carruthers would stand up to the world. Fuck the odds. Joel Carruthers would survive. It was time to seek out David. He'd flush him out of hiding and bring him back home. Where he belongs. Where he should have never left in the first place.

How though? He looked out the window. He needed a sign. He wasn't going to a foster home. No way. Joel saw no divine signs. No beam of light illuminated the path, no neon sign flashed an arrow in the right direction.

He fixed his objective concretely in his mind. It was time for action. In a mood of euphoria now, he formed the steps he needed to take. He could make plans. He could carry them out. He focused on his one goal, finding his brother. The sun peeked pink on the horizon. It was dawn already. He downed the rest of his coffee and sprang out the door, running all the way home. He was anxious to get going.

CHAPTER 28

Joel dialed Scott's number. "Hey," he said, "any news?"

"Some. I don't know what it means though."

"What? Anything's a help."

"I was talking to Jennifer. She heard he went to Boston."

"I know that. *Where* in Boston?"

"If he wanted to come back, he'd be here already." Scott gave a little laugh, "David pretty much does his own thing."

"Yeah but he needs to know. He deserves to know. Does Jennifer think he knows?"

"Knows? Knows what?"

Joel ran his hand through his hair. "About Dad."

"If he's been in touch with anyone from Amherst at all, he knows."

"He wouldn't know and not come home. He wouldn't leave me and Mom alone with all this going on."

"Why don't you leave it alone? Drop it, don't even think about him for a week or two, he'll be like a cat and come back when he gets good and hungry." Scott paused for a few seconds then went on, "Jennifer thought Cambridge, and she's pissed. It's not *where* so much as *who*."

Joel moved to the window and looked out. "Who?"

"She heard he might have tagged up with Ellen again."

"Just what he needs." Joel took a deep breath. Up on Forest Road, he saw the yellow flashing light of the snowplough clearing the roads. The snow had stopped.

"I hear snippets. I don't know if any of it is true."

"David's got to be talking to someone. You and I both know he'd burst if he wasn't talking to someone. Not for this long."

"Don't know, Joel, I'm getting this third or fourth hand. For all I know David could be lurking in your fucking basement right now. I'm telling you what I've heard. Somewhere around Harvard Square."

"Reliable?"

"Far as I know."

"I'm going to Boston." Joel stood up, jammed the phone between his shoulder and ear, grabbed his knapsack and threw in some clothes.

"Jesus, Joel, don't you think—"

"That he doesn't want to be found? That if he wanted to come home, he'd be here already?"

"Well, yeah, and he's staying away on purpose. That he feels responsible. You know, the fight, and then with your Dad…" Scotty took a deep breath. He exhaled slowly. "And with Jennifer on his case."

Joel put a pair of woollen mittens into the bag. Joel hated it when his hands got cold. He tossed in an extra pair of socks. He reminded himself of the way his brother packed the last time he saw him. Throwing things in a bag without even thinking. He looked at the hockey card David had given him the night he left. He stroked it, as though for good luck. Or maybe if he rubbed it in the right way, it could tell him where to start looking for David.

"This is as close to finding David as I've come since Dad, since Mom, since everything. I'm going."

"It's thirdhand information, Joel. For Christ's sake, slow down. Please. If he ever was there, he'll be long gone by the time you get to Harvard Square. And Cambridge, Boston, fucking New England is huge when you're looking for one guy."

The house was quiet, all those noises—the breaking glass, the bottles flying, the Charlie Parker saxophone solos wailing on the record player—all the sounds that used to upset him to the point of having another seizure—these were replaced by silence. It was early afternoon and the house was like a church at midnight, sullen and undisturbed.

"Beats staying here," Joel said into the phone. "I'm heading to Boston, Scott. I'll track him down. Or Ellen. I'll find somebody he's hung around with. He deserves to know."

"You sure?"

"I'm leaving as soon as I get off the phone."

"If I was you, Joel, I'd give him some space. He needs some time to sort through everything. To process it all."

"For fuck sake, Scott, what do you think I need? I'm standing here dealing with this mess. You try sticking your father in a coffin without your brother around. Fuck that, You try talking to your goddamned mother in the hospital and have her stare at you with a blank look in her eyes and drool rolling down her chin. Fuck."

"Don't you have an aunt or somebody in Quincy who can check it out? Save you from going."

"I'm heading there tonight. I don't know why you're against this. My father's sister used to live there years go. What part of 'I want to talk to my fucking brother' are you not getting?"

"I'm going on record saying you should leave him alone. I know David as well as you, probably better. There's things you tell your best friend that you don't bother to tell your kid brother."

"Have you been talking to David?" Joel was yelling now. "Scott, tell me the goddamned truth."

"Jesus no, Joel, no. I'd tell you if I was. For sure."

"Promise?"

"Fuck off."

"You coming then?"

"I'll see if I can get an address for you. Warren. Winthrop, Washington. Something like that. I'll doublecheck."

"Terrific," Joel said, "that's close enough. You coming?" Joel zipped up his bag, opened his wallet and checked inside. "I'm heading out now."

"Got to work in the morning, otherwise I would. Taking your Dad's car?"

"Yep."

"Will it make it?"

"I'll hitchhike if I have to. I'll go get some gas and swing by your place on the way out of town. Track down that address for me."

Joel threw his bag in the car, turned the key. The engine was sluggish and cranked lazily for a few turns. Finally it sputtered to life. The smell of stale beer lingered, a vestigial reminder of his father's presence in the vehicle.

After Joel paid for his gas, he shoved the rest of his cash in his pocket along with a handful of change. He headed for Scott's. The sun was high in the clear sky. The weather forecast called for more snow tonight. Joel hated driving in the snow. He just wanted to get on the road, swoop into Beantown, grab David and come back home.

Joel pulled up in front of Scott's house. He honked the horn. "Come on, come on," he said out loud, "hurry up." Joel cranked the heater in the car full blast.

Still no Scott. Joel hopped out and ran up and banged on the front door. "Scott! What did you find out!" Joel ran back to the car to keep warm. He honked again.

Scott came out the door and waved to acknowledge Joel. He was still on the telephone. Then he held up one finger and hollered out, "One sec," and ducked back inside.

Joel turned on the car radio but kept the volume low. He could hear the engine stutter; it was making a weirder noise than usual that sounded like fast ticking. He started to anticipate seeing David and thought about everything that had happened. What was he going to say to him? Tears welled in his eyes. How would he break the news? Did David know already? It would be easier if he did.

He honked the horn two more short bursts. Scott finally ran out to the car.

"Time's a-ticking," Joel said, "I want to get there and back before that snowstorm starts. The weather forecast sounds brutal."

"You sure you want to do this? Have you thought about what you'll do if you find him and he doesn't want to come back? What then?"

"Did you get an address?"

"Sort of. The top floor of an apartment building." Scott shook his head. "I don't know the apartment number. But the building is 200 or maybe 300 Franklin Street. It's called the

Elsinore Arms. Why don't you wait till tomorrow? They said that David told them he was hitting the trail again."

"No. I'm going now. See you when David and I get back." Joel roared away and headed for the Trans Canada.

The highway was smooth, but the car's engine lurched every now and again. With the sound of the tires speeding along against the hard asphalt, Joel couldn't tell if the engine was still making that ticking sound or not. And he didn't care. His foot stayed steady on the accelerator. The miles rolled by quickly. So far, the roads were bare, no snow yet. His mind jumped ahead to Boston. Finally, things were going right. He could make it to Harvard Square. He felt the relief already. He could breathe easy for the first time in days. He would manage to find Franklin Street. He would make it to the Elsinore Arms. Then he'd wait for him. He'd wait all night if he had to. But he knew he'd find David quickly.

Joel glanced at the dashboard clock. "In ten hours," he thought, "me and David will be heading back home." And soon, then, they'd be sitting in their mother's kitchen. No doubt crying at first, but maybe sharing some beer and take-out burgers. And yes, even laughing perhaps.

Joel could see the remains of the old railway car foundry. He shuddered seeing the crumbling bricks again, where he had run, drunk, after the garage fire. The busy streets of downtown gave way to subdivisions, and the subdivisions gave way to farmland. One question plagued his mind. Would David come home?

Joel didn't even know for sure if David was still in Boston. Maybe he did take off again. He could be in New York, or anywhere.

He kept the accelerator engaged and the needle of the speedometer exactly at the speed limit. He didn't need the cops to slow him down with a speeding ticket.

Joel noticed an acrid smell. The *tick-tick-tick* became louder. He heard metal grate on metal. He slowed down. The ticking was very fast now. He put on his signal and let the car slow to a crawl. The engine clanked hard three times, followed by a loud *bang!* The engine shuddered. The gauges went dead. As the car lost all power, he struggled with the steering wheel to coast off the highway and onto the exit ramp for Sackville.

"For fuck sakes," he muttered. He felt sweat run down his forehead. He wanted a cigarette. That feeling of needing to cry returned full on. He wiped his eyes.

"Fuck!" he screamed, and banged his hands against the steering wheel.

Joel popped the hood and got out of the car. A metal rod poked through a jagged hole in the metal casing. He looked up and down the highway. Behind him was Sackville's Tantramar Regional High School. Should he start to walk home? That would take him hours. The sleet was driven so hard by the wind it stung his cheeks.

The north wind does blow.

He couldn't walk home, not in this. Maybe a taxi? He decided to walk up the ramp, there was a gas station and a restaurant at the top of the hill. He could get there and then figure out a plan.

He was soaked from the sleet when he arrived at the restaurant. A car with a roof light sign that said *Sackville Cab* was in the parking lot. He walked over to the driver's side door.

The cabbie rolled the window down a crack. "Can I help ya, bud?"

"How much for a ride to Amherst?"

The cabby gave him an estimate. This fare would take a dent out of his money. Joel opened the back door and got in. "Palmer Court, in Amherst, please."

The taxi pulled out of the parking lot and headed down the ramp onto the highway toward Amherst. Joel looked across at his father's broken-down vehicle on the ramp on the other side of the highway, its yellow hazard lights flashing as it sat there motionless.

"That your car broken down there?" The cabbie asked as they headed down the ramp to get on the south bound lane of the Trans Canada.

"Yep. It's toast."

"Want me to call a tow truck for you?"

"How much will that cost?"

"Depends where you want it taken. Amherst?"

"No, I don't care—a junkyard, I guess."

"They'll pick it up for free if you let them keep it."

"Really? Yes, please then, would you call a tow truck."

The cabbie picked up the handset of his radio. "I'll ask dispatch to call one."

The cab sped up as it merged onto the highway carrying Joel, alone, back home to a dark and empty house.

Chapter 29

Joel flipped through an old *Reader's Digest* while he waited in the reception area. He wondered how his mother's doctor at the hospital was able to get him an appointment with his neurologist so quickly. He usually had to wait months to get an appointment. This time he goes to visit his mother in the hospital and they send him downstairs to the neuro clinic. They tell him Dr. King will see him right away. Maybe it was that social worker pulling some strings.

Dr. King opened his office door. "Joel, come on in."

Joel hopped up on the examination table, and Dr. King did all the usual tests.

"Okay, have a seat and let's talk about your options, Joel. I know you've had a hard go lately. And the seizures, more frequent, more severe."

"There's no way I'm taking any more pills, if that's what you mean by options."

"Pills are one option. I'm not saying you—"

"No. Absolutely not. I'm sick of pills. I'm sick of being sick."

Dr. King wrapped the blood pressure cuff around Joel's arm. "Let me check your pressure."

"I'm already on three different medications."

"Please keep still, Joel, for a moment." Dr. King pumped the ball on the cuff.

"It's not like I'll die from it or anything." Joel held his arm straight out and kept it still.

"You know your condition. We talked before about the risks, the complications."

"But where will it end?"

"Your blood pressure is high."

"No wonder," Joel laughed.

"A higher dosage might do the trick."

Joel looked at him and wanted to scream. Instead he asked, "Does it have to be more medicine, though, Dr. King?"

"Look how far you've come in the past six months, Joel. This is the kind of progress we talked about all along. Six months ago I thought we may have had to consider more drastic interventions. I was worried we might have to pull your driver's license, that you wouldn't be able to go to school, that work would be out of the question."

"Work is fine. So is school."

"Yes, that's what I mean. You've made great progress."

"And now you throw a 'but' in there..."

"But you've had a lot of stress in the past little bit. We just need to manage your illness a little more aggressively."

Joel stood up. "You're not the one who has to shove a handful of horse pills in your gob twice a day."

Chapter 30

Joel walked back home from the hospital. He heard children laughing and their squeals of delight as they sledded down the hill. Their faces wrapped in scarves against the cold and their matching mittens flashing as they sped down. Fathers and mothers waited at the bottom of the hill. They sat on frozen park benches with Thermoses of hot chocolate and bags of marshmallows. Some of the older kids had a boom box blasting out "Two Princes" by The Spin Doctors.

Everyone knew the hill and the fields at the base as The Pitch. Joel and his friends dubbed it the Shit Pit. Some called it that because of the sloppy, snowy mess that greeted you at the bottom of the hill after a snowy day of sliding. Others thought that it was because a few who shot out of control going over the 'mother bump' and went straight up into the air, needed to change their pants once they landed.

David and Joel went there many times. He remembered the cold and the snow, but most of all the fun of freedom. The snow would stick to their woollen mittens, little ice balls clinging to their cuffs. It froze their skin and made their hands turn red, then white with cold. But that was never a bother. Even when their cheeks would flare red, they continued to slide down the hill time and time again.

Radio Flyer sleds, toboggans, the two-seaters, the three-seaters and even the four-seaters would go down the hill sliding fast and catching air on their way to the bottom. They bumped and coasted their way down. Passengers would be thrown off. Laughter abounded. They would land in a heap of snow, giggling and anxious to run back up the hill, pulling the toboggan behind them to do it again.

Joel thought about his brother, and smiled. He and David had spent hours, full days, together at The Pitch. Soaking wet mittens and boots clogged with snow. It was a great place for escape. A few hours of time being a kid, enjoying freedom, getting a thrill from risking life and limb over those gigantic mounds and bumping and plummeting down the hill and waiting for the final thrill of the thump at the end. The Pit was their favourite place to go by themselves. They could be boys and have fun. The only tension and screams were when they slid down the hill.

Joel noticed some parents there with little kids. No parents were with the older kids. They were there on their own. Just like he and David used to be. Why did that social worker think he needed to be taken care of? He'd be fine on his own.

And there was no way he was going to a foster home.

Chapter 31

Joel stuck his key in the lock of the door to the bookstore and turned it. He punched his code into the alarm panel next to the door while balancing his coffee in one hand and propping the door open with his knee.

"Hey Joel," Maria said as she came up behind him. "You don't look so hot this morning. You're pale."

"Good morning to you, too."

"Your hair is sticking up all over the place." She gave a soft laugh.

"I don't feel myself this morning. I couldn't sleep at all last night."

"You should have called in sick this morning and stayed home in bed. Man, are you feeling okay?"

Joel went behind the desk and downed the rest of his coffee. He flipped open a file with 'special orders' marked on it. He started to flick through the pages.

"I couldn't," he said, "the old man's not coming in today and he needed me to open."

He glanced down at the packing list of a new shipment.

"Too bad you're not feeling well. We could go for supper after we close up today."

"I'm just tired. Once the coffee kicks in, I'll be fine. I'll be fit as a fiddle."

"Okay," Maria smiled. She grabbed a stack of books to put out on the shelves.

The shop was busy all day. Saturdays before Christmas meant a constant flow of customers. Joel and Maria barely had a chance to speak to each other between serving customers and ringing up sales. Pritchard would be happy with the day's take, Joel thought as he counted out the bank deposit. After Joel locked up the shop, he and Maria walked to the bank and made the night deposit. They went next door to the Cozy Corner Café. The jazz playing on the stereo was soft in the background. A crackling fire in the fireplace threw a warm ambience. The clatter of cups and spoons spinning in beverage mugs was soothing and relaxing. The aroma of freshly ground coffee beans and rich, dark chocolate was pronounced and delicious.

They selected a couple of dark Colombian coffees. Maria lead the way to the back of the shop and picked a table for two, right next to the fire. The heat felt good.

She let Joel slide her chair out for her before she sat down.

"So what do you do when you're not at work?" Maria gave an exaggerated shrug trying not to reveal her interest in him.

"Believe it or not," Joel said, hanging his head, "I like to read a lot, go figure, working in a bookstore and all." He looked across the table at her. Her face was warm and kind.

"What kind of books do you like?"

"I'll read anything." He took a mouthful of his coffee. "Novels, but also religion, philosophy, history, you know, the stuff other people find dry and boring. I just finished *In the Skin of a Lion*, and *The Stone Angel*. Also a new book just out is supposed to be good, I haven't started it yet—*No Great Mischief,* I can't wait." Joel felt his face redden, realizing he just droned on and on about himself. He looked at Maria.

Maria nodded. "I like history and religion and all that boring stuff too. But," she swirled her coffee, "I don't do much reading for pleasure these days. Or much of anything else for pleasure come to think of it. Just go to class and write papers."

"When you do read for the heck of it, what do you read?"

"I just read *The Great Gatsby*."

"Interesting," Joel sipped at his coffee. "What did you think?"

"I liked it, but it made me sad at the end."

"I had to read it in grade ten and I hated it."

Maria smiled, "I sense a 'but' coming."

"Yep. But read it again for my enriched class this year. I loved it. I think two years made all the difference for me. I see why a guy would build a mansion and throw all those wild parties to get the attention of a Daisy."

Maria laughed. "It really is the classic American story, though, isn't it?"

"Have you read Hemingway? *The Old Man and the Sea*?"

"Loved it. Also felt sad for Santiago at the end."

"What about Joseph Conrad? Anything by him?"

"No, I don't think so. Not that I can remember anyway."

"I have some good ones by Conrad." Joel took a drink of his coffee. "He's great, especially if you love the sea and ships."

"Thanks anyway, but I have a whack of assignments due. Plus I suck at returning things I borrow."

"Yeah me too. Once I get something, I keep it."

Engaged in their conversation and sipping their coffees, they were unaware of voices rising outside. Two or three of the other patrons stopped talking and looked outside. Joel and Maria looked out the window.

Two guys, one in a blue 'NSCC' jacket the other in a black leather jacket with 'Mount A' across the back, were staggering and pushing each other. A crowd circled around them, but gave them lots of space. They looked drunk, very drunk. Drunk and enraged to the point where ration and reason had vanished completely.

The guy in the NSCC jacket smashed the one from Mount A in the stomach. He doubled over, and before he could regain his balance, NSCC connected with a horrifying jab to his face. Sirens screamed in the distance. In slow motion, with blood spurting from his nose, Mount A tried to straighten up and make a fist. But the other guy slugged him again, hard on the jaw. He tottered and crashed through the plate glass.

Crack! His head hit the floor. Joel thought it looked like a scene from a 3D movie: a body flying out from the screen and into the audience. Jagged chunks of glass crashed down. Maria gasped and turned her head. The couple at the table nearest the window had jumped out of the way just in time. Their table was flipped over and a coffee mug, still intact, spun aimlessly on the floor.

The guy outside stared through the broken window at his victim lying on the floor. "Let's go!" one of his friends said, pulling at his sleeve. They ran off down the street.

Joel and Maria stared at the guy on the floor. Joel felt like he was going to throw up.

Blue and red lights flashed, lighting up the café. Two police officers, with radios squawking, walked in. The kid with the Mount A jacket didn't move. Blood pooled beneath his head. Paramedics arrived and started working on him.

Joel looked at Maria. He knew she wanted to go home now, but the cop had motioned to them to wait. Neither of them wanted to see any of this.

"Do you think he's dead?" she whispered to Joel.

One of the police officers crouched over him and talked to the paramedic who was feeling for a pulse. The medics started an IV in his arm and put an oxygen mask over his face. They loaded him onto a stretcher and slid him into the back of the ambulance.

The ambulance's air horn blasted several shorts bursts while it crawled through the intersection.

"I feel sick," Maria said.

Joel nodded. "That was plain gross."

"I can't believe that went on." Maria dodged the broken glass as they left the café. "What could it possibly have been all about?"

"Yeah, what would be that important to fight over and end up like that." Joel pointed to where the ambulance had just driven away. "That poor guy, he's dead, or half-dead."

"I don't think the ambulance would have taken him if he was dead." Maria looked at her watch. "I've got to head home."

A police officer held up his hand. "You folks saw what happened? I'll need your names and contact information."

They gave their names.

"Carruthers? You must be Roger's boy. You're the spitting image of him."

Joel nodded.

"I'm sorry about your dad. He was a great man. I've worked these streets for a long time. Roger always gave the immediate sense of order and calm. The guy was a genius medic. Nothing rattled him. The hotter the call, the more chaos there was, the more calm, cool and collected Roger was. Roger the Dodger, he dodged all the garbage. Nothing ever rattled him. We all miss him. The whole county does."

"Thank you," Joel smiled. "All I saw and heard was these two guys fighting and the next thing one comes flying through the window and cracks his head on the floor."

"Right, that's the picture we're getting." the cop said. "And you?" He turned to Maria and she nodded, looking shaken. He jotted something in his notebook. "Okay, thanks," he said. "I don't think we'll need anything from you. We'll be in touch if we do."

Joel stopped after walking for a few steps. He turned around and walked back toward the café. "Sir," he called out, "is he dead?"

The cop turned around and faced him. "What? Who?"

"Is he dead? The guy? Is he dead?"

He shook his head and frowned. "He wasn't when he left here. But he'll have one hell of a headache in the morning, that's for sure."

Maria and Joel headed down the street and turned onto Queen. A streetlight flickered and buzzed above them.

"Do you think he told the truth?" Joel asked her.

"Who? Who told the truth?"

"The cop. Do you think he told the truth?"

"He only asked us our names and stuff. What truth?"

"No, do you think he was saying that the guy wasn't dead, I don't know, to keep the gossip down, you know, till next of kin are notified. Isn't that how they do it?"

"I think he got punched, went boom, and knocked his head. I'm sure, like the cop said, he'll get up in the morning."

They continued walking. The yellow glow from the streetlamps was certainly more soothing than those flashing police car lights outside the café.

They passed the old graveyard. Some stones were so weathered and worn they gave no hint of who lay under them. Joel swept his eyes across the names as they walked. Only now could Joel put his thoughts into words.

"Have you ever thought about eternity?" he asked.

Maria did not respond.

"Eternity? Forever? Have you thought about it? About your place in it?"

"Nope," she smiled. "I'm only thinking about getting home. It's getting late."

"I remember when I was a kid, eight or nine, I remember sitting on the porch looking up at that church steeple. It was so high up and so heavy looking made out of stones. The bells seemed to touch the sky. I remember trying to grasp the idea of eternity. My next-door neighbour had died of a heart attack and I couldn't figure it out. I'd start thinking about eternity never ending, just going on forever. I couldn't figure it out. So I'd try to stop thinking about it. But that was like trying not to think of a white horse. You remember that old joke? Don't think of a white horse."

Maria laughed, "It's all that gets in your mind. A white horse."

"That guy back there, let's say he's not dead, but if he was, his eternity would have started as soon as his head cracked open."

"Well, thank goodness for his sake, it didn't." They laughed. "Not tonight anyway. He'll have a major headache in the morning that will feel like it's forever."

They walked a few blocks in a comfortable silence.

"It's a pleasant night," Joel said. He reached for her hand.

"It's getting a little cold." Maria shoved her hands deep into the pockets of her overcoat.

They walked on, winding past Miller Lake. Joel reached down to the edge of the shoreline and picked up a rock. It was an oval-shaped piece of slate worn smooth by the constant action of the water. He hefted its weight. It was a simple rock, but in the right hands with the right spirit it could be a tool or even a weapon. He turned it over in his hand. It was as big as his palm, reddish pink with flecks of white in it.

"See this rock?" he said, holding it up towards Maria. "It proves it."

"Proves it?"

"Yep. Proves there's a God."

Maria laughed. "It does, does it? Do tell."

"I know," Joel laughed. "I know but hear me out. You take a rock—basic, cold, inanimate, trace of white flecks through it, et cetera et cetera, not important in the grand scheme of things. But go deeper, ask a few more questions." He looked over at Maria and held out the stone for her to take. "Go ahead, take it, touch it." He pushed it into her hand. "Hold it."

"You're on something, aren't you?" she laughed. "Your medication is whacked. You're whacked."

He held out the rock to her. "Go ahead," he laughed, "take it."

She took the rock into her hands.

"Go on, feel it, know it." Joel said, still laughing.

"Ha-ha. He without sin throws the first one... isn't that what they say?"

"Ha, yep. Guess I better not touch it then."

She flipped the rock over and rubbed her hand on it. "Yep," she said, "smooth, cold, not talking, not breathing, not moving. Definitely a rock."

"Now look beyond," Joel said.

She looked at the shore of the lake where Joel had picked up the rock in the first place.

"Look beyond the rock in your hand. Think of the questions the rock would ask if it could. It would ask the same things we would. Think of yourself as the rock, you would ask 'where did I come from', 'why am I here', 'what is my purpose'—"

"And who is this big warm giant hand that snatched me from my home and is now strangling me?"

Joel laughed.

Maria laughed and returned the rock to Joel. "You are nuts. Take your philosopher's stone!"

Joel held the rock up with a mock reverence. "And, our friend Rocky here, is asking 'where am I going in this life?'" Joel launched the rock with all his might toward the lake. "To the water, my little, hard, cold friend." He laughed again.

The ripples where the rock hit the water circled wider and wider. "And see that's about the same as our impact. We'll make a few ripples on the surface, and then we'll sink to the bottom. All the big questions—why are we here and where are we going—are the same for us as for Rocky."

Maria shook her head and laughed again. "And how does all that prove there is a God?"

"I guess it doesn't prove God as much as it proves we're all in this together. People, rocks, all of us, together. And all of us have these questions. We all want to know."

Maria laughed. "You, Mr. Carruthers," she tapped on his forehead, "have rocks in your head."

"It's what every religion tries to answer, each in its own way. It's caused a lot of wars, too, over who's right, who's wrong. Supreme being, master planner, yin-yang, divine force, great spirit, creator, whatever." He picked up another rock. "See this one." He held it out to her. It was brown with flecks of black in it. "Same questions." He flung it far out over the water.

"Come on," Maria said, and grabbed his hand. They walked along the path by the river. Joel relished the connection. They walked along and turned off the path, back up toward the road.

"I've got a question for you," Joel said.

They stopped and Maria looked in his eyes.

Joel looked back, deeply. "Do you think... that if you stop believing in God, that God still believes in you?"

She squeezed his hand tight and they walked on toward her building. The lights of the parking lot glowed ahead in the distance.

"Hey, did you hear that?" Joel asked.

"Hear what?"

"Like someone in the bushes," he said, "or walking on the fallen leaves. Someone sneaking up on us."

"I didn't hear a thing. Probably the wind. You're spooked from all that God talk."

He looked over to where he thought he heard the sound and scanned up and down. "Guess so," he said.

The moonlight trailed like a phosphorus yellow glow behind them. Out on the lake they could hear the distant calls of a pair of loons.

"Calling each other," Joel said.

"Um," Maria said. She buttoned up her coat and pulled her woollen cap down over her ears. "That wind is really cold."

"Coming right off the lake," he said.

She looped her arm though his and she nuzzled in close as they walked. "Lots of stars," she said.

Joel looked up and nodded. He cocked his head again. "There, again, do you hear it?"

"I don't hear anything."

"Like footsteps, soft footsteps, like sneakers squeaking on wet pavement, like someone walking behind us." He stopped and peered back to where they had come from. "You sure you didn't hear it?"

Maria shook her head and shrugged.

"Christ," he said, "I must be losing my mind."

They arrived at the wrought iron fence that ringed Maria's apartment building. It was a four-storey building, with dingy yellowed siding that had streaks of a green mossy mould near the eaves. He drew her close. "Good night," he said. Joel wanted to say something else and he tried to form the words in his mind, but he couldn't articulate them.

Maria looked at him and smiled, "Night, Joel. See you tomorrow." She headed toward her building.

Joel leaned back against the fence and braced himself with his hands on either side. He watched her go in and close the door behind. He stood there feeling the cold air on his face. After a long time he pushed himself off the fence. He listened closely and heard the trees, the leaves swirling in the wind, he heard the distant loons, the soft whooshing of traffic from the highway—but he did not hear footsteps. Joel brushed the flecks of black paint and rust from the fence off his hands and headed home.

Chapter 32

Joel stood in the empty kitchen; it was missing both people and activity. His mother had moved so effortlessly around it and, seemingly like clockwork, supper appeared without fail on the table. It would be nice to return the favour, he thought. Hospital food sucks and the mashed potatoes are like glue. A home-cooked meal would be a great idea.

He looked in the fridge. There was a casserole that Pierre from next door had sent over before his father's funeral. That was almost a week ago now, so Joel threw out what was left. A dish of mac & cheese that Scott's mother had dropped off was also several days old, and there was not much left. He had lived on that since his mother took sick. All that remained in the fridge were a few onions with green sprouts coming out the top. In the bottom drawer there was half a bag of carrots that had little yellow stringy shoots growing along their length. He tossed those too.

He headed out to the grocery store. He'd been there many times with his mother over the years. Sometimes his mother or father sent him by himself, but it was always with a list, and usually with very specific instructions. But going on his own, deciding what to buy, turning over cuts of meat like he'd seen his mother do, selecting the produce, was new to him. Somebody else had always done that.

He wandered around the butcher aisle feeling like a newbie. He stopped at several displays of meat. He wasn't even sure he knew what to look for in a cut of meat or even in a tomato for that matter. There were so many choices—pork, beef, chicken, seafood—he didn't know where to start. He was unsure what was at a good price, what was a good value or not. He walked up and down the meat section again, and eyed the roast beef. His mother liked roast beef.

Roast beef it was then. So now he had to pick out a package of it. He picked through the selection in the case. He remembered his mother commenting on the fat that marbled through a cut of meat. He couldn't remember though; did she say it should have a lot or a little?

The butcher, from behind the counter, asked if he needed help.

"No thanks," he muttered, embarrassed. He grabbed a package and put it in his cart. He should be able to pick out a cut of meat. Maybe the social worker was right.

Joel loved roast beef dinner. His mother made it with potatoes and gravy. Yes, and with peas and carrots too. He went to the frozen food section and scanned the shelves behind the glass. A bag of frozen peas would do the trick.

He wheeled back to the produce section and grabbed a small bag of potatoes. For as long as he could remember one of his chores when he got home from school was to peel the potatoes, cut them up and put them in a pot of water. Add a few pinches of salt. That part would be easy. He picked up a bag of carrots; he was used to peeling and cutting them up too. That would be a snap.

Maybe horseradish instead of gravy. His father had loved horseradish, and smothered his meat with it. But his mother loved gravy. He'd get some horseradish, then, and if he screwed up the gravy he'd have horseradish for backup. He rolled down the condiment isle and found it. All these decisions for a simple dinner. How hard was everything else going to be?

He stopped and thought about what else he would need. They usually had dessert on special occasions. And when they did it was pie or cake that his mother would have baked. He pushed his cart toward the bakery section, passing the selection of rolls and breads. His mother always had fresh-baked rolls or biscuits for dinner on Sundays. He added up the price of everything he had already and decided against them.

He picked the smallest, freshest pie he could find and placed it in his cart. He looked over his items, and headed back to the frozen food aisle again and grabbed a small tub of vanilla ice cream. He double-checked his cart and tallied everything up in his head, then rolled toward the check out.

Once home, he put the bags of groceries on the counter. The grocery store was one thing, but now the kitchen seemed like foreign territory to him without his mother to give him instructions.

He pulled down the book from atop the fridge that he'd seen his mother refer to countless times, *Betty Crocker's Cookbook.* He flipped through the pages. Anything he had tried before his mother was close by for advice. Not now, though. The slop they pawned off as food at the hospital was outrageous. How could anybody, especially someone sick, be expected to eat that and get better?

He flipped through *Betty Crocker's* and found the instructions for roast beef. He put the meat in a pan and added the spices and the other things the book said. He put it in the oven and closed the door. He set the oven to the right temperature.

Peeling potatoes was a breeze. He was much more comfortable with that chore. Preparing the carrots was familiar to him as well. He poured some peas in a pot with some salt and water, and unpacked the last of his groceries. He held out the horseradish and smiled as he remembered how they all made fun of his father for drowning his meat with it. Suddenly he remembered the ice cream. He had forgotten about it, still there on the counter next to the pie. He put it in the freezer and slammed the door.

Joel checked the cookbook again and started his ingredients for the gravy. He chopped an onion and noticed how easily the tears flowed down his cheeks. He blew his nose with a tissue and didn't remember onions being so powerful the last time he chopped one while his mother was making supper.

Joel had everything ready to go, waiting for the meat to cook. He went to the living room to watch TV while the roast was in the oven. He flipped on an old black and white movie,

The Third Man with Orson Welles. Joel had loved him from the time he saw *Citizen Kane*.

Once the movie ended, Joel checked the roast with a meat thermometer as he had seen his mother do so often. He readied the vegetables and finished his gravy. He tasted it. A bit salty, but not too bad for a first attempt. He took out the meat and sliced it. He remembered how his father would always swoop in at the last minute and carve the roast.

He rooted around for some suitable containers to transport the meal down to his mother in the hospital. He poured the gravy into the thermos bottle he occasionally used for his lunches. He packed everything up in an empty cardboard beer box and tossed in some cutlery and some salt and pepper packets he saw in the silverware drawer, no doubt remnants from some take-out meal. He found a few paper plates and put those in too. He placed the ice cream in a separate bag; he didn't want it to melt again by putting it in with the hot food. He looked around the kitchen, making sure he'd turned everything off. Feeling satisfied with himself, he went to the door to put his boots on. He heard the big diesel engine of an ambulance pull up out front. He looked out the window and Jenkins was coming up the walkway. Snow was falling fast and melting when it landed on his jacket.

Joel opened the front door. "Mr. Jenkins. Hello, come in."

"Thanks, Joel." He stepped inside. "Sorry to drop by unannounced, I can only stay a minute, we're on our way to the hospital to pick up a patient to transfer into the city." He ran his hands through his hair to brush off the accumulated snow. "I just wanted to check in on you."

"Thanks. I'm doing okay."

"One of the other crew mentioned about your mother. I just wanted to see how you're doing, to see if you needed anything."

"No, I'm fine. Mom's getting better. I was just heading down to visit her."

"It smells good in here. Something cooking?"

Joel laughed. "I tried to cook a roast beef dinner for my mother. I'm taking it down for her. The last time I was there they were feeding her some disgusting mush."

"Hospital food is notorious."

"I couldn't even tell what it was supposed to be."

"If you want, if you're ready to go, we can give you a lift down to the hospital."

"In the ambulance?"

"Yeah, is that okay?"

"Yes, but I thought Dad always said you weren't allowed—".

"I won't tell anyone if you don't."

Jenkins slid open the side door and told Joel to hop up in the back of the ambulance. "Joel, this is Robert Miller."

"Nice to meet you."

"Have a seat there," Jenkins said, pointing to the chair that was at the head of the stretcher.

Joel got in and sat down, holding his beer box full of food. He set the bag with the ice cream on the stretcher.

Jenkins got in the front seat and pulled away from the curb. "When we have a patient in the rig, we call that the A-seat. A for airway. It's where your father worked all his miracles."

Joel nodded. He looked around at the cabinets stocked full of medicine and supplies. He looked at the equipment—the defibrillator, the suction machine, the immobilization gear. His father had referred to them all countless times.

"Your dad is really missed," Jenkins said as he turned the ambulance onto Forest Road. "Isn't your aunt still here?"

"No, she moved to San Francisco."

"How are you making out? Tell me the truth."

"I'm doing okay."

"Your food smells great. If that's any indication, you must be."

"Sure does," Miller said.

"And school? How's school going?" Jenkins asked.

"That's okay too."

"You're not skipping are you? You're going to class every day, right? Getting your homework done?"

"It's fine."

"You're going to get all the credits you need? You're on track to graduate in June?"

"Yep. Provided finals are okay."

"They will be, do you think?"

"Should be. I'm not worried. The school's on my case for missing so much time. You know, first Dad, now Mom."

"Keep up your schoolwork, Joel." Jenkins turned onto Willow Street. "It's important."

The snow started falling heavier and flakes became hard ice balls that tinkled on the windshield. "What about David? Have you heard from him?"

"Not yet. I tried to get to Boston to get him. But Dad's car conked out on me."

Jenkins laughed. "I'm not surprised. That old beast was ready for the junkyard."

"That's where it is now," Joel laughed. "I managed to get a guy from the junkyard to tow it there just to get rid of it."

"Just as well, it was falling apart. It wasn't safe." Jenkins clicked the windshield wipers to a faster speed. "I kept telling your father that."

"It was wobbly to drive. That spring clanking in the back made me nervous. Never made it far enough to pick up David, though."

"He knew you were coming for him? He was expecting you?"

"I'm heading back there. I want to visit Mom first though."

"He knows you're coming? He's coming back home? That'd be great."

"Well, not yet."

"Why doesn't he just hop on a bus from Boston and come here? You can meet him at the station, it would save you the trouble of going there."

"I need to tell him. I need to break it to him."

"He still doesn't know about your dad?" They arrived at the hospital.

"Or Mom. I'll be talking to him soon, though."

"That's good. I'll drop in on you and your brother in the next few days."

Jenkins pulled in front of the ambulance bays at the hospital and switched on the revolving lights. "We've all been there, Joel, seeing things we wish we could un-see, or that we wish we never saw in the first place." Jenkins put the ambulance in reverse. "If you get flashbacks or you find yourself spiraling down or—" The ambulance beeped as Jenkins backed it slowly into the bay. The red and white flashing lights and the backwards motion made Joel instantly woozy.

"Please, please reach out to someone. Me, your priest, a teacher or guidance counselor at school, your doctor. Anyone you're comfortable with. Promise me you'll talk to someone, okay?"

"Okay." Joel closed his eyes and waited for the wave of nausea to pass. It did, and he nodded and smiled, "But I'm okay, Mr. Jenkins. I'm fine."

Jenkins shut off the engine. He scribbled something in his notebook and ripped out the page. "Here's my phone number. If you need anything, if you run into any snags, you give me a call. I put dispatch's number on there too. You can call them if you can't reach me. They'll be able to get a hold of me."

"Thanks." Joel took his box and the bag with the ice cream and climbed out the side door of the ambulance.

"I'm looking out for you, Joel. Your dad would have done as much for me if it were the other way around. A lot of us cared so much about him. And then with your mom and everything... well, we can help you through this."

"Mom's getting better."

"Sure, but she has a long road ahead of her."

"Thanks for the lift."

"Anytime. You can go through that door," Jenkins said, pointing, "that will take you inside to the main entrance, right to the elevators."

"See you later." Joel took a few steps toward the door and then turned around. "Was this the same ambulance that my father would've worked in?"

"This is 505. Yes, we worked in 505 a lot. And 510 and 512."

"Thought so." Joel headed to the door.

"I'll pop by when I can," Jenkins called out. "Stay in touch."

Joel opened the door to the hospital, clutching his beer box and the bag with the ice cream swinging by his side. He found the elevators and went upstairs to his mother's room. She was asleep and looked comfortable. A bouquet of roses stood on her bedside table. Joel read the card: *Rest up, sweetie! Love, Penny.*

Joel went to the window and looked out. The sun was bright, so he opened the curtains wide. The room felt a little cheerier as the sunshine flowed in.

His mother stirred in bed. He leaned over and gave her a kiss on the cheek. The words the doctor had said rang in his mind. *Don't expect sudden improvement. It's going to take time to heal.*

"Hey, Mom." he said, looking at her face. Her eyes were closed. "It's me, Jo-Jo. How are you feeling?'

She nodded her head slightly. "Good." She tried to wave but could only move her hand an inch off the bed.

"You hungry?"

She smiled.

"I don't mean hungry for the slop that they try to pass off as food here. I mean for a real meal." He took the container out of the beer box. He held it up for her to see. "I did some cooking," he laughed. He felt the bottom of the plastic container. "Still warm." He opened the Thermos bottle and poured the gravy over the mashed potatoes and slices of roast beef.

He pulled the hospital bed tray closer and cranked it up in height. He moved the chair closer to his mother. He cut off a little piece of the roast beef. "Open up," he said as he brought a forkful to her mouth.

She opened her mouth and chewed in slow, deliberate motions. She couldn't take her eyes off Joel.

"Funny how the tables are turned," he laughed. "I guess it's payback."

He fed her some of the vegetables. She chewed like she had to concentrate on every movement. Even eating was a struggle, Joel thought. He dug up a big forkful of the mashed potatoes smothered in gravy and brought it to his mother's lips.

He waited while she swallowed it down. "Is it good?"

"Yes." Her speech was slow and cautious. "Yes, it's good."

"I learned from the best," he laughed. "The best, and Betty Crocker. I had no clue how to do the gravy. But I figured it out. It's not too bad is it?"

"Great," his mother said. Her eyes smiled.

He fed some more to her, and he was glad she was eating. It made him feel like he was contributing to her recovery. Joel felt something was finally going right.

After a few more bites, Joel sensed a wave of frustration wash over his mother. She tried to grab at the fork and feed herself. She clutched at Joel's hand and knocked a forkful of mashed potatoes onto the bed.

"Goddamn," she said.

"Mom," Joel laughed in mock indignation, "what are you doing cursing? If I said that you'd wash my mouth out with soap."

"You can't."

"Then you can't either."

"Can't help it," she said, "slipped out."

Joel forced himself not to show any reaction to his mother's speech which was so different from normal. He pushed himself to make sure he understood everything she said, no matter how twisted and slurred her words sounded to him. Joel picked up the lump of potato she had knocked onto the bed and tossed it in the trash can beside her bed. He wiped the gravy from her chin with a tissue.

He cut up another piece of meat. She chewed it slowly. He fed her several more forkfuls of the meal.

His mother raised one hand up off the bed. "No more," she tried to smile.

"You full, Mom? You hardly ate enough for a bird."

His mother nodded.

Joel ate his own supper. His mother dozed off.

"How about a piece of pie?"

She opened her eyes. "You made pie?"

"Ha-ha. No way." He laughed with her. "I drew the line at gravy. That was bad enough. I bought the pie at the grocery store."

"Oh," she chuckled.

Joel sliced a piece of pie and spooned some soupy ice cream on top. His mother closed her eyes again. He shrugged and ate the pie himself.

A nurse came in. She stood at the foot of the bed and looked at his mother. She made some notes and checked the IV pump. "She's made some improvements over the past 24 hours," the nurse said.

"I can see a difference since yesterday. She knows who I am. And most of what she says makes sense today."

"She tires easily." The nurse put a new bag of saline on the IV.

"She ate some supper."

The nurse looked over at the array of containers and leftovers Joel had packed up. "You brought that from home?"

"Yes. She seemed to like it."

"We do have her on a special diet. You shouldn't bring any other food."

"I'm sorry I didn't know."

"Low sodium, low fat, that kind of thing."

"I didn't know. I never thought." Joel's face reddened.

"Shouldn't be a problem. I'm just glad she ate something."

"Her supper last night looked like mush. She never ate a bite. I want her to get her strength back."

"I know you do." The nurse pulled out a plastic bag from under the nightstand next to the bed. "These are your mother's clothes and her jewelry. When she's ready to be discharged we'll get you to bring her some clean, fresh things from home." She passed the bag to Joel. "Take these home to wash them. And put your mom's jewelry somewhere safe." She went to the patient's room across the hallway.

"I will, thanks," Joel said. He looked in the bag and took out the smaller clear plastic bag that was labelled *CARRUTHERS, GLORIA JANE*. Inside, Joel could see his mother's watch, two small hoop earrings, her wedding band and engagement ring, and the gold cross chain that she always wore around her neck.

Joel opened the bag and took out the cross, making sure he didn't kink the chain. He rubbed the cross between his fingers. He knew it was given to her by his father years ago and she wore it constantly. He thought about placing it around her neck. She could use some divine intervention. But she thrashed around often enough that he was worried she might snag the chain and snap it.

The crucifix was light and cool on his palm. He traced the figure with his finger. The watch and earrings didn't hold the same meaning to her as this gold cross did. Her rings did, of course, and he gently slid those back into the bag.

He undid the clasp on the cross's chain. He put it around his own neck and clipped it closed. He patted the chilly gold as it lay against his chest.

He sat there as his mother slept. He pulled out the book he was reading, *A Year of Lesser,* and immersed himself in the story. His mother drifted into a deep sleep and emitted a soft snore. After he finished a few chapters he checked his watch. He wanted to get on the road. Outside the snow was falling faster and the wind was picking up. He started to pack up the empty supper containers and his mother's bag of belongings. His mother opened her eyes.

"Hi," she said.

"Hey, Mom. You fell asleep."

"Oh."

"I need to get going." He leaned in and gave her a kiss.

His mother's eyes lit up. She nodded. "David," she said.

"I'm working on it. Soon, both your boys will be visiting you."

His mother smiled. "Good."

"Okay, Mom," he squeezed her hand, "see you tomorrow."

Chapter 33

Joel tossed and turned all night long; in the distance he could hear a siren wail—an ambulance heading for the hospital. He flitted in and out of sleep, in and out of consciousness. The darkness of night had wrapped the room in a mantle of gloom and murk.

Outside, the wind rustled the branches of the silver maple so that they scraped against the side of the house and his window. He pulled the covers further up over his head and tried to sleep. Joel's mind was spinning in overdrive, processing everything that had happened to his father, his mother, his brother.

His sleep, if he could call it that, was fitful, and it provided no rest. His eyes felt heavy and he wavered between slumber and wakefulness. The wind howled outside. He sat up in bed. The tree groaned as it grazed the glass. Inside, the house was still and quiet, with none of the familiar sounds.

Joel eventually went back to sleep. He dreamt he was immersed in a dark forest. The forest was shadowy, cast in an eerie gloom. He dreamt he was walking through the forest, weaving around trees whose branches were brittle and looked as though they were made of dark brown glass. The forest floor was a dry black sand. Joel found himself running through it, his feet bogged in the sand. He ran past trees that looked dead. They were dry and fragile; there was no way they were alive. Yet the trees had life. As he passed by them, he could see each tree had a face in its trunk. The trees were people that Joel recognized. He was gripped with a wave of dream-induced realization that the woods held many secrets and he was being tested. He started searching the faces on the tree trunks looking for his father.

"Dad," he called out. "Dad? You in here?"

The trees murmured in response. "There. Over there."

With their branches creaking, the trees all pointed to the north side of the forest. Joel began walking, his steps heavy in the dry sand. As he passed by, trees pointed with their brittle branches. "Keep going. He's over there." Joel could see trickles of sap flowing down their trunks as they spoke.

Joel tossed and turned in bed. The ice pellets beat against his window. The wind pushed the tree branches and they creaked against the siding.

He dreamt he walked through the forest, stumbling in the direction the trees showed him. He came to a tree, newer, much younger than the rest. Not as many branches, its trunk showing some signs of green. A wind rustled through the forest and the branches creaked and groaned with the movement.

Joel saw the image of his father, his face locked in the trunk of a tree. The wind picked up and blew hard. A few twigs snapped off and blood flowed from the wounds. When the blood flowed, his father, the tree, could speak.

"The north wind does blow, Joel, and there will be snow." The blood flow slowed and so did his father's words: "And what will robin... do then... poor thing..." His voice trailed off as the trickle of blood slowed to a few drops and then stopped.

"What? What do you mean?" Joel asked in the dream. "What are you telling me?"

The wind circled and howled and as it blew it picked up a few flecks of the gritty, black sand and blew them in Joel's face. The wind roared and whipped around the tree that was his father. It snapped off another twig. A trickle of blood seeped from where the twig had been.

The wind whipped around and snapped another twig from the tree that was now his father.

"He'll tuck his head under his wing to keep himself warm," the tree said. Blood trickled from where the last twig snapped off. "Keep yourself warm, Joel, keep your head warm, stay out of the wind."

"Wait!" shouted Joel. "Where is David? Where is he?"

The blood from the broken branch dripped one drop at a time.

His father uttered a single word with each drop: "City."
Another: "Go."
Then another: "Safe."
"Go."

The flow of blood stopped. The tree with his father's face stood still. The wind had settled down and Joel could see hints of the pink break of dawn on the horizon.

He sat upright in bed. His T-shirt was soaked with sweat. He was breathing hard, like he had run a long distance. He got up out of bed. His feet were cold on the bedroom floor.

Chapter 34

Joel made it to school as the bell for first period was ringing. He ran into class and sat down. He managed to put in an appearance at every class.

He bumped into Zack after history. "Hear anything?"

"Nothing," Zack said. "Radio silence."

"Think you can get your Dad's car?"

"Maybe after he gets home from work," Zack said, "and that's a big maybe."

"Call me tonight when you know."

Joel sat with Maria at lunch. She was madly working on her paper for English.

Joel took a sheet of paper and wrote out half a page. He had to refocus his thoughts. Whenever he was with Maria, Tal Bachman's new song, "She's So High," played in his mind.

"Told you, Gatsby may like Nick, but he uses him to get to Daisy. Here," he said, sliding the loose-leaf towards her, "use this in there somewhere. But put it in your own handwriting."

"Awesome, thanks." Maria read the notes. "You're so clever, Joel."

Joel munched on an apple. He didn't want to spend any money on cafeteria slop. He was mad at himself for being in too much of a rush to bring something from home.

"Cookie?" Maria offered him a homemade chocolate chip.

"Love one." He grabbed one and shoved it whole into his mouth.

"That new?" Maria indicated the crucifix around his neck.

Joel's hand instinctively covered the gold cross. "No, it's been around for a while."

"I've never seen you wear it before."

"I just felt like putting it on."

"You're not going all super religious on me, are you?" She laughed.

"Nah," Joel laughed with her, "it's my mother's. I'm just keeping it safe for her till she gets better."

"You're sweet, Joel."

The last class of the afternoon ended, and Joel walked toward the main doors. He hoped word got to the social worker that he was in school, that he attended all his classes. Joel made a point of walking by the office three separates times that day. He wanted to be seen by the secretary, the vice principal, by anybody that could vouch for him that he was at school and doing fine. He needed witnesses.

Joel walked down the front steps and started for home. The fresh air felt good.

"Hey, Joel," Jennifer, David's girlfriend, called out.

"Oh, hi, Jen." Joel stopped walking.

She came up beside him. "Mind if I walk with you?"

"Sure." He cinched the shoulder straps of his backpack and started walking again. "Be my guest."

"Did you hear from him?"

"Nothing," Joel said, "but I know where he is. I tried to head down the other day, but I had some issues."

They turned onto Queen Street.

"Do you have time for a coffee? I need to tell you something."

"I'd love to, but I'd have to hit a bank machine first."

"It's on me," Jennifer said. "Let's go to the Nook & Cranny."

"Sounds good."

They went into the café and Jennifer ordered them each a Chai tea. "My mother always says tea is the best to warm you up." They sat next to the fireplace.

Jennifer poured some sugar into her tea. "It's crazy," she said, "I'm going crazy. I need him."

"You and me both."

"I know, Joel, I'm sorry, but you don't understand."

Joel stirred his tea and smiled.

"I feel so isolated without him." Jennifer put down her mug. "It's like I don't know where to—I, I haven't got a clue…"

"Did you know Dad and David got into a big fight before he left?"

Jennifer shook her head.

"I thought they were going to kill each other. David is so much bigger than Dad now. He towered over him. Dad could barely stand up as it was. He'd been drinking all day and David—"

"Were they yelling at each other? David call him names again?"

"David hit him. Right in the jaw. Almost knocked him out."

"Oh my God. You call the cops or anything?"

"I thought about it. I always thought about calling the cops. Every time Dad got on one of his tirades, I'd almost call 9-1-1. But then I'd stop. I'd wonder, Will he turn on me for calling?" Joel stared into his mug. "He knew every cop out there. He'd get super embarrassed."

"But still, it's not right. How was David? Did he hurt him?"

"I know there is no way the cops would have ever arrested my father. They would've taken David before they took their paramedic buddy." Joel took a drink of his tea. "This is perfect for a chilly day."

"You don't think David would have got a concussion, do you? I'm grasping here, but you don't think he got amnesia or anything?"

"If anybody got a concussion it would have been Dad. David clocked him pretty good. And that's the night Dad," Joel swallowed hard, "when Dad died."

Jennifer nodded. "And that's why you think David took off?"

"I know that's part of it."

"Yeah." Jennifer swirled her tea and took a drink.

"He'd been talking about going to Boston for weeks. That's all he could talk about." Joel stared down into his tea. "I thought he was joking. You know, talking big. Did he mention it to you?"

"Boston?"

"Yeah."

"Yes, but he said not right away. He wanted to set something up, get himself squared away here first. He wasn't talking immediate, he said he wanted to do it right, so he could make a go of it."

"A job first, you mean?"

"A job, a place to stay, a plan. A longterm plan."

"He told me everything was set up. That he was going to go there first and then maybe move on to New York."

"He hasn't contacted you at all?"

"Nothing," Joel shook his head.

Jennifer frowned. She stared into the fireplace. The gas flames licked at an imitation log.

"I need him back here." Joel thought about his mother, the empty house.

"Me too."

"If he doesn't turn up back home, they're going to put me in a foster home."

"Aren't you a bit too old for a foster home?"

"Not according to the stupid fucking law I'm not."

"Eighteen," Jennifer nodded, "I guess, makes sense."

"It's fucking stupid."

Jennifer drank her tea. "I need him," her voice trembled. "I have decisions to make that I can't do by myself."

Her words made him anxious. Joel felt a wave of fear and panic wash over him.

"You haven't heard from him? Please, Joel, please tell me the truth. It would kill me if David were just telling you to say that."

"That last time I talked to him was after he slugged Dad."

"Honest? I won't tie him down to anything. You'd tell me, wouldn't you Joel?"

"If I knew anything, I'd tell you." Joel started to piece together what she was really inquiring about.

"I know he wants his freedom," Jennifer whispered, her voice cracking. "Free of me, free of Amherst, free of any responsibilities. I just need to hear it from him. I just need to tell him."

Joel struggled to find words. He looked down at his cup. It was nearly empty now. He tilted it in his hands, swirling the tea leaves, hoping they would spell out an answer, or advice. Instead, they looked like miniature sparrows flying in a perfect circle. "You're having a baby, aren't you?"

Jennifer nodded. "David needs to know. He deserves to know. I need him to weigh in here."

All he could think about was how pissed off his father would have been, and how his mother would be angry at first but then would secretly buy things for a baby, a grandchild. She'd make plans to take it on walks to the park and to the beach.

"How long?" Joel asked.

"I need to make some decisions quick. I need to tell him before I tell my parents. My father is going to freak. I want David there. It'll make things go smoother," Jennifer sighed. "Or at least it'll be two against two and not me alone against my parents."

"David never was one much for owning up to things. Are you thinking David could protect you?"

"Something like that. I don't think I'll be kicked out or beat up or anything like that. But I want to show them that I can, that me and David are old enough, mature enough, to handle this."

"David always bails out at the first opportunity, though, he never sticks with anything."

"That we can handle it together, that we can deal with it like rational adults. And I fucking well can't do that when he's run off to Christ knows where."

"He's in Boston. I have a line on where he is."

"Take me with you. I want to go get him."

"I'll go and bring him back. I promise. You don't need to be going on the road right now. I need him back too or else they're shipping me off to live at some stranger's place."

"I'm coming with you, Joel. I think I've got more riding on this than you do."

Joel drank down the last of his tea. "You keeping the baby? Have you thought about a—"

"I think my parents will have an easier time accepting it. I mean, plus I can't, I couldn't go through with it. I have nightmares already. I just couldn't. I understand why some girls do it—I get it—but I just—no." Jennifer shook her head. "No." Tears welled in her eyes.

"I meant adoption. Would you put the baby up for adoption?"

She laughed. "I'm sorry, these are all the things going on in my mind. I've been wracked with guilt and worry. I want David here. I need him. I'm getting to be too far along to consider abortion. My main decision now is to keep it myself and raise it or give it up."

Joel nodded.

"And if the baby looks anything like David," Jennifer smiled, "how could I possibly do anything but keep it?"

Joel looked at Jennifer. He thought she looked so pretty. Her long blonde hair and deep blue eyes made her and David look like a couple straight out of Hollywood. He thought back to the time he nearly walked in on them at the shack. Was that when it happened? He remembered seeing them on the couch. He tried to look at her and felt his face reddening.

"I'm sorry, Joel. Look at me all so self-absorbed. After everything you've gone through. Your dad. Your mom. And he is your brother."

"Mom's getting better. I'll track David down and bring him home." He tried to look at Jennifer and focused on her hair, her lips, anything but her eyes. "With Dad it's still so strange. Some days it's like he's working on shift somewhere and will be back the next morning. Other times, it hits full on that he's gone."

Jennifer nodded. "I'm sorry you have to go through all this." She swallowed the last of her tea and slipped on her jacket. "I always thought I'd be happy about a baby. I've always wanted kids; all I ever wanted was to raise a family and stay at home. I never saw myself as a career woman or some free spirit who never settles down." She frowned and shook her head. "I didn't expect it this soon. And I didn't expect to do it solo." She zipped up her jacket and pulled on her mittens. "I was stupid, but," she patted her belly, "I'm not going to let that affect this little unplanned surprise."

Joel stood up. "I'll bring him back," he said, pulling on his toque. "David needs to be here."

Chapter 35

The phone rang and Joel jumped. The shrill ring shattered the silence of the house.

"I got my father's car." It was Zack.

"Great. Pick me up."

"You'll have to come here. Scott and I had a few nips already, so I shouldn't really be driving."

"Seriously?" Joel was pulling on his boots, cradling the phone between his shoulder and his ear. "Whatever. I'll be right over."

When Joel walked up to Zack's house, Zack and Scott were sitting in the car with the engine running. Joel got in the driver's side. The heat in the car was welcome. He took off his toque and gloves, and shook his head at them.

"You guys crack me up." He could smell alcohol mixed with the faint odour of pot. "Is that all you guys do, drink and smoke?"

"We need to make a little stop before we get on the road."

"I need you guys to be able to stand up when we get to Boston." Joel backed the car out of the driveway. "I may need you to help me convince David to come home. I may need your muscles, Scott. You need to be okay with it."

"Little Jo-Jo, you need to pull into the NSLC before we get going. We need some road pops."

"Only my Mom gets to call me Little Jo-Jo. And my aunt. But that's it."

"Right, Big Jo-Jo," Zack laughed. "Stop at the liquor store, we need supplies."

Joel waited in the car while Scott and Zack went inside. The rain turned to ice pellets, and they bounced off the hood and windshield of the car.

"Drive, Joel, drive!" Zack yelled as he hopped into the car. He threw the two forty ouncers of rum on the floor. Scott jumped in the back and slammed the door. He laughed and turned around to look out the rear window as they drove away.

"Step on it!" Zack yelled again. "Get this thing going as fast as you can."

"What's your rush?" Joel backed the car out of the parking spot. "Didn't they give you a bag for the booze?"

"They wouldn't serve us because"—he laughed—"they claimed we were drunk. They tried to kick us out."

"Didn't stop us, though," Scott added from the back seat. "Took the booze and ran."

"What! Are you shitting me?" Joel looked in the rear-view mirror back at Scott. "What in hell were you thinking."

"I was thinking I wanted some more rum," Zack burped.

"You've got to go back, take that booze back and apologize," Joel said. He slowed the car down.

"You step on the gas pedal and drive like a son of bitch." Zack made a fist and shook it in Joel's face.

"Assholes. You're fucking crazy." Joel pushed Zack's hand away. "Get your fist out of my face." He stepped on the gas and turned down Maple Street. The sleet pelted the windshield. "Where do you idiots want me to go?"

Zack turned around. "See anything out the back, Scott?"

"Not yet." Scott scanned the road behind them. "Hurry up, Joel."

"The highway. Head for the highway," Zack said.

"For fuck sakes." Joel turned onto the ramp and got on the highway. "We were supposed to go get my brother and you jerk-offs pull this shit. Did you hold them up too?" Joel asked, his voice shaking from a combination of anger and fear.

Zack snorted. "What do you think, we're stupid?"

"You want an answer?"

Scott laughed. "No, we just took the booze."

"Well thanks for roping me into this shit." Joel felt the rear end of the big Chrysler fishtail as he drove through heavy slush. "It's slick," he said. Behind them they heard sirens in the distance.

"I'm stopping for them," he said. The car slid again, and the rear wheels spun. Joel pressed the gas hard and the car straightened out. "It's too slippery to drive. I'm stopping." He took his foot off the accelerator and eased onto the brake. The car veered on to the shoulder of the road and missed the guardrail by inches.

"You can't stop, Joel. Get to the next exit and we'll lose them in Springhill."

"We'll lose our lives if we keep going. I'm pulling over right here."

The other cars on the highway slowed down. "Look at everybody else, they're stopping too. It's so icy. This is nuts. We're going to kill ourselves."

The police car was five hundred feet behind them, and its flashing lights flicked in the rear-view mirror. "I'm giving you guys fair warning. I'm stopping at the bottom of this hill. See that bridge? I'll never make it up there anyway." The hill was a steep incline that the sleet had turned into a skating rink. "You can jump out and run or whatever. I'm not into this shit, you crazy bastards."

Joel slowed the car down as he approached the hill, put on his signal, and pulled to the side.

"You're a prick, Joel," Zack said as he jumped out before the car could stop. He ran down the snowbank and headed toward the river clutching the two liquor bottles.

Scott hopped out too. "Thanks for the lift, you bastard," he yelled. He stumbled away from the car and disappeared over the bank.

The cops were a hundred feet away. Joel shut off the engine and put on his four-way flashers. He sat in the car, his hands perched on the steering wheel, and waited for them.

The other cars on the road slipped and slid. At the top of the hill, Joel could see a red Chevrolet coming over the crest. A blue pick-up truck was behind it. The little red car hit a patch of ice and slid sideways down the hill. The driver of the pick-up truck jammed on his brakes. The brake lights glared in the driving sleet. The truck spun out of control and clipped the car hard. The crunch sounded like thunder. The red car spun. Twice. Then a third time. It bounced off the front of the truck, ricocheting into the guardrail of the bridge, its front end crumpled. The blue truck spun and stopped. It was in the wrong lane. Other cars, coming up to the crest of the hill, tried to slow down but skidded and slid out of control down the hill. But nobody else crashed.

Drivers stopped to help. Joel stepped out of the car. He fell, hitting the road hard. It was a sheet of ice.

The cop pulled his cruiser behind Joel's car and stepped out. The red and blue lights flashed. Joel felt like he was watching a movie. All he was supposed to do was drive to Boston and get David. And those two jackasses did this to him.

"Stay put," the cop said to Joel as he snapped handcuffs on him. The officer spoke into his radio. "Send an ambulance and fire, we've got an MVC. Springhill exit, southbound."

Another police car pulled up, and the cop got out and trudged over to Joel. He patted him down and shoved him in the back of his squad car.

The cop went over to the red car buried in the guardrail at the far side of the bridge. From the back of the police car Joel looked out across the bridge. The scene was surreal: a red car smashed into the guardrail of the bridge, a truck lengthwise across the highway halfway up the hill, and hunks of raw and bloody meat scattered on the highway around the blue truck.

The two people inside the truck wore orange vests and there was a rifle rack in the back window of the cab. Hunters, Joel thought. The mess splattered on the road was their catch of rabbits. Joel felt sick but was glad the guts on the road weren't human.

The passenger of the truck was trapped. The driver of the truck got out and tried to help him.

The wind bit into Joel's cheeks. He wished he could close the front door the cop had left open, but his hands were cuffed. The cop didn't stay at the red car long. He walked up to the truck and spoke to the driver, then the passenger. He spoke into his radio. Then he walked over to the red car again. The wind blew him back, and he hunched over and took baby steps so he wouldn't fall.

Joel watched from the back of the police car. Bitter cold air howled in through the open front door. More sirens approached. They sounded official and reassuring. Lights flashed along both directions of the highway. An ambulance was coming from Springhill and a fire truck was coming from the other direction. And more police cars from both directions.

The firefighters arrived and grimaced as the icy wind tore at their faces.

The ambulance pulled in and parked at an angle. One paramedic went over to the truck. The other went to the red car that had disintegrated into the guardrail and poked his head inside. Joel wanted to close his eyes and make all of this go away. Instead he watched, locked inside the back of the police car. He watched in horror and fascination.

The guy in that car must have died instantly. He would not have felt a thing. It was a solid hit—first the truck slammed him, and then he smashed into the guardrail. Nobody could survive that. Joel knew the guy was dead because the paramedic that went over to help him stayed a few seconds, a minute at the most, and then went to help the other paramedic and the firefighters trying to free the guy in hunter orange trapped in the truck.

The firefighters hooked up an array of big, heavy tools powered by a generator. They worked to free the guy from the twisted truck.

A fire truck at the top of the hill blocked the road. Another big red engine, with its lights flashing, did the same on the other side of the bridge. Joel was locked in the back of a police car watching everything. He was freezing. When they got the passenger out of the truck, they put him on a long board and slid him onto a stretcher and took him to the ambulance. A paramedic escorted the driver into the other ambulance.

The cop, the one who had arrested Joel, came back to the car holding some papers. He spoke into his radio.

Joel knew the guy in the red car was dead. He could see from the back of the police car. The guy was young. He wore a blue parka, and the hood was twisted around and hung down on his chest. That was the one peculiar thing. Except for that, he looked like he was sleeping, his head tilted on the headrest. Joel couldn't believe that all this happened in a matter of seconds, and before his own eyes. In seconds, a guy had dead. That's all it took.

The police officer had closed the car door now. He was busy outside talking to people and writing in his notebook. Joel began to warm up; the heat was on full blast and felt good.

Joel saw a big blue sedan creep up to the fire truck blocking the bridge. A man got out of the sedan. He wore a red and black checked lumberjack vest and a pair of fuzzy brown slippers trimmed with white fake fur. He was slow and surefooted on the ice as he walked over to the red car. He walked like he knew he wouldn't slip. Or if he did slip, like he didn't care. He looked inside the car. His mouth moved. Joel knew he must be yelling. The wind howled, and Joel couldn't hear anything the man said.

The man left the red car and went over to the paramedic who was helping the driver of the truck into the side door of the ambulance. He spoke to the paramedic. The paramedic ignored him and escorted his patient inside the truck. The man in the brown slippers was yelling. His mouth opened wide, his lips moved fast. His forehead furrowed.

The paramedic shut the side door of the ambulance. The man in the slippers yanked it open. A gust of wind blew hard and slammed the side door and bent it back hard on its hinges. It buckled. The paramedic reached out and tried to close it, but he couldn't. He got out of the truck and slammed the door to close it. The man in slippers moved to the double doors at the back of the ambulance and banged on the doors with both fists. The paramedic walked over to stop him. The man turned and grabbed the paramedic's arm and pointed at the red car. The cop walked over to the back of the ambulance now. The man in slippers was screaming at the top of his lungs.

The wind buffeted the police car Joel was locked in. The bridge swayed in the wind. Then the wind died down. Joel heard the man in slippers.

"Help him! Why aren't you helping my son?" he screamed. He pointed with both hands at the little red car crushed into the guardrail of the bridge.

The paramedic talked to him. He was calm. The man in the slippers listened. It was the first time since he left the red car that he was silent.

The paramedic said something and touched the man's arm. He looked him in the eyes, nodded, and spoke a few more words.

The man in slippers fell to his knees on the frozen highway. His hands trembled as he held them to his face. His chest heaved.

Joel knew the guy in the crushed red car was dead. And now, the man wearing the brown slippers with the fake white fur, his father, knew it too.

"We got your two buddies," the officer said as he escorted Joel up the stairs into the police station back in Amherst.

"I didn't know what they were up to," he said to the officer. "I didn't know they were stealing from the place."

"Wait till we get inside, then we can talk." They walked inside the station and the officer opened a door to a small room. He pointed to some chairs and led Joel to one at a small round table.

"Okay," the officer said, "why don't you tell me what happened."

Joel told him how he was driving because his friends were drunk, and that he waited in the car outside the liquor store. He told the officer how Scott and Zack were all giddy and laughing and how he panicked when he knew what they had done. And how he stopped at the bottom of the hill because he did not want to run from the police and the roads were bad. He told him how Zack and Scott hightailed it through the woods, and how Joel just waited for the police to come get him. And then the crash happened on the hill.

The cop stared at him. "How do you know these guys?"

"I've known them all my life. They're my brother's friends. They've done some stupid things but never anything this stupid."

Another cop, holding a small device in his hands, walked into the room. He motioned for the one speaking with Joel to join him outside the door where they whispered a few moments.

The first cop came back in. "Your friends, if you can call them that," he said to Joel, "have verified your side of the story. We're going to hold you here until we get a statement from the clerk at the liquor store."

"Right now though," the cop holding the little machine said, "we'll have to give you a breathalyser test. We'll see if that's okay before we do anything else."

"It will be," Joel said. "I told you I was driving, I wasn't drinking."

The cop held up the machine and pointed to a tube on the side of it. "Blow hard into here till I say stop."

Joel did as he was told. The machine beeped. "Okay stop." The cop looked at the screen for a second and the machine beeped again. "Zero point zero."

"What's going to happen to me?" Joel asked. "Am I going to jail?"

"Lucky for you, if the clerk's story jives, we won't be charging you with theft. But there'll be a few motor vehicle act charges. Speeding, running a red light. You know you went right through the intersection at Main and Maple without even slowing down?"

"Yeah, sorry about that. I couldn't believe they robbed the place."

"You might get careless and imprudent for that. You'll be safe from resisting arrest." He smiled at Joel and put his hand on his shoulder. "You did the right thing by stopping, son."

Chapter 36

Joel left the bookstore and headed towards Mrs. Payne's house. He passed St. Francis church and noticed the manger scene out front. It looked so festive with a coating of snow. A few evergreen trees were propped up around it, making the re-creation of the stable look like a camping trip or a walk in the woods. It felt simple to Joel. It felt peaceful. Every year before Christmas his mother would go to confession and drag him and David along.

"It's good to get your soul washed clean for Christmas," his mother would tell them. As soon as they were old enough to go to confession, she'd shoo them into the confessional. "Don't leave anything out."

Afterwards, Joel and David would compare the list of prayers the priest told them to say as penance. "I got five Hail Mary's, how many did you get?" he would ask David.

Pretty much even, the boys would giggle. Then suppress the laughter when their mother glared at them. She took it so seriously.

Every lamppost on the street was decorated with lights in the shape of holly or a star. The town looked festive, in a simple straightforward way. Joel liked things simple, as they had been for as long as he could remember. As he walked on and the overhead decorations lit up, gold and red and green lights twinkled. It was warm and quaint, the falling snow the perfect backdrop. Joel took it all in and wondered if his mother would be able to get to confession before Christmas. She'd like it if she could. But he realized nothing was simple anymore.

As Joel walked up the hill toward Payne's house, the snow started to fall in soft, fluffy flakes. He waved to Siggy Smith on his usual bottle-collecting route.

"Hi, Siggy," Joel called out as he passed by.

Siggy kept his head down and didn't look up at Joel, but he did raise his hand in a quick wave. He pushed his shopping cart along. "Oh brother, bottles and cans," he muttered, repeating the words over and over.

Joel passed Siggy, and noticed his hands gripping the push bar of the shopping cart. His hands were red and looked raw. He felt bad for Siggy. Parker greeted Joel at the door and brought him inside.

Mrs. Payne glanced at him as he came in. She was sitting in front of a music stand, playing the violin. It sounded full and sweet and warm to Joel.

Parker whispered to him, "Have a seat."

Mrs. Payne moved in a steady rhythm, creating a beautiful sound with her instrument.

Joel strained to read the title on the sheet music: *Brandenburg Concerto No. 3, J.S. Bach.*

Joel was mesmerized by her playing. As he listened, he scanned the room. He noticed the photos on the mantle. One of a much younger Mrs. Payne and her husband on a sailboat, with a younger man, obviously their son, smiling between them. Payne continued playing her piece.

Joel marvelled at how she could draw such emotion, such feeling out of pieces of tightly wound gut. She finished the Bach piece and returned her violin to its stand.

Joel clapped. "That was beautiful."

Mrs. Payne set the bow on top of the piano and came over and sat in her armchair opposite him. Her face radiated a combination of pleasure and exhilaration tinged with a whisper of exhaustion.

"I'm played out," she said. "Literally. I'm not as young as I once was." She took a few deep breaths.

"I had no idea you could play like that."

"Years of lessons. And practice. What else does an old lady have but time for practice?"

"My brother and I listen to a lot of music. We always focus on the lyrics, you know, we rely on the words they are saying to give you the meaning of the song." He looked over at the violin.

"You get the meaning from the words. The music, the melody, hangs in the background and drives the song forward." He saw the sheet music on the stand. "But with that, it's just four strings and you manage to bring out a huge range of emotion."

"That's one of my favourite pieces to play. So deep, so textured."

"I'm envious. I can't play anything like that. I pluck away at the guitar and, in my mind, I'm using it as a background for whatever song I want to come up with." Joel went over to the violin. He looked at the sheet music. "I can't read music. I wanted to try to learn saxophone. But Dad took his to a pawn shop just before he died." Joel pointed to the photo above the fire. "This your son?"

The fireplace crackled, and the warmth spread across the room.

"Dear Christopher. The love of my life. I still miss him."

"I'm sorry. I didn't mean to—"

"Do not apologize. I love to talk about him."

"How old was he when he…?"

"He'd be a middle-aged man now. I think of all that he has missed out on. That's the regret I have now. I feel his absence."

"Dad always said he found losing young people was the hardest."

"I think of Christopher when I see an orange sunset over the water. Or when I smell coffee with cinnamon. Or when I hear 'When Doves Cry.' Or any Prince song. Christopher loved Prince." Mrs. Payne looked toward the fireplace. "I'm always missing him."

Parker came in carrying a tray of cheese and crackers and a pot of tea.

"Something to nibble on, Mr. Carruthers."

"Sometimes it just seems like Dad will walk in the front door. I don't forget everything that happened. It's just that I get lost until I remember the old familiar routine is gone."

"Oh Joel, I know. And I don't mean to minimize the pain that you're feeling. That's not my intention." She lifted the cover off the teapot and peered inside. "That cliché is true. Time does heal old wounds. It doesn't remove the scars, but they do heal. It's like a hole in my heart, there's scar tissue and it's closed over, but you know there is a piece gone."

She poured two cups of tea. "Memories remain fond. As you get further away from the event, the shock, the horror, fades, and you try to move forward one step at a time. Indeed, you try to stand your ground, not fall backwards. You try to dodge the overwhelming grief that crashes towards you like a sorrowful crescendo." She passed Joel the teacup. "Those are the days when the only prayer you can utter is 'take me too.'"

She spread some blue cheese on a cracker and ate it.

"The grief, in the beginning, permeates your entire life," Mrs. Payne continued, taking a sip of her tea. "How you eat, how you sleep, how you talk to others. Even how you walk down the street."

Joel took a drink. "My house is so quiet," he said. "Even the phone ringing or the wind outside rattles me."

"I do have regrets." Mrs. Payne balanced her saucer on her knee. "Christopher was a human being after all. Full of the same evils and vulnerabilities as the rest of us. My regret, though, is the things he never had the chance to do." She took a sip and stared at the photos on the mantlepiece. "Travel. Or the pride of ownership of having your own home. A man's castle, you know. Or the pleasure of cooking a Christmas dinner for your own family. Or playing Santa Claus for your own kids. Or reading a bedtime story to your child and assuring them they are loved as you tuck them in at night. I only have regrets of what never was." She looked at Joel. "And then I think how grateful I am to have had him in the first place."

"I can't even think about my father yet. I think about my brother."

"You're right to focus on the living." She set her cup down on the table. She held out her hands toward Joel. "As I sit here with these blue-veined and wrinkled hands"—she tugged at tufts of her hair—"and this head of curly white hair, all I can do in these twilight years I have been given is be grateful." She sighed, "So grateful."

Joel sliced off a sliver of camembert. "Dad said that he could hear the music, but that he could never play it." He popped the cheese into his mouth. It tasted sour and creamy—and he realized he was starving. "Charlie Parker said it actually, I guess."

"Music is more than a hobby," Mrs. Payne smiled. "It's more than something you let happen to you. Especially when you play it, when you create it, or when you re-create something someone else has created. It becomes a part of you, if only for an instant. You feel the rhythm. The beat lives in your fingers and toes."

"I always have to hum along or tap my foot. I can't help it."

"Something in a piece of music grabs hold of you. It manifests itself physically inside of you. You go from being a passive listener to being an active participant in the experience. You become one with the music, the same way a dancer does."

Joel sipped his tea. Then he put the cup down and walked back to the fireplace to let his eyes move over the photographs on the mantelpiece. The flames from the fire danced yellow and orange. Joel looked at the albums that were arranged on the shelf next to her stereo. He picked up *Hits*. "My mom loves this album."

"Joni Mitchell is an amazing woman," Mrs. Payne smiled. "She's a huge talent."

"Your son play anything? Any instruments?"

"He was so talented." She shifted in her chair, rearranging the cushion behind her back. "Violin, cello, bassoon. He was learning the oboe when he died. I'll always remember the day he got his acceptance. He was so nervous before the audition. I was never worried a bit." Mrs. Payne smiled. "A mother knows."

"Audition?"

"Yes. He was accepted to Berklee."

Joel nodded. "Cool. Great school."

Mrs. Payne looked at him with a wide smile. "Joel," she moved to the edge of her chair, "you should learn to play saxophone. What about your father's?"

"I thought about it, but I'm flat broke since Dad, since Mom, since everything."

"Joel, allow me to support your, shall we say, education in the arts." She took her cheque book from the drawer of her desk. "It will be my pleasure to assist you."

"Thanks, Mrs. Payne," Joel said, shaking his head, "but no, I couldn't."

"You can, and you will." She signed the cheque with a flourish.

"No, I can't. It's not—"

"I'll hear none of this." She passed him the cheque. "You're buying your father's saxophone back."

Chapter 37

Joel walked out of the bank after cashing the cheque from Mrs. Payne. It felt great to have a wad of cash in his pocket. He walked over to Church Street and into the pawn shop where he had been with his father. It seemed so long ago.

Big Bobby was sitting behind the counter, his eyes focused on a television in the showroom. There were fingerprints in the dust that coated the screen. A *Coronation Street* episode blared on the television. The picture was snowy, and the volume was loud.

Joel looked around the showroom. He saw his father's saxophone propped up with the other musical instruments. He felt his chest tighten.

"I'd like to buy that saxophone."

Big Bobby put his fingers to his lips. His eyes fixed on the television. Joel went over for a closer look at the instruments—acoustic guitars, electric guitars and bass guitars dangling tantalizingly from racks along the wall. Amplifiers stacked one on top of another. Joel stood there and wished. He wished he could afford to buy one of each. Even just an electric guitar with an amplifier would be amazing. He had claimed his father's old acoustic guitar as his own about a year ago. He learned to play, picking away at it and jamming with his buddies from school. An electric guitar would be so cool.

The credits rolled on the television and the theme music played. The trumpet piece sounded lonely and tinny to Joel.

Big Bobby called out, "Okay, now what did you want, kid?"

"That saxophone," Joel pointed, "I want to buy it."

"Oh. I remember you. You were in a few weeks ago. Your old man was into the sauce. He gave that beast a funny name."

"Birdie blue. I know," Joel smiled.

"Yep. Dude was very particular about that." Big Bobby laughed and walked out from behind the counter. He picked up the saxophone and closed the case and brought it back to the cash register and rung up the sale.

Joel counted out the bills from his wad of cash.

Big Bobby slid the saxophone toward him. "Enjoy it, kid. It's got great tone."

Back home Joel opened the saxophone case. He remembered the last time he saw his father play the sax. It was that afternoon when the power company came to cut the power. His father was so drunk he couldn't play it and dragged it out to the car to take to the pawn shop. That seemed like forever ago.

Joel lifted the saxophone from its case, revealing a few sheets of crumpled sheet music, "In the Mood" and "'Round Midnight." Under those was an old photograph. Joel remembered seeing this picture before, but he never thought about it much. To him it was just a picture of his dad when he was younger.

He studied the photo. His father was wearing a suit jacket and narrow tie. He was standing with four other men, all about the same age. Twenty-five or thirty, Joel thought, but he didn't know for sure. They were posing outside a club. The neon sign said, "Starlight Jazz Club." The "j" in jazz was a saxophone. He wasn't sure where the club was. It looked like it was on a busy city street. Was it Halifax maybe? Or New York? He didn't know. Who would have taken the picture?

In the photo, Joel's father stood with one hand on the saxophone case. He held the horn to his chest. He was looking directly at the camera. His smile was so wide he looked like he had just conquered the world. The four others were all smiling too. They were having fun. One guy, with a curly black beard, held up a trumpet like a trophy. The second, lanky with a huge head of hair, posed with a bass guitar. The other, with a friendly, round face, his head back in laughter, held his hands out, as though he were playing an imaginary piano. The last guy, with curly hair, and the same height as Joel's father, tapped a pair of drum sticks together. They were having a blast. They were all so happy. They all wore matching black suits with those narrow ties that looked so dated and lame. Joel's friends would call them 'retro.' He was sure his father would have described himself as mod or cool. He put the photo on the coffee table.

Joel picked up the saxophone and polished the bell with the soft black cloth from the case. He tried to remember the fingerings his father had shown him months ago. Joel felt the action of the keys. They were cold; the brass absorbed the coldness of the house. He pressed them. They made a soft *pfft* sound as the felt pads sealed over the valves. He held out the horn and looked it up and down.

He rooted around in the case and found a new reed. He changed it the way he had seen his father do so many times. Then he raised the mouthpiece to his lips and drew a deep breath as his father had taught him. "The secret is air, embouchure and aperture," his father had said. It all comes down to those fundamentals. That's it. Joel could still envision him with the mouthpiece dangling near his lips as he talked.

Joel formed his lips like his father had shown him and breathed out like he was blowing out birthday candles. He moved his fingers on the keys. He practiced the scales in the key of b flat. The sound of the instrument was big and bright, and its notes filled the room.

Not half bad, he thought.

He played again, going up and down the scale. He changed position and played the scales again. This time he took it slower and concentrated. Joel liked what he heard. He tried a few more times.

Eventually he tired of playing scales and wanted to try a melody. He thought of his father's favourite song by Charlie Parker, "Lover Man." He took a moment to remember how it went in his head. He put his lips on the mouthpiece and blew, fingering what he thought the opening notes were. He was close, but what he produced did not sound like "Lover Man." It was pleasant, but it wasn't the melody he was hoping for.

He tried again. The music sounded good, but still not the song he was attempting to play. He slid back into more comfortable territory and worked on playing the scale. It was rewarding to play something he was familiar with, something he knew he could get right. After several attempts, he managed to get all the way through the scale without a mistake. He tried "Lover Man" again. It sounded better, but still not quite what he wanted.

He thought of another favourite song of his father's, "Blue Skies." He had heard that for as long as he could remember.

He tried to play it, but it didn't sound recognizable. He thought of something easy. He played "Twinkle, Twinkle Little Star." He went slow and hit all the notes. But it sounded choppy. He blew again and tried another verse. Then he put the sax back in its case. A few lessons would be great.

He picked up his guitar and strummed it. He tuned it; the coldness of the house had contracted the strings and they sounded flat. He was much more comfortable playing guitar. His hands flowed across the frets, and he played all the scales he could think of. Joel was a natural on guitar. He ran through a bunch of different chords, alternating the rhythm, and he became lost in the music. It felt good. It was a release.

The house was quiet and still except for the sound of Joel playing the guitar. He finger-picked the notes of a G chord. He sped up, switching from G to C, then added in an F. He got into a rhythm. He flew through the chord changes with ease. The music sounded natural and complete.

An impulse to sing struck him. He sang out a few words.

Sometimes I look in the mirror.

He played some chords around these words and sang them out again. He repeated the words, strumming more music to accompany them. He tried a different pattern, changing the rhythm. He sang again. His voice startled him in the empty house. He was surprized how strong and clear it sounded.

Sometimes I look in the mirror
And see there's no one there.

He tried alternating the chords and experimented with different rhythms. He tried singing different words. He sang out snippets of phrases. He started playing and singing again. The start of a song flowed out of him.

No one there to say hello.

He put the guitar down and ran upstairs to his room. He grabbed the notebook he had once used to jot down ideas for songs. He bounded back downstairs, then stopped, returned to his room and retrieved the *Roget's Thesaurus* from his desk.

He returned to the living room and wrote out a few verses. He picked up the guitar and strummed it. He tried a lead break in the key of C, his fingers sliding up and down the fret board. He thought that worked okay. He made a note in his journal, wishing he knew how to read and write music.

He worked on another verse and wrote it in his journal. He scratched out some words, added some others. He read it back to himself. He wrote a second verse then a third.

He played the guitar and sang the words. He changed the order of some lines and scratched out others.

He worked on the song for an hour. His voice started to feel hoarse, but he continued working. He felt a joy in making something, in creating something new, feeling a release of tension in the process.

He went back upstairs to his room and rooted around in his closet. He knew it was in there somewhere. He checked the boxes on the floor. Then he looked up on the shelf. There it was. He pulled down his brother's tape recorder and some blank cassettes.

He went back to the living room and started a fresh page, creating a neat and legible copy of the song he had just written. He set up the microphone on the coffee table. He used his mother's Blue Mountain pottery eagle—a souvenir, she had often reminded him, of her honeymoon in Boston—to keep his notebook open to the page he was working on.

He strapped the guitar around his neck, then pushed the 'record' and 'play' buttons down at the same time. The machine whirred to life. Joel started playing a bright folk-rock rhythm pattern on his guitar. Then he sang, projecting his voice toward the microphone. He sang loud and clear while he played:

Sometimes I look in the mirror
And see there's no one there

No one there to say hello
No one there to listen to my cries
No one there to answer why

How can I linger in the streets?
With no one to guide me; no hand to hold
No one to share these times—sweet or cold

Sometimes I look in the mirror
And see there's no one there

How can you live it up in the wild city?
Do you know, and do you care?
In this empty room, I'm snared in pity

How can I assemble these puzzle pieces?
With no picture to use for clues
In silent shadows, my lonely prayer increases

Sometimes I look in the mirror
And see there's no one there
I see there's no one there
I see no one there.
No one there.

Chapter 38

The lights were on at the bookstore when Joel arrived. Pritchard was already there. Joel went to the staff room and hung up his coat. Maria wasn't in yet, but she would be soon. She would make the day bearable. He plugged in the kettle and made a cup of instant coffee. He took a drink and grimaced.

He moved out front to take up his place by the cash register. A couple of shipments had come in. Joel needed to phone the customers and let them know that their special requests were in. Some would offer their credit card numbers to pay for the titles and say that they'd be in later. Pritchard encouraged Joel to suggest that, because he wanted people to come into the store. They'll buy more if they come to the shop in person.

The wealthier customers wanted their purchases delivered to their homes or offices. Pritchard charged for the delivery—a service fee, he called it. If it were up to Joel, he would bring them the book for free, just to see someone get a book they wanted to read.

Pritchard only trusted Joel to deliver the books. He was excellent with customers, even the most pretentious ones. He made them feel good about their exquisite taste in literature.

Joel wrapped each book order with brown kraft paper from the large roll and sealed the edges with masking tape. A neat package. He placed the customer card on each package showing the their name, address, the title and the price.

He went to the back room with his empty coffee mug. He poked his head into Mr. Pritchard's office. "I'm going out on these deliveries," he said. "Is there anything else you need while I'm out?"

"Joel, step into my office please." Pritchard was reading a newspaper that was spread out on his gleaming wooden desk.

The account ledgers Pritchard normally pored over were pushed aside to make room.

"Close the door. Sit down."

Joel sat down in the chair in front of Pritchard's desk. It made him feel like he was at the principal's office.

"What's this I'm reading in *The Daily News*?" Pritchard tapped at a photo in the newspaper. It was the accident scene from the highway.

Joel shuddered at the memory of it.

"You're blurry, and, of course, there's no names in the article. But that's you in the back of that police car, isn't it?"

"My friends were stupid."

"I've heard rumours."

"I was stupid."

"It won't look good to our—to my—customers. You know what the people in this town are like. This does nothing for my shop's prestige."

"I know." Joel hung his head.

"This is a small town. People like things neat and orderly. Just like their picket fences and their gardens. They like their quaint little downtown with its Christmas lights and they like to talk with their neighbours after church on Sundays, they like shops they can walk to. They like our book shop where we can get books for them from anywhere in the world. They like their local little daily newspaper that brings them the news of the world, edited by the people that understand them." Pritchard wiped his spectacles. "What they do not like, Joel, is being served by people they can't trust. People that have done questionable things, objectionable things."

"I'm sorry, Mr. Pritchard. I've learned my lesson."

"People don't need to buy our books to live. It's not like they are groceries or wine. With so many choices out there, I don't want to give our customers, *my customers,* any excuse not to spend their money here."

"I know."

"I can't risk the reputation of my business on you."

"Mr. Pritchard, please."

Pritchard placed his now clean glasses on his nose. "Truth is Joel, you're good at your job."

Joel looked at Pritchard. He looked tiny behind his enormous desk. "Nothing like that will happen again. I promise."

"Perhaps it won't. But consider yourself on notice. One more slip up and I'll have no choice. The problem isn't your ability or your work ethic. It's not your knowledge of books. Those are above reproach. Public perception, Joel, is everything. If there's any hint of impropriety, it'll be game over."

"I won't let you down." Joel's face reddened. "Mr. Pritchard, you can count on me."

"I'm banking on it." He slapped his hand on the desk. "Now run those special orders to our best customers. Where are you headed?"

Joel listed the customer's names and addresses, all near downtown.

"Hurry back. I need you here to sell books to the gaggle of Christmas shoppers we'll get today. They, and their pocketbooks, will be out in droves." Pritchard stood up and looked out his window onto Albion Street. "And while you're out, pray for snow. Soft and pretty snowflakes make them feel like they're in a goddamned Currier and Ives Christmas card and they'll buy buy buy."

Out front, Joel gathered up the packages he had to deliver. "Hey," he said to Maria as she settled in at the cash register. A few early shoppers had trickled in, and they were browsing the aisles. By lunch time Joel knew the place would be a frenzy.

"Good morning." Maria yawned.

"I'm heading out to make these few deliveries. Want me to bring you back a real coffee?"

She stifled another yawn. "That'd be awesome."

Maria was gazing through the big showroom window by the cash desk that overlooked the street as Joel returned less than an hour later. The snow fluttered down. The street was busy with cars and taxis. The sidewalks were packed with shoppers rushing from store to store, gripping their packages and bags.

Joel came in from the street. He stamped the snow off his boots. He passed Maria the coffee.

"Thanks, Joel. You're a doll."

"I'm thinking of having a few people over to my place. You know, let loose a bit."

"Good idea."

Joel's mouth was dry. "You want to come?"

"Maybe. Can I bring Patricia too?"

Maria had opened some cartons of books, and now she was unpacking them and putting them on the cart. "Mr. Pritchard wants these displayed as soon as possible." She put her hands on her hips and twisted her neck to mimic Pritchard. She scrunched up her nose and said in as nasally a voice as she could muster, "Buy, buy, buy!"

"Anything new and interesting come in that order?" He looked through the packing slip to read the titles. "Nope. Just the usual."

A few more people entered the store and milled around. They wandered up and down the aisles, reaching for whichever books were most prominently displayed. They didn't show much thought; it was too close to the big day to find a joy and satisfaction in gift giving. Their patience was stretched, and they snatched up whatever looked right. They shopped in desperation.

The shop also had a few customers that had come in with the intention of scratching a few items off their gift lists, but instead ended up intrigued by a book they would buy for themselves. A customer asked Maria for some help and she pointed him toward the cookbook section. Another customer, a man with greying hair, caught Maria's eye and asked her where he could find books about birds. Joel could hear him while stacking the shelves. The guy really thought he was something. Maria was chatting with him as he tried to remember the name of the book he was looking for.

"It had a red cover," he said.

Joel could feel his heart beating in his chest, pounding out its own miniscule protest. He wanted to scream out loud, but remained silent instead.

He rang up a sale for two young children that had come up to the cash. Joel looked at the two kids and smiled. They put up their money and he stuck the books in a bag. "Thank you," they said, and left.

Joel stood on his tiptoes to see who had cornered Maria this time. He looked again at the back of the store. He couldn't see where she was. It didn't take that long to find a guy a book. He started out from behind the counter and made his way to the back of the store.

He turned around the corner and walked along the back. Maria was crouched down in the reference section. Joel felt the customer was studying her and not the books. He hovered at the end of the aisle to watch.

Maria passed the customer a book. "We have some general interest coffee table-type books too." She stood up. "If you're looking for field guides, they're in the science section."

Joel hurried back to the front of the store. He took his place behind the cash register before Maria figured out he was spying on her. Mr. Pritchard came out of his office. "Joel, Mrs. Payne telephoned." He pushed his round spectacles up his nose.

Joel turned around. "Oh, yes."

Mr. Pritchard was holding a slip of pink paper. "She's quite interested in finding these books. She wants you to call on her."

"I'll phone her in a few minutes."

"No," Pritchard replied, "she was quite specific. She was adamant that she wants you to call on her."

"I'll call her as soon as this rush settles down."

"No, call *on* her, as in visit her," he clarified. "In person." He passed the slip of paper to Joel. "She's a peculiar old bird, that one... but we will bend over backwards for her, won't we, Joel?" He turned to go back to his office. "You'll take care of her then, my boy, won't you."

Maria's customer came up to the cash with a big armload of books.

"Did you find what you were looking for, sir?" Joel forced himself to sound pleasant.

"Yes, but I wouldn't have without the help of this lovely lady." He towered over Maria and looked down at her and smiled. "She knows her stuff."

Joel scowled. Maria gave him a look that said *smarten up*.

"Thank you"—the man bent his head down to read her name tag—"Maria, is it? Thank you so much for your help."

Joel gritted his teeth. Maria took the books from the customer and placed them on the counter, and Joel rang them up. It was a significant sale. Joel gave the customer his total and swiped his credit card. Maria held the door open for him as he left.

"Bye. Thank you," she said, and looked at Joel. "What was all that about? That was my best sale of the day. Probably ever. Why were you so rude to him?"

"I'm sorry, I didn't realize." Joel busied himself at the till. "Old Pritchard will be happy with that sale. Nice work!"

Maria laughed. "Yep, he wanted birds and butterflies and I gave them to him."

CHAPTER 39

Joel's guests started to arrive, but word must have kept spreading, and people showed up at his house that he didn't know. They were friends of friends of friends. They were strangers to him. He had invited six people.

They had the television in the living room cranked as loud as they could, music videos blaring.

Scott and Zack were shooting tequila at the kitchen table. They were just two of the people who invited themselves over.

"Did you pay for this?" Joel picked up the bottle of tequila and held it up to the light.

"Yes, yes, I did, smart guy."

"You got ripped off. No worm."

They laughed. Joel poured himself a shot and drank it with them. He made a face. "How could anybody drink this shit? It tastes like fire starter."

"How in the hell do you know what fire starter tastes like?" Scott doubled over in laughter.

Joel wandered over to another groups of kids hanging out the back door smoking pot. Joel took a puff, exhaling slowly.

"Make sure you keep the door closed," he gasped. "I don't want any smoke getting inside."

"No problem, but I thought you live by yourself, so who cares?"

"My mother will be home any day now. If she smells smoke, she'll have my nuts in a wringer."

"Okay, man. Cool. Got it, door closed."

The music blasted in the living room. A couple who Joel didn't know headed upstairs.

"Stay out of my parents' room," Joel yelled up after them. "Actually, stay out of both bedrooms. They're off limits." Joel ran up the stairs and closed both bedroom doors, and the couple sat down on the top steps.

Joel recognized one of the kids in the living room from a grade below him at school but couldn't remember his name. He was sitting on the living room floor, staring at the window. "I've got the munchies," he said.

"Let's order some pizza," said another guy sitting on the floor with his back against the couch. "Who wants to chip in?"

They pooled their money and phoned the pizza shop. Thirty minutes later, Joel opened the front door and scanned the street. Sometimes the delivery drivers couldn't see the numbers on the houses on Palmer Court.

Pierre came out from next door. "Joel, all is well over there?"

"Everything's great."

"Having a few friends over, eh?"

"A few," Joel laughed, "plus a few mystery guests."

"You're not going to let things get out of control, are you? Everybody will stay safe, yes?"

"Yes, Pierre, we're fine. Everyone's fine. We're all having a good time."

"But don't let things get crazy. If you need me to throw the hammer down, I'm right here."

"We'll be fine. Thanks though."

The pizza delivery turned onto Palmer Court and slowed down. Joel stepped onto the driveway and waved his arm at the driver. He pulled up in front of the house.

Afterwards, a group of kids went out the front door to have a smoke, leaving the front door wide open. Joel felt the cold breeze and closed the door. "Hey guys, please keep the door closed. It's freezing out."

He turned up the thermostat. The furnace beneath him rumbled and roared to life, but only momentarily before cutting out again. He cranked the thermostat further, but nothing happened. He went downstairs to the basement. It was dusty and had a smell of fuel oil, old laundry and rotting potatoes. He studied the furnace and eventually found the reset button. He pressed and released it, and the furnace roared back to life. But just as he started up the stairs the furnace fizzled out and went silent. He pressed the button again. Nothing, not even a click. Joel looked over at the fuel tank. He checked the gauge on top. It read empty.

The doorbell rang again and Joel bounded up the stairs to answer it. It was Maria and her friend Patricia. They's brought a grocery bag with some CDs in it.

"Come on in," Joel smiled.

Maria turned and waved to her father in the car. He drove off.

"You were allowed to come after all."

"I told my dad your older brother's home, in case he checks up. He didn't want me coming over if it was just a bunch of kids throwing a party with no parents around."

She sat down on the couch and pulled a vodka cooler from her purse. "I brought this," she smiled.

"Can I put something else on?" Patricia plunked herself down on the floor beside the stereo and reached for the bag of CDs.

"Sure," Joel said. He made the rounds again to make sure everyone was having a good time. There were now at least two dozen people in his house. He helped himself to somebody's bottle of rum on the kitchen counter, mixing it with Coke.

He made his way back to the living room to find Maria sitting on the couch listening to the new Pearl Jam album. The television was still on, but the sound was off, and the stereo was turned up full blast. The bass reverberated through the old house.

Joel slid in next to her. "What's up?"

"All good." Maria put her cooler on the coffee table. She reached for Joel's hand and held it. "It's getting cold in here. My hands are like ice."

"You're right. I'll light a fire." Joel crouched in front of the stove, balled up some newspapers, and placed them inside. He arranged some sticks of kindling on top of the newspaper. Then he turned the damper, struck a match against the hearth, and touched it to the newspaper. He waited for the paper to burn and the kindling to ignite. Then he placed three pieces of split firewood in, waited till those caught, and closed the door. The fire glowed warm and orange, visible through the smoke-streaked glass of the woodstove door. Joel stood up. He felt woozy. He waited a second before he moved, afraid he would lose his balance.

Patricia and another girl Joel didn't know were dancing in front of the television set. Maria was sitting in the armchair. Joel squeezed in next to her.

"You're squishing me." Maria moved over to sit on the arm of the chair.

Joel leaned in closer. "Having a good time?" His words sounded loose and out of control. He found himself yelling over the music.

She nodded. "Pretty chill."

He gazed into her eyes. He felt dizzy. He had trouble controlling his movements; his head bobbed more than he wanted it to. He leaned over and tried to kiss her.

She pushed him away. "You're drunk. Stop it."

He leaned toward her again.

"Joel, I mean it." She pushed him again. "Not here. Not now."

"You want something to drink? Those guys have beer. They owe me."

Joel pushed himself up, bracing himself against the back of a chair. "I'll get you a beer." He stumbled toward the kitchen.

He found two beers in the fridge and claimed them. He also grabbed one of the pizza boxes from the kitchen table and brought it with him, staggering back to the living room. His head was swimming. He shoved the pizza box towards Maria. "I brought you some pizza." He grinned and held up the two bottles of beer. "And some refreshments."

"You're fucked up." Maria looked at him and shook her head. She put the pizza box on the coffee table and slid it under the wing of his mother's Blue Mountain eagle. "Sit down before you fall down."

"Let's dance." Joel pulled her to her feet. "Put on some Goo Goo Dolls," he said to Patricia. Maria resisted being pulled up.

"I don't feel like it."

Patricia put on "Iris." Joel tried to pull Maria to her feet again. She didn't budge.

"You can barely stand up," she said.

"Come on, let's dance." Joel moved his feet awkwardly. Patricia started dancing close to him, clapping her hands to the music.

Joel felt the rhythm of the music move through him. He swayed to it, feeling the bass boom and thud in his chest. He pulled Maria's arm again.

"Come on, time to dance."

"Joel, no." Maria yanked her arm away.

The room spun. Joel drank down his beer and teetered in the middle of the floor. He yelled over the loudness of the music, "Want another beer?" He put one hand out to steady himself and held up his empty bottle with the other.

Maria shook her head. "I'm still drinking my cooler."

"I'll drink this one then." He tipped back the beer he had brought for Maria.

"Slow down or you'll make yourself sick."

"It feels good to let loose."

"You won't be feeling so good tomorrow." She folded her arms across her chest and shivered. "Your fire's going out."

Joel opened the stove door. He poked around at the ashes, twisted the damper control on the stovepipe, and the fire sprang back to life. "There we go," he said, leaving the door open a crack. He tried to get to his feet again, wobbled unsteadily, and finally stood straight. "I need some fresh air," he said, making his way to the kitchen.

He went out to the back door. The smokers were there, passing a joint around.

"Jesus, I hope the neighbours don't smell that. They'll call the cops on us or something." Joel reached for the joint and took a drag.

"I'm sure it's not the first time your neighbours have smelled pot," Scott said. "Besides, they won't care, as long as we don't do anything to disturb them." He took the joint. "If anything, they'd call the cops with a noise complaint."

"Or a selection of music complaint." Zack motioned toward the house. "Seriously? Spice Girls? That crap is offensive," he said, and they all laughed.

Joel went inside. He opened the fridge in search of another beer, but there were none left. The rum was still there on the counter, so he reached for a glass from the cupboard and poured himself a tall one. The bottle of Coke was empty. He took some ice cubes from the freezer and added some water from the tap. He drank the rum down and tried to put the glass in the sink, but he missed, and it slipped to the floor and shattered. "Damn," he said. He got the broom from the closet and swept up the mess.

He returned to the living room to find Patricia sprawled out on the floor, eyes closed, nodding to the music. Maria was still on the armchair, so he stumbled over and plopped down next to her.

"Joel, stop." She sat up on the arm of the chair again.

Joel tried to say something profound, but managed only to sigh instead. He put his arm around her and kissed her.

"Knock it off." She wriggled away.

Joel locked his arm around her and kissed her again.

"Come on, no. Not now."

He kissed her once more, then hoisted himself up on the arm of the chair. He wanted to grind his hips against hers but couldn't coordinate it.

"Ugh. You reek like booze."

He buried his face in her chest.

She tried to push him off, but he was too heavy. "Joel, get off me," she gasped, "you're crushing me."

"You're so..." he hesitated, "you're so gorgeous."

"You're hurting me," she said.

Joel tried to kiss her again, holding her tight.

"Stop!" Maria squirmed free, rolling off the arm of the chair and hard to the floor, grazing her head on the coffee table on the way down. She rubbed her head. "Why'd you do that? You hurt me."

Joel slid down into the armchair. He looked down at Maria and shook his head. He tried to focus on her face, but his eyes wouldn't work properly. He moved his head back instead.

"You okay?"

"I'll live." She rubbed her head.

"I'm sorry." He closed his eyes, sinking further into the chair. His arms and legs felt loose and rubbery. "Sorry," he repeated. "Don't know what I was thinking."

"Don't be a jerk."

"Sorry." His eyes were still closed. "I need a nap."

Joel woke up several hours later. He was cold. He looked over at the woodstove and the fire was out. Maria was sound asleep, stretched out on the couch, her overcoat pulled over her like a blanket. Patricia was nowhere to be seen. Joel got to his feet and headed upstairs to the bathroom, squeezing past a couple at the top of the stairs. He didn't recognize either of them.

He went into the bathroom, relieved himself, and turned on the hot water tap. The water was ice cold. He waited a few seconds for it to warm up, but it didn't. He cupped the cold water in his hands and splashed it over his face. Joel felt a combination of discomfort and relief. He felt more alert, but his head was definitely starting to throb. He splashed some more water on his face and wet down his hair. He studied himself in the mirror.

Joel went back downstairs. He stood over Maria as she slept on the couch. He stood there a long time just looking at her, watching her chest move gently up and down. He sighed and shook his head, then walked out to the kitchen to find two guys smoking at the kitchen table. There were empty bottles everywhere.

"You guys can't smoke in here."

They dropped their cigarettes into empty beer bottles. Joel looked at the clock on the stove, then went back to the living room.

"Maria," he whispered, shaking her shoulder. "You should probably be getting home. It's late."

"How late?" she said. She was groggy.

"After two."

"I'm dead meat."

"Come on, let's get going."

"Oh my God."

"Come on. I'll walk you home." Joel reached for his jacket.

"You don't have to." She slid her arms into her coat. "Did Patricia leave?"

"I don't know."

They walked out together into the briskness of the night. The soft glow of the streetlamps lit their way along Palmer Court.

"You better not try anything like you did earlier. I'll kick you in the balls if you do."

"I'm sorry. I was a jerk. I was so hammered."

They walked along and turned onto Forest Road. In the distance they coud see a man walking a small dog.

"It's freezing," Maria said.

They walked downtown and past the farmer's market with its empty stalls. Ahead, Christmas decorations twinkled along Main Street. A single taxi drove past. They walked on, past the high school and onto Maria's street. Her apartment stood at the end of the road.

"How's your head? Is there a lump?"

"It's fine. It's nothing."

"I'm sorry. I was a complete jerk," he said. His forehead was starting to ache. He wished he'd grabbed his toque before they'd left.

"Don't worry about it," she said.

Joel's face burned red. "I was such an idiot. I'm sorry I hurt you."

"Forget about it, Joel. You were hammered, it wasn't you."

They arrived at Maria's building to find a racoon scrambling around in the garbage bin. Otherwise the place was quiet.

"This'll be fun," Maria said. "I hope they're sound asleep." She turned and hugged Joel. "Thanks for walking me home."

"For sure. I'm just—I'm really sorry. That was so fucking stupid," he said.

Maria pressed a hand to his lips. "Shush." She stood on her tiptoes and kissed him on the cheek. "It wasn't you, it was the booze."

"Okay, thanks." He held the door open and smiled at her. "Good night."

Maria waved once and stepped inside. Joel watched her climb the stairs. He wished he had a cigarette, but settled for a piece of gum instead. He could see his breath in the cold night air. He envisioned her opening the door and creeping silently into her room. He thought of her slipping out of her clothes and into bed. He smiled at that, but then found himself thinking of the boy in the car accident instead. He banged a fist against his head, trying to shake the image of the boy's father in his slippers.

He kept watching Maria's apartment, waiting for a light to come on. He knew which window was hers. Third floor, last on the right. He watched and waited for a sign she was all right, thinking about his being drunk and trying to kiss her and knocking her to the floor. He imagined kissing her again, and this time she didn't try to stop him. She pulled him close and pressed her lips against his instead. He could feel her hot breath. He buried his face in her hair, and could smell the soft scent of it on his cheek. He kissed her again, without interruption.

Joel stood there a long time, waiting to make sure she was safe. He hoped she wasn't getting in trouble with her parents. He kicked at some snow on the ground, turning his collar up against the wind. There were still no lights on in Maria's apartment. She must have crept in. No lights meant her parents never woke up, so they wouldn't know what time she got home. She must be in bed by now, he thought. He bowed his head and started walking toward home. The wind tore at his face, and he shivered and picked up his pace.

The street was awash in soft yellow light and the gusts of wind were numbing. Joel took the shortcut through the park.

He walked with shoulders hunched, his ears burning from the cold.

The north wind...

He tried to think of Maria warm in bed, but found himself picturing the young man in the car accident instead. And about the young man's father, in his slippers, moving about on the ice.

Chapter 40

Joel arrived home to find that a crack in the storm door's window had spidered all the way across the glass. He groaned when he saw it. Inside, the house was as cold as it was outdoors.

No one was in the living room. Joel crouched in front of the woodstove and lit a fire. Once the fire was going he sat and warmed himself by it.

Joel was thirsty and his throat felt dry. He went to the kitchen. His guests that had been at the table before he and Maria left were nowhere to be seen. The back door was wide open. He slammed it shut and clicked the lock. He got a glass and turned on the tap. Nothing. He went upstairs. The couple that had been on the landing was gone. He decided to look in his bedroom to make sure there were no lingering guests. It was empty. He checked his parents' room too, but there was no one there either. He went to the bathroom and tried the taps, but no water flowed.

He went down to the basement. He tried the laundry tub tap and a trickle of water dripped out. He looked up at the copper pipes in the ceiling above, hoping to find an obvious answer as to why there was no water. He went to his father's workbench and found a flashlight, shining it up at the pipes. They were covered in frost. His head pounded and the room spun a bit when he walked. He was worried about a seizure. He moved the flashlight beam along the copper line to where it entered the house from outside. Joel found a neat split in the pipe about four inches long. Through the gash he could see the pipe was blocked with a cylinder of ice.

He returned to the living room. The fire was going well now and he put in some birch logs and they flared up right away, the bark igniting and crackling as it burned. Joel breathed in the pleasant aroma of the birch.

He went to the closet and pulled on a thick woollen sweater Aunt Penelope had given him last year. He went upstairs and hauled the blanket from his bed and grabbed the pillow. The cold radiated off them.

Back in the living room he turned off the lights and stretched out on the couch and covered up. The heat from the stove was comforting. Through its glass doors the fire glowed a cheery, soft orange. The fire crackled, and Joel closed his eyes. In the ceiling above the wood stove he thought he could hear water dripping.

His sleep was fitful. He woke up and flipped over on the couch, then drifted back to sleep. He dreamed he was in a farmer's field. There was a smudge fire burning back near the tree line. It was a corn field, and its dry empty stalks stood around him like a fence. He walked through them and came upon a scarecrow. It was dressed in a tattered and dirty paramedic uniform. The scarecrow had a round head that was made of black cloth. Lengths of yellowed straw sprang from the scarecrow's neck, ankles, wrists. Joel dreamed he kept walking. The scarecrow followed him. Joel turned around and looked at its face. He realized it was his father. They walked along, and the scarecrow hurried past Joel and lead the way. Joel stumbled along behind his father. They arrived at a cemetery. The scarecrow stopped. They were in the midst of tombstones. They stopped before one. It was broken and crumbling. Three big pieces of smashed granite lay in a heap at its base. Broken beer bottles and shards of glass littered the ground. Joel stared at the tombstone and the broken glass. A hoard of rats scurried over the shards, jagged pieces twinkling with the reflection of the moonlight. Joel dropped to his knees. His lips trembled. He was trying to form a prayer, but no words came out. He woke with a start.

In the corner of the living room the embers in the stove glowed a dull red. Joel threw the blanket off and got up. He looked around the room and went over to the window. It was coated with a thick layer of frost. Joel scraped at it with his fingernail. He looked out and saw the big bucket truck from Nova Scotia Power. Someone was walking around to the side of the house. Minutes later the lights flicked once and then went off.

Joel heard the refrigerator in the kitchen shudder and then the house became completely quiet except for the hissing from the logs burning in the stove.

He bounded upstairs to his room, rummaging around for some presentable if not clean clothes. His breath was visible in the air.

As he undressed he glimpsed himself in the mirror. His hair was sticking up, a dishevelled mess. His armpits stunk. Joel wrapped a towel around his waist and went downstairs. He stirred the coals of the stove and added a few pieces of kindling. The fire roared back to life. He headed to the kitchen and popped a tray of ice cubes into a pot. His teeth chattered.

He carried the pot with the ice to the living room and placed it on the woodstove. Maybe after he got washed and dressed he could walk to the bookstore. He could sit in the back room for a few minutes, or in Mr. Pritchard's office, and hog the heat from the radiators and get warm. There was lots of hot water there. He could brew a pot of coffee, too.

He swished the pot of ice cubes. They were melting now. Joel noticed a steady dripping of water hitting the stove. The drops sizzled when they landed. He looked up at the ceiling and saw a wet spot spreading. The drips were coming from a large and sagging bulge that had bubbled up beneath the paint.

There was a knock on the door. Joel went to the window to peek through, but it was too thick with frost. He couldn't see anything.

Another knock, louder and longer this time. He stood there a moment, hoping whoever it was would go away.

"Joel? David?" said a voice.

Joel stood to one side of the door and opened it a crack.

"Good morning, Joel." It was the social worker. Joel tried to fill as much of the doorway as he could.

The social worker peered inside. "Just here to see how you and David are doing."

"Oh, he's not home right now."

She checked her watch. "Where is he? Awful early to be going anywhere."

Joel moved away from the door. The cold wind blowing on his bare skin was painful.

"May I come in, please. You can go get dressed and I'll wait downstairs."

"Umm, I was just—"

She pushed the door open and stepped into the living room. "Please go get dressed. I'll wait right here." She closed the door. Her eyes went to the sizzling drips on the wood stove and then to the wet spot bulging in the ceiling. Then she looked at the pot of water now steaming on the stove. Finally she looked at Joel.

"There's a leak in the bathroom. David's going to fix it."

She surveyed the living room and its assortment of empty pizza boxes and beer bottles.

"Go get dressed, Joel."

She walked out to the kitchen. Joel followed behind, one hand clutching his towel. The social worker sniffed the air, a stale combination of cigarette and cannabis. She looked at the bottles on the kitchen table.

"It's freezing in here. Is your heat working?" She headed towards the door leading to the basement. She stepped over a pile of broken glass, the broom and dustpan propped beside it.

"We had a few friends over last night. They got a little rowdy. I haven't had a chance to clean up yet."

She opened the door to the basement.

"We have a little leak down there, too." Joel stood at the top of the basement stairs. His feet were aching with cold. He clutched his towel. He was so cold now he could feel his testicles tighten against his body.

"Get dressed, Joel," the social worker repeated from the basement. "Now."

Joel gripped the towel tight around his waist and headed upstairs.

Chapter 41

The social worker turned onto Regent Street and stopped in front of a yellow bungalow with painted white shutters. In the front yard there was a single spruce tree wrapped in Christmas lights.

"Okay, Joel," she put the car in park, "this'll be your new home for a while."

They got out of the car. Joel followed along behind, his backpack on his shoulder. The social worker had let him gather a few essentials from the house before she whisked him off. Joel had sat in the waiting room of her office while she made some phone calls. She would arrange a place for him to go on an emergency basis, she had told him. Joel didn't understand that.

He kept his head down and stared at the deck while the social worker rang the doorbell. Joel noticed how symmetrical the screws on the deck boards were, how they were spaced evenly. He noticed how the boards were stained a dark brown and how none of them looked rotten or cracked.

"Oh, wonderful!" a woman of about fifty said as she opened the door wide. She had short, grey hair and wore heart-shaped, diamond accented earrings. "Come in."

They stepped inside. The warmth of the house blanketed him. He peered into the living room and saw a huge beige brick hearth with a blazing fireplace. Above the mantlepiece, a gold clock covered with a clear glass dome spun in silent rhythm.

"Joel, these are the Wilsons."

"I'm Donna." The woman held out her hand.

"Hello," he said, awkwardly shaking it.

A man, also about fifty, rose from an armchair beside the fireplace. He folded the newspaper he was reading and placed it on the coffee table. He came to the door. A ring of grey hair circled his otherwise bald head. "Hi, Joel, I'm Gerald. Come on in and get settled."

The social worker passed Joel her business card. "Call me if you need anything." She pointed to a number on the bottom of the card. "This is a twenty-four-hour emergency line if you need me afterhours. Somebody's always on-call."

"Okay." He stuck the card in the back pocket of his jeans.

"I'll check in on you from time to time. Make sure you get back on track at school. You have that reading list we got from your school?"

Joel tapped his shirt pocket. "Yep."

"Good. School is the most important thing you can focus on right now." She put her hand on the doorknob and looked at Mrs. Wilson. "Let me know how things go."

"We will." Mrs. Wilson smiled and waved as the social worker walked to her car. She turned to Joel. "Let me show you to your room." She led him down the hallway.

Joel noted the pictures on the walls, mainly those of younger versions of Mr. and Mrs. Wilson. In one they were leaning on hiking poles in a forest surrounded by mammoth trees. In another they were sitting in kayaks in the middle of a lake, smiling wide for the camera. A third showed them in front of the Eiffel Tower with the same big smiles.

Mrs. Wilson pointed to a bathroom as she walked down the hall. "This is yours. You'll have it all to yourself. Gerald and I have our own." She opened the door at the end of the hallway. "And this is your room."

"Thank you." He stepped inside and plunked his backpack down on the bed. A comforter stretched across the bed. It was yellow and matched the curtains pulled back from the windows. There was a desk with a gooseneck lamp and a small radio alongside a wooden dresser that looked like an antique. Out the window, Joel saw a naked oak tree in the middle of the yard, and a row of cedar shrubs along the back.

The room was neat and orderly; it even smelled clean. It reminded Joel of a hotel room, or the examination room at the doctor's office. Everything felt like it belonged.

"Come on, Joel. I'll show you the kitchen."

Joel followed behind her.

"You can use the kitchen, but you have to clean up after yourself." She opened the fridge. "You can make yourself a snack with anything on this shelf," she said. "But you have to ask if you want to use anything else."

Joel nodded as he looked inside the fridge. It was neat and orderly, like the rest of the house. There were no beer bottles.

"A few rules," she said as she closed the fridge door. "No drinking and no smoking. You have to be in bed by eleven and lights out by midnight. You can have friends over, but phone calls and guests have to be in the living room only."

"Okay."

"I'll drive you to school in the morning, and pick you up at four in the afternoon. Any questions?"

"No. Sounds great. Can I take a shower?"

"Sure, there are towels in your bathroom. Put your dirty clothes in the laundry hamper when you're done. In fact, why don't you give me all the clothes out of your suitcase. I'll wash and dry everything for you so you can start fresh."

Chapter 42

Joel rang the bell at Mrs. Payne's house. Parker brought Joel into the main room where she was reading the novel he had delivered his previous visit. A bowl of popcorn and spool of twine sat on the table beside her.

"Joel? You're not in school?" She bookmarked the novel.

"No. There's too much to do. I just came... I wanted to say goodbye."

"Goodbye? You taking a trip?"

"They put me in a home."

"You mean they placed you in foster care? Because of your mother?"

"Yes." He felt his voice tighten and he fought back tears. "And it's a house, not a home. I mean the people mean well, but they're so, I don't know, like having me there is a business transaction. It's like a cold, stark hotel room more than a home. And David," he added. "I may have led them to believe he was home. You know, looking after me."

"And he is not home, correct?"

"I told them he was there. If I didn't, they would have made me get a goddamned babysitter."

"And now?"

"I have a goddamned babysitter."

"They put you in a foster home. And you came to say goodbye?"

"I'm not staying there. They seem nice enough and everything, but I'm not staying. I'm heading to Boston. He's living at a place on Franklin Street."

"Taking after your brother, are you? Following in his footsteps?"

"No. Going to get him and bring him home."

"How are you going to get there? Walk? It's a ten-hour drive by car."

"I don't know. Hitchhike, I guess."

"That's no way to travel, Joel."

"Bus, maybe. Or train."

"You'd have to go to Montreal. Then transfer to a train or bus going to the States. Do you know your way around Montreal? Would you have a place to stay?"

"No. I've never been to Montreal. I don't know how. I just know I'm going. I need David. Plus, I need to tell him some things. Things he needs to know. And I'm not living with a new family, no matter how nice they are. They are just so matter of fact—like they treat me fine—but I just don't get the sense they care what happens to me one way or the other."

"You need to be rational, Joel. You need to think things through and make a decent plan."

"I will. I just wanted to come by and say thank you. I got Dad's saxophone back. Thank you for doing what you did. I really appreciate it. I don't know how I'll ever repay you, but I will." He got up from his chair.

"It was my pleasure, young man. It was the right thing to do." She turned and called, "Parker!" and waited for him to come in. "Parker, would you please make our young friend here something to eat. He looks half starved. We don't want to send him on a long journey without sustenance."

"Yes, ma'am."

Joel devoured some sandwiches and cookies, and downed a glass of orange juice. "My mother bakes molasses cookies just like these." He held up the cookie and took a big bite. "Delicious."

"You can think better on a full stomach. Less distraction," Mrs. Payne said.

"I'm sorry. I just need to get David back here."

"You're adamant about going, aren't you?"

"I'm going."

"Nothing I can say or do to change your mind? And that address is in Cambridge, by the way, just across the Charles River from downtown Boston."

"I'm not staying with the foster people. I'd rather die trying to get David than stay here and do nothing. Dad would want me to. And Mom."

"If I can't convince you not to go, maybe I can make your journey a little easier."

She snapped off a piece of cookie and put it in her mouth.

"Easier?"

"I want you to take my car."

"I couldn't. But thank you."

"Why not? I'm not using it. I can front you some gas money." She called to Parker again, and whispered something to him. He returned a short time later and passed her a sheaf of twenty-dollar bills.

"I'd rather—"

"You don't have a plan, Joel. I'm giving you one. You know where he is, right?"

Joel nodded.

"You drive down there, get him, come back and you return the car to me. You get your brother, you don't have to stay in foster care. God knows he's probably desperate to come back anyway but let his ego get in the way."

"I couldn't, Mrs. Payne. I appreciate it, a lot, but—"

"Why can't you? You can and you know it. Here's the thing, young man, in you I see the same spark that my Christopher showed. You have the same drive as he did, the same unrelenting optimism. I can't do a damn thing for him anymore, but I can for you. This trip will help you become your own man. Help an old lady feel useful again, Joel. Take my car, get your brother. Be on your way."

Joel bent down and gave Mrs. Payne a hug.

"Stay safe." She clutched his hands in both of hers and squeezed tight. "Parker, get him our map. He's going right by my old alma mater. My old stomping grounds."

Parker took out the map and passed it to Mrs. Payne.

"See, take the I-93 here, and head south. Look for Route 16, it will say Mystic Valley Parkway. Doesn't that have a nice ring to it? Anyway, keep going down here"—she traced her finger on the map—"and it'll take you right to Harvard Square. From there you can walk to your brother's place."

"I can't thank you enough."

"You can thank me by driving carefully and coming back with your brother. Safe and sound. That's all the thanks I need."

"For sure. Thank you. We'll be here."

Parker escorted Joel through to the kitchen and down a small flight of stairs and out into the garage where he detected the faint smell of gasoline and grass clippings, like the wad that cakes inside the mower blades by the end of summer. He could feel his heart thumping in his chest as waves of both excitement and nervousness washed over him. He hopped into the blue Thunderbird and turned the key in the ignition. It was so quiet and luxurious inside that he couldn't even hear the motor running. He rubbed his hand along the plush burgundy upholstery. It reminded him of Mrs. Payne's living room drapes. He held out his hand to Parker. They shook hands.

"Thank you, Mr. Parker."

"Mr. Charles," he smiled at Joel. "Parker is my first name. Parker Charles."

Joel laughed. "You must like music, don't you?"

"Of course. That's one of the reasons I like working for Mrs. Payne so much. Other than that, she's a gracious old doll. She always has music playing somewhere in the house. Take care, Mr. Carruthers." Parker pushed the button and the huge garage door rolled up. He passed Joel a slip of paper. "Here's the phone number. Call if you run into any snags."

Joel had to listen closely to make sure the engine was still running. He pressed the gas and it revved smoothly.

"Heated seats," Parker said as he reached in and clicked the button for Joel.

Joel smiled. He could get used to this.

He backed the blue Thunderbird out onto Victoria Street, gave the horn three quick taps and waved to Parker. Moments later, he turned from Forest Road onto Palmer Court. He needed—no, wanted—to get some things from the house before it collapsed. The social worker had only let him take a few essentials.

He pulled up in front of the house and parked. Pierre opened his door.

"That was some soiree you had last night."

"I hope it wasn't too loud for you."

"Your friends were busy."

"I'm sorry, Pierre. I guarantee you that's the last time that will happen. I only invited six people over."

Pierre laughed. "Word spreads fast when teenagers find out there's no parents home. Spreads like wildfire."

"It got a little crazy."

"Fancy new car," Pierre nodded at the Thunderbird. "You are getting rich without me knowing about it?"

"Rich friends."

"Rich friends, eh? That's almost as good as being rich yourself."

Joel went inside. The house was as cold inside as it was outside. He ignored the mess, but noted the chunk of Gyproc from the living room ceiling that had fallen across the woodstove. The fire had long gone out.

He went downstairs and got some empty suitcases. Then he went to his parents' room where he opened his father's top bureau drawer and looked at his *Star of Life* medal. He picked it up and felt its cold, shiny metal. He touched his mother's cross around his neck. He shoved the medal in his jacket pocket.

Joel took the jewelry box off his mother's bureau and placed her rings in one of the suitcases. Her took her photos as well, photos of her and his father, and of her with David when he was a baby, and more photos of him and David. He placed them all in the suitcase.

He went to his room. He took the hockey card David had given him and put it in his pocket. Then he loaded that suitcase in the trunk of the car.

He took another empty case and headed back to his room. He took his journal that he wrote songs in and put it in the suitcase. He tossed in the books from his bedside stand. He scanned around the room. He jammed in a few pairs of jeans, some shirts, and socks and underwear. He picked up his pill bottle, shook out two pills, and popped them in his mouth and swallowed. He stuck the bottle in his jacket pocket. He looked around again: the rest he didn't care about. He could get by without the rest of his books or clothes. He lugged the suitcase down to the car.

He grabbed his guitar and his father's saxophone and put those in the Thunderbird too.

From the living room, he carried two milk crates of his father's albums out and packed them in. He scooped up the remaining photos from the living room and his mother's Jesus statuette. He tucked the broken arms that his mother had tried to glue back on into his pocket. Maybe he could fix it. He took the towel he had on that morning when the social worker had arrived and wrapped up his mother's most precious memento, the Blue Mountain pottery eagle. He set it carefully on the floor in the backseat.

He stood at the front door and surveyed the room. He didn't want anything else from here. David didn't either, or else he would have taken it. And his mother, what else would she want? He had her jewelry, her photos, and the eagle, the pictures of her boys, and her Jesus figurine. That's it. He loaded everything into Payne's car.

Joel backed out of the driveway and down Palmer Court. He saw Pierre in the window and waved. He turned onto Forest Road and pressed the accelerator—the engine was smooth and powerful. Joel headed for the highway.

He took the ramp onto the highway and headed north to New Brunswick. He cranked up the music. Mrs. Payne—or who knows, maybe Parker—had a great selection of CDs. Joel drove thinking of how great it would be to bring David back, get things back on track, have life sorted out and making sense again. He crossed the Tantramar Marsh, past the Nova Scotia welcome centre, a mocked-up lighthouse where in the summer a bagpiper beckoned tourists. He drove past the radio towers for CBC's short-wave service and crossed into New Brunswick.

The roads were clear and the sun was bright. The car showed the outside temperature was minus ten, but inside it felt warm and comfortable.

Joel sped past Moncton. The Petitcodiac River flowed in the distance. Its brown mud flats were coated with ice. He drove along, the time passing quickly, and he sang along to the music. He passed by the vast farmlands outside Sussex, covered with a recent snowfall. He could see deer tracks in the snow, but he saw no deer.

He drove towards Saint John with its tall refinery stacks sending steam into the air. He drove across the bridge and past the pulp mill belching out its sulfuric waste. Eventually he pulled in at a diner outside of Lepreau where he ordered a hamburger and French fries. He took a large coffee to go and got back on the road.

An hour later he was in St. Stephen, and wound his way through its tiny downtown core. He drove across the St. Croix River and waited his turn at U.S. Customs.

"Where you headed?' The board patrol officer looked over Joel's driver's license.

"Boston."

"What's going on in Boston?" The officer peered in the back seat.

"I'm picking up my brother."

"What's under the towel?"

Joel twisted around to look in the backseat. "Oh, I forgot to take that out. It's my mother's."

"How long will you be in the U.S.?"

"We'll be coming back tomorrow."

"Travel safe."

Joel drove away from the border crossing trying to recall Mrs. Payne's instructions. He turned onto North Street and drove till it turned into Baring Street. He drove further and saw the sign for Bangor—Route 9. Airline Road. He turned left and pressed down on the accelerator.

He stopped for gas in Bangor, ordered another coffee to go, and got on the I-95. The Thunderbird sailed down the highway and Joel lost himself in *Appetite for Destruction*. He had laughed when he pulled that CD from the case. Was it Mrs. Payne's or Parker's? He nodded his head to "Sweet Child O' Mine."

The miles flew by on the Interstate where the Thunderbird seemed to perform even better at higher speeds. Signs for Waterville, Augusta, Brunswick clicked by as he moved steadily south.

The Thunderbird roared past Portland where the traffic started picking up. There were cars and trucks everywhere now, and Joel began to get nervous. He made sure to stay in the far right lane and stick to the speed limit, or even a little less. He started yawning, and knew he needed rest.

He crossed into New Hampshire and pulled into a rest stop. He used the washroom and bought a can of pop from a vending machine, then dozed off in the car.

Back on the road, he soon passed a huge billboard: Welcome to Massachusetts. He kept watch for the exit Mrs. Payne had told him about. Soon Joel saw the exit for the I-93 and went south. Then he turned onto Highway 16, Mystic Valley Parkway. His breathing relaxed—it was still a busy road, but not as packed as the interstate had been. He followed the Mystic Valley Parkway exactly as Mrs. Payne had told him, driving down to Harvard Street. Eventually he turned onto Palmer Street and laughed out loud.

He found a parking lot. The sign said ten dollars, and Joel hesitated with his blinker on. Should he park and pay the money or find someplace else? Behind him a delivery truck blared its horn. Joel jumped. Now the truck was trying to squeeze by the Thunderbird, so Joel turned reluctantly into the lot. He shook his head. Maybe his mother had paid for parking in Halifax when she took him there for a specialist appointment, but parking was free everywhere in Amherst.

He parked and got out. He could feel his arms and legs shaking, and hoped it was from the long drive. He found a coffee shop and went in to use the restroom.

"Can you tell me which direction it is to get to Elsinore Arms?" he asked.

The clerk pointed out the window. "Down three blocks and turn left."

"Thanks."

Outside, Joel saw a Salvation Army Santa ringing his bell. Pedestrians crowded impatiently at every corner. A car beeped its horn as it zipped by. Joel stepped back from the curb. He noticed the lampposts had Christmas decorations on them just like back home, candles and wreaths and twinkling lights. Darkness began to envelop the city. Joel peered into every restaurant and bar he walked past. They were all jammed with people, their conversations loud enough to compete with the music. The Boston Bruins game was on every television. Joel kept walking from bar after bar, where the laughter of the patrons spilled out into the street. He kept walking, wondering where he might find his brother amongst all these people.

He kept walking.

Chapter 43

Joel made his way down the street with the map Mrs. Payne had given him still folded in his pocket. He formed in his mind how he would word things to David.

Dad's dead. No matter how he phrased it, it was so final. How did they say it on TV or in the movies? *Sit down, I've got some bad news. Terrible news. Dad has passed away. Dad has died.*

Nothing seemed right to Joel. He was still trying to absorb the shock and grief himself. Granted, he had experienced his father's funeral and received the words of comfort from friends and extended family. All that helped make it real. Almost like his father simply hadn't been around the house. To Joel that felt normal; it wasn't unusual. It seemed like he was off at work somewhere and he'd be home when his shift was over.

He walked down Massachusetts Avenue and turned onto Hancock, a narrow one-way street lined with parked cars on one side, leaving barely enough room for those on the road. The sidewalk was concrete, and the houses were an arm's length away from each other. Each house had a tiny patch of a front yard, boxed in by a small picket fence, a rock wall or a green vinyl chain-link. He turned onto Franklin Street and felt his heart jump in his chest. He was close now. With street names like these—Putnam, Green, Pearl, Auburn—he could almost be back in Amherst.

Wasn't there a town of Amherst in Massachusetts, too? This place was larger than his hometown, but it had a familiar look. The biggest difference was the volume of cars and people and their constant movement.

The houses on Franklin were sprawling wooden two- and three-storey homes. They were painted yellow and white or grey. Most had some decorations for the holidays. Some had strings of lights stretched across the roofline. Others had a

Christmas tree twinkling in their living room window. Dark green wreaths covered almost every door, each festooned with red holly berries and bows.

Joel walked along the sidewalk. How would he bring up that other issue with Jennifer? What was he going to say? How was he going to say it? *By the way, your girlfriend is having a baby.* How do you break that news? Or should he say, *You need to call Jennifer,* and let her tell him. *You have to call Jennifer. Now.*

Joel slowed enough to scan the numbers on the doors. He felt the veins in his head throb with every heartbeat as he drew closer to his goal.

The traffic had all but disappeared now, this far from Massachusetts Avenue. He was in a quiet residential neighbourhood, its population overwhelmingly students or people associated with the nearby universities. Tucked between Harvard and MIT, it reminded Joel of the south end of Halifax. He and his brother once attended a hockey game at St. Mary's University. David parked the car and they walked down quiet streets with huge wooden homes. South end Halifax was virtually identical to this area of Cambridge.

Joel continued along Franklin Street. The sidewalk buckled unevenly. A cat darted past him and vanished into the narrow alley between two houses. Parked cars lined one side of the street. Joel noticed the street signs: "Resident Permit Parking Only." Every parked car displayed a sticker.

A couple walking a small poodle shuffled past Joel, and the dog sniffed at his pant leg. The woman holding the leash smiled. Joel smiled back. Joel had expected a cold and distant aloofness—in Amherst everyone knew, or knew of, everybody else—but the friendliness surprised him here.

In the distance he heard church bells. A place this big probably has church services all the time. He checked his watch: five o'clock. Maybe it was a wedding. He kept on walking. The pleasant chimes ended and the last tone of the bells hung in the air with sullen authority. Or a funeral, he thought.

Joel walked on. His throat felt dry. He felt a knot in his stomach and he needed to burp. His heart thumped in his ribcage; he could feel the blood coursing through the side of his head. He fought off a headache, but it was growing in scope, invading every corner of his brain. It was taking over.

He arrived at 216 Franklin Street and drew a deep breath. Trembling visibly, he walked up the three wooden steps onto a long porch. Three doors faced him. The last one on the right, 216, was painted a vibrant red. He couldn't see a doorbell. He took off his glove and knocked on the door, rapping the wood with his bare knuckles.

He felt a lump in his throat. How would David react? Would he be happy to see him? Would he be surprised to see his little brother standing on Franklin Street? Getting from Amherst to Boston all by himself.

Inside, he heard movement. The lock on the door clicked and Joel took a deep breath. The door opened a crack, and a brass chain looped across the crack. A young woman with shoulder-length black hair and glasses peeked out.

"May I help you?"

"Hi, I'm looking for my brother." Joel thought the woman looked familiar. "I was told he was staying here."

"You're looking for Dave?"

"Yes, David. David Carruthers. I'm Joel—he's my brother." Joel's lips trembled.

"He was, but he's gone now." She frowned.

Joel looked down at his boots, hoping to avoid eye contact.

"Come on in out of the cold." The woman closed the door briefly to unclip the chain. Then she opened the door wide. "You look frozen."

"Thank you." Joel stepped inside. The woman looked to be a few years older than David, and Joel recognized her now from Amherst; he was sure she had a sister in his grade. He recalled that she had gone away to university, and figured she must be studying here somewhere. Joel understood the connection now, how Scott was able to provide this address. How David must have been in touch with someone back home. So he knew, or should have known. He knows everything, Joel thought, and still hasn't come home.

"Your brother was staying here, but he left a few days ago."

"I've driven a long way to bring him home."

"You drove down from Amherst? By yourself?"

"Yeah." Joel looked down at the floor, at the water pooling on the hardwood under his boots. "I didn't have much of a choice." He looked up at the woman. "You're from Amherst. Your sister is Meaghan, right?"

"Yes, you probably go to school with Meaghan. I'm Linda."

Joel nodded. "Do you know where he went? Did he go home?"

"He didn't say. He just said it was time for him to move on. As far as I know he's still washing dishes at Legal Sea Foods. You might be able to track him down there."

"Legal Sea Foods. What's that, a fish market?"

"It's a seafood restaurant. It's down on the waterfront, near the aquarium."

Joel shook his head.

"It's downtown. Take the Red Line to Downtown Crossing, switch to the Green Line and get off at Aquarium station. Once you come up out of the subway, you'll see it right there."

"Can I drive there? I've never taken the subway."

"Oh man, you don't want to drive in that mess. Your car's around here somewhere?"

"I parked up by Harvard Square."

"Leave it there. Do yourself a favour and take the subway. Here, let me show you. I'll get my map."

"I have one here." Joel unfolded his map of Boston. Linda pointed to a red line.

"We're right here. Go to this station and take a train heading to Braintree. Get off at Park Street. Then switch to the Green Line, take a train for Lechmere and go one station, get off at Government Centre." She traced her finger on the map. "Then take the Blue Line, heading for Wonderland. Get off at Aquarium."

"I'm going to be lost for a week."

"It sounds worse than it is. It's easy. You'll be fine."

"I don't know." Joel frowned and looked at the map.

"It might be easier for you to get off at Park Station and walk the rest of the way downtown. Go down Tremont Street, and then down State. Keep heading towards the water. You can't miss it."

"You sure driving's not a good idea?"

"The traffic is nuts down there. Some drivers around here don't have any patience."

"Ok, thanks a lot. Do you think he'll be back here? I mean I could come back."

"No, he won't be back. He's gone for good. He took everything he had with him and left a few days ago."

"Seems like a pattern."

"Look, Joel, I think being here was too close to home for him. I talk to my Mom all the time. I hear what's going on at home. I talk to Meaghan. I still have friends there." Linda put her hand on Joel's arm. "I don't know everything, but I know you guys have had a hard go of it. You've been through tough times. I think being here was too close to home for him."

Joel nodded.

"He works from four in the afternoon till close. You'll be able to see him. You have loads of time to get there."

"Thanks for all your help. I appreciate it." He folded up the map and shoved it in his pocket. "I'll head for the Red Line."

"Get off at Downtown Crossing and head for the water. There are signs and maps all over the place. You'll be fine."

"Thanks." Joel looked at the ground again. "Did David mention anything to you about going home?"

"Not a word about Amherst. Nothing."

He nodded. "Thanks a lot. I appreciate it."

Linda smiled. "Tell him I said hello."

Joel stepped out into the cold. He headed back down Franklin Street towards Harvard Station to catch the Red Line into the city.

He entered the station. He was impressed by its gleaming tile floors and the sleek stainless-steel interior design. Joel hadn't expected that, not with the hundreds, maybe thousands, of people rushing everywhere. He wove his way through the crowds towards the escalator that lead down to the train platform.

A few minutes later, he got off the train at Park Street Station, walked up the concrete stairs and popped out in the middle of the Boston Common. He looked around and wondered which way it was to get to the waterfront. He started walking. The air here was crisp and cool, but it didn't have that unbearable chill like back in Amherst. In fact, for a late afternoon in the middle of winter, it was almost pleasant.

People pushed past as he gazed up at the architecture all around him. The business of the city fascinated Joel, so different from what he was used to in Amherst, where his whole world revolved around a few streets and a handful of people. There were more people milling about Brewer Fountain than would ever be in all of downtown Amherst. He understood the attraction David had to this city. Get out of the town that holds you back, keeps you down. See the whole wide world. He understood that phrase now, *the whole wide world*. And this was but one city, in but one country. How great would it be to travel, explore and experience the rest?

Cars and buses zoomed past. Despite the cold, people moved about on bicycles and skateboards. He walked along the sidewalk and looked up the pedestrian paths of Boston Common. He decided to walk in there. It looked quieter and less frenzied than the street.

He was right. People were walking leisurely through the park. Grey squirrels with broad tails scampered across paths and dashed up trees. He walked past the Visitor's Centre.

In a clearing, surrounded by a wrought iron fence, stood a huge fir tree decorated with lights. It was the biggest Christmas tree he had ever seen, reaching high into the air, its impressive array of white lights twinkling against the twilight sky. He stopped to read the plaque beside it. *Nova Scotia*. So this was where that tree went every year. Joel knew from history class that Boston had stepped up after the Halifax Explosion of December 1917. When Halifax had been levelled with thousands killed and more injured, Boston had come to the rescue with doctors, blankets and food by the trainload and Nova Scotia sends a Christmas tree every year as a thank you.

He kept walking, down past the bandstand towards some street vendors. One cart had jerseys, hats and scarves from the Bruins, the Red Sox, the Celtics and the New England Patriots. Other carts offered warm cashews and pretzels. They smelled delicious. He bought a pretzel—it was huge, with massive chunks of salt on top. Joel hadn't realized how hungry he was. He chewed as he walked. Another cart offered T-shirts and sweatshirts from MIT, Yale, Harvard and Boston University. The nearest university to Amherst was Mount Allison in New Brunswick, or the few in Halifax.

He continued down past the Frog Pond where a handful of skaters circled. Music played from the loudspeakers. He kept walking past baseball fields, idle now except for a few dogs out for a run. Beyond those, tennis courts stood quiet for the season. He walked parallel to Beacon Street, crossed over Charles Street, and wandered along the pathway. He wasn't paying attention to where he was going. He was lost in thought. He passed some bronze statues of a mother duck and her eight ducklings trailing behind. Someone had placed little red and white caps on their heads.

The path lead across the pond. It was frozen, the ice smooth and clear. Ahead, the swan boat pavilion was shuttered and silent. Joel remembered David joking with Jennifer once: "I'm going to pedal you around the pond in a swan boat." The boats had been put away for the winter. Joel crossed the footbridge above another section of the pond, its engineering reminding him of the bridge crossing the harbour in Halifax or the one across the Northumberland Strait to Prince Edward Island. Metal brackets spanned the distance between solid stone columns. The lampposts were covered with a coppery green patina.

Joel stopped in the middle of the bridge and peered down into the pond. The ice was translucent. In its midst, the ice gave way to water where a flock of geese swam in silence. Joel stood on the bridge and stared down at them a moment. He felt grateful for their presence.

He crossed the bridge and walked out onto Arlington Street, focused on finding David. What would he say to him? How could he make sense of everything that had happened? He walked down Commonwealth Avenue, a wide boulevard with a park-like space in the middle, where paths pushed past enormous trees with naked branches. Joel was swept up as he walked, fascinated by the breadth and busyness of this city. At every street corner something caught his eye. He walked along; the waterfront must be getting close. Joel was starting to feel the coldness in his feet and hands. Finding a place to warm up might be nice, but he wanted to find David.

At Clarendon Street, Joel stopped to admire a huge granite sculpture, what appeared to be a sweeping wall of water flowing from a hose. A large bronze firefighter's jacket and helmet were perched atop the wall. A plaque indicated the memorial was for some firefighters who'd died battling a hotel fire nearby. Joel read the inscriptions. He felt his throat tighten. It could have been, and probably was, something his Dad would have said at some point.

The worst is a death, but you learn to let it go. You wouldn't be able to do your job.

Joel swallowed hard and carried on to the next intersection, turning down Dartmouth Street. He must be getting close now. He pulled out his map and studied it, folding it smaller so that it wouldn't flutter in the breeze. He found the Boston Common, and looked for Dartmouth Street near the waterfront. He couldn't find it on the map. He must have gone the wrong way then, when he came up the stairs from the subway station. He refolded the map and put it back in his pocket. His hands felt frozen. He kept going down Dartmouth Street, looking for a place to warm up.

At Copley Square he found Trinity Church. It was the biggest church he'd ever seen. He gazed at the steeple spiralling up into the sky and mouthed a little prayer. He needed to find David.

He turned around and found a library, a good place to warm up and get his bearings. He passed some panhandlers on the steps, maybe two dozen of them, thinking how his hometown had but one homeless person he could think of. The library was enormous, and looked like a palace, with two statues flanking the front entrance. He walked through the huge front door, and the bustle of the city faded behind him. Inside, two massive marble lions lay on either side of a sweeping staircase bathed in warm yellow light. He found a reading room and its row after row of big solid tables, each lit by a brass lamp with an emerald green shade. He felt like he was in a cathedral. For Joel, being here was something of a religious experience.

He wandered into a café, bought a coffee, and made his way out to the courtyard. On the far side he found a set of gleaming polished stairs leading to another reading room. He sat next to the window, sipped his coffee, and for a moment forgot all about his father and mother and David and needing to find him. He delighted instead in the books that surrounded him. The heat of the coffee warmed his hands and he wished he could stay here in this room. Surrounded by these books he felt at home, he felt part of something bigger and more noble than himself alone.

Eventually, though, he had to go. He retraced his steps through the park, and found his way back to Park Street Station. He hurried down West Street, stopping briefly at Brattle Books to admire the shelves of books on the street. He checked his map. Then he headed down Washington and turned onto Milk. He could smell the salt in the air now as he crossed the green belt, passed the Grain Exchange and arrived at Rings Fountain. Ahead was Legal Sea Foods. It was not what he'd expected. He'd not expected such a fancy place. He studied his reflection in the window, wondering if he was fit to enter. He looked down at his jeans and boots, and ran his fingers through his hair. Then he shrugged, opened the door, and walked in.

A young woman in navy-blue shirt and grey trousers hurried past him with two platters of red, steaming lobster. "Someone will be with you in a second," she said.

Another woman came up. "For one?"

"Yes, um, no. I didn't come in to eat."

"A seat at the bar then? I'll need to see your ID."

"No, I'm here to see my brother, if I can. He works here. He's a dishwasher."

"Who's your brother? We have a few dishwashers here."

"David."

She smiled and cocked her head. "David..?"

"Carruthers. David Carruthers."

"One sec," she said, and disappeared through some double doors.

Joel stood there, wondering what he would say to his brother. Wondering how it would go. Soon the woman returned with a man in a blue shirt and grey tie. He was large and his face was ruddy. "You're looking for Carruthers?"

"He's my brother. I need to see him."

"He doesn't work here."

"This is Legal Sea Foods, right?"

"Oh he did work here. But he quit. Didn't give me any notice either."

"Quit?"

"Yep. After his last shift. At least he finished the shift. Sometimes these jerks walk out and leave me holding the bag."

"He's not here?"

"Afraid not. He's gone."

Joel felt his face drain. His legs started to tremble.

"Hey kid, you alright?" The man pulled out a chair at the nearest table. "Here, have a seat." He motioned to the waitress. "Get him some juice or something, kid's going to pass out."

Joel sat down. He rubbed his face with his hands. He could feel the tension around his head. "What the fuck," he said.

"Here you go." The waitress placed a glass of orange juice before him. "You in some trouble or something? Can we call anybody?"

The man nudged the orange juice toward Joel. "Take a drink, kid. You need some sugar."

"He's not here?"

"No, he's long gone."

"He didn't say where he was going?" Joel took a sip of juice. "Did he say if he was going home?"

The man shook his head. "All he asked was if I could mail him his last cheque when it was ready. You want the address?"

"That'd be great."

A few minutes later the man returned with an envelope. "He even put a stamp on it."

Joel looked at the address, scrawled in David's handwriting: *David Carruthers, c/o Ashley Martin, 35 Oxford Street, Portland, Maine 04101.*

"Oxford Street," Joel laughed. "That's funny."

"You sure you're okay, kid? You look like you're going to drop."

Joel downed the last of the orange juice. "I drove all the way from Nova Scotia to bring him back home."

"Nova Scotia? As in Canada? Are you kidding me right now? That joker told me he was from California."

Joel laughed. "He's definitely not from California."

"Wicked."

Joel got up, pulled out his wallet, and took out a five-dollar bill. "For the juice."

"Don't worry about it, kid. Hope you find your brother." The man passed Joel the envelope. "You take this to him. He was a good worker, a nice guy, but definitely had some stuff going on. Good luck," he said.

"Thanks," Joel said.

Chapter 44

Joel crossed State Street without looking. A car screeched to a stop and blared its horn. The driver rolled down his window and shook a fist at Joel. "Hey buddy, watch where you're going!"

"Sorry," Joel muttered. He hung his head and kept walking. He wandered down Atlantic Street, walking alongside a park. A group of kids laughed and romped in the snow. Joel didn't notice them either. He kept walking, head down, following the sidewalk that skirted around Christopher Columbus Waterfront Park. He was unconcerned with where he was going. He was on Cross Street now. He couldn't decide if he was mad or hurt, and didn't notice the crowds on the sidewalk were getting thicker. Cars and trucks were slowed or stopped. Horns beeped and buses belched exhaust. Joel barrelled his way down Cross Street.

Finally he noticed he was heading in the direction of a bridge. He stopped and pulled out his map. Cross Street and North Washington. If he could get to North Station, he could get a subway back to the car. He walked over to Beverly Street and all the way down. He was thinking about David.

Joel walked to the end of the street, where it came out at Causeway Road. He checked for traffic and darted across to find a group of people in Bruins jerseys milling about and posing for pictures. They were clustered around a bronze figure of Bobby Orr, his arms outstretched like a superhero in flight. "The Goal" the plaque below noted. It was the same image as the hockey card David had left for him. He reached into his jacket and pulled it out. He looked at the statue, and then at the card, and felt the hair on the back of his neck stand up. He realized he was standing outside Boston Garden, the very place it had happened all those years ago. It would be so nice to share this, he thought, to experience this moment with David, and with their father.

He stuffed the card in his pocket and pulled out his map, feeling felt the moist warmth of tears on his cheeks. Wiping his face, he headed for North Station.

At the station, Joel found the line to Downtown Crossing. He switched to the Alewife train and disembarked at Harvard Station. He circled around the block a couple of times, trying to remember where he had parked Payne's car. Eventually he found it, and doublechecked his map, estimating how far it was to Portland. He'd be there in two hours, two and a half at the most.

He stopped at a gas station and filled up, and soon he was cruising north on the I-95. The traffic thinned with every mile north. He crossed the Massachusetts-New Hampshire border and eventually the Piscataqua River Bridge into Maine.

He took the exit to Portland and found Congress Street and then Maine Mall Road, but couldn't find Oxford Street. He drove around in circles a while, and eventually stopped at a corner store for a pop and a chocolate bar.

"Is Oxford near here?" he asked the clerk. "I've been going around in circles."

The clerk nodded. "Yeah it's tricky. It's a one-way. Turn left at Lincoln Park."

Joel found Oxford Street and slowed down, looking for number 35. There it was, a two-storey white walkup, with at least six different units visible from the street. An orange and white sign in the front window declared, ROOMS FOR RENT.

David must have been in contact with someone from home, Joel thought. This staying away had to be deliberate. Maybe he felt responsible in some way for their father's death. Maybe he couldn't face the grief. Or maybe he couldn't deal with their mother being sick. Still, Joel thought, you can't spend your whole life running. You face it, you deal with it, and then you move on. If Joel could deal with it, then so could David. He no longer wondered what he was going to say to his brother.

Joel pulled over to the side of the road, got out, and made his way up to the door. The screen was ripped and hanging, and the window was cracked. He banged on the door. He could hear movement inside. The door swung open, and the stench of stale cigarettes, garlic and cat litter struck him hard. A man in shorts and T-shirt stood before him.

"Hello. I'm looking for David Carruthers."

"David ain't here."

"Oh okay. When do you think he'll be back?"

"Buddy, he's gone."

"Moved out?"

"Never moved in. Still owes me rent too."

"How long ago was this?"

The man shrugged. "He was here yesterday, chumming around with his little gal pal. Told me he'd be right back with the rent and his stuff, and I ain't seen hide nor hair of him since. Meanwhile I got an empty room that ain't making me any money."

"Any idea where he might have gone?"

"Buddy, there's a train to Boston, and there's a Greyhound to New York. I have no idea." A foghorn sounded down along the waterfront. "Or maybe he's waiting for spring to hop on the Cat and head back to his old stomping grounds. No fucking clue."

"Is there an Ashley Martin around? Can I talk to her?"

"Try Lookin' Good."

"Huh?"

"Lookin' Good," the man said. "It's a laundromat on Congress. She works the late shift there."

"Where's that."

"Down to the end of the street here. See that steeple? It's right there, other side of that church."

A few minutes later, Joel pulled up in front of the Lookin' Good laundromat where a young woman with blond frizzy hair and a short red leather jacket stood smoking a cigarette.

"Hello," Joel greeted her as he walked past and into the laundromat. The woman followed him in and stepped behind the counter. She slipped off her jacket and picked up the remote for the television mounted high in the corner of the room.

Joel wandered up to the counter.

"Quarters, honey?"

"Are you Ashley? Ashley Martin?"

She scowled slightly. "And who might you be?"

"You know my brother, I think. David. David Carruthers."

"Oh you mean Mister Pack-of-lies?"

"He left your name and a forwarding address—"

"I know the little weasel," she interrupted. "You're his brother, are you? I hope you're not as flakey as he is."

"You know where he is? I checked that place on Oxford Street, he's not there."

"No, he's not. We were going to travel together, out to the west coast. We were going to fix up my van and head for California. I'm a sucker."

"California?"

She nodded. "He said he'd help me get my van back on the road. Said he could do the brakes, fix the radiator, a few other things. We met up when I was down in Boston visiting my sister. We hit it off right away."

"Any idea where he might have gone?"

"He talked a good talk, and—like a fucking idiot—I believed him. I told him he could get a room in my building. We could work on the van and hang out."

"Did he happen to mention home? Our mother? Or our father?"

She shrugged. "He's got some issues, your brother. He spills his guts when he drinks. He said he had to get going. Said he didn't want to be around people. I don't know what changed. In Boston he couldn't be around me enough." She shook her head. "I tell ya, I'm a sucker for jet black hair and blue eyes."

"Well, did he happen to say where he was going?"

"Na. Though he did say something about getting into a fight with his old man, and how he could never go home."

"Anything about our mother being sick?"

"No, nothing like that. Said he wanted to go off by himself. Wanted to be a 'hermit in a cabin in the woods.' Far away from 'everyone and everything.'" She shook her head. "All I know is, he took what little stuff he had and booked. No note, no kiss goodbye, nothing. I'm a sucker," she added, turning her attention to the television.

Joel pulled up to the marina where the catamaran sailed to Nova Scotia in the spring and summer. He got out, walked to the end of the pier, and stood staring at the choppy, grey water. Waves lapped against the concrete pier. This is ridiculous, Joel thought. He needed to get back home. He needed to get back to his mother. And Mrs. Payne would want her car back soon. Maybe a foster home wouldn't be so bad after all, he thought. Maybe he could tolerate it for a year. The Wilsons seemed like okay people. Stick it out till he turned eighteen, less if his mother recovered, and work his ass off at school. Maybe get a scholarship to Mount Allison University, or Acadia or Dalhousie. Joel returned to the empty parking lot at the base of the pier.

He would move from Amherst when the time was right. In the meantime, he would buckle down and do his schoolwork. He would keep to himself, and keep himself busy reading everything he could get his hands on. He would excel and get top marks. Besides, his mom would soon be released from the hospital. He would live with her, and they would get a new place. Yes, he would do all of this. Because this search for his brother had become a dead end.

He enjoyed the drive up the coast; it reminded him of home. After driving for a couple of hours, he stopped at a takeout in Rockland, the self-described "Lobster Capital of the World." He laughed, knowing a few fishing towns on Nova Scotia's south shore would take umbrage with that. He ordered fish and chips, and took his meal back to the car. He stayed in the parking lot gazing out over the harbour, cranked up the music, and ate.

When he finished eating, he closed his eyes. My job is to exist and to breathe till it passes, he thought. He braced himself, and started rocking back and forth, slouched there in the front seat of Payne's car. The rhythmic motion of the seizure gripped him hard.

His only thought was to abandon all hope. Then the great shuddering of his body would start. He felt like he was gliding up, high up, until he was looking down upon his body. Joel looked down upon his quivering mass, twitching there in the space behind the steering wheel of Payne's car. He felt like he was folding. He didn't want to go back. He wanted to stay away, detached, and float here in this warm, serene air high above himself. But his soul was folding back into itself and back into this distorted body. He folded down and slammed back into himself. The shaking stopped. Joel came back to the sound of his father's voice.

The north wind does blow, and where will poor robin go.

Joel remained there in Payne's car, dazed in his postictal state. It hadn't been as bad as usual. The medication must have helped. Eventually he dozed off, thinking about what he needed to do when he got home. There was so much to do when he got home. He slept there in the car for hours.

In the morning, he went into a gas station washroom to clean up and change clothes. He bought the biggest coffee they had and got back on the road. The drive along the coast reminded him so much of home. A few hours later he pulled up to the border crossing at St. Stephen.

"You're a Canadian Citizen?"

"Yes."

"Where do you live?"

"Amherst."

"Bringing anything back with you—tobacco, alcohol?"

"No, sir."

"Mind if I look in the trunk?"

"By all means." Joel popped the trunk, and the guard leaned forward slightly.

"Travel safe," he said.

Joel motored down Main Street and followed the ramp for New Brunswick Highway 1, heading towards Saint John.

He pulled in at Magnetic Hill outside Moncton and filled up with gas with Mrs. Payne's money. He bought another large coffee and made his way east. The roads were clear, and the weather was fine. He'd be home in a couple of hours.

He motored through the New Brunswick-Nova Scotia border where the sign announced, "Welcome to Nova Scotia." He picked out a fresh CD to play. *Fire in the Kitchen* by the Chieftains, about as Nova Scotia as it gets. Rita MacNeil's "Come by the Hills" came on. The flute resonated in Joel's soul. He smiled at the memory of his father's contempt for local music. It's so hokey, he'd so often said.

It felt good to be returning home. Maybe living with that family won't be so bad after all. Then his mother would got out of the hospital and they would get a place without stairs that was smaller, cheaper, and just right for the two of them. He could get on at the bookstore full-time. Hadn't Pritchard said he wanted to step back, do more community things, get ready to retire? Yes, he could work there full-time, and as soon as his mother was able, she could go back to work too. And there must be some sort of insurance money. Something to help them get back on their feet.

And David. He knew now that David had no desire to come home. What did his brother know? Joel wasn't sure. Where could he be? Nova Scotia was small, certainly, but large enough when you were looking for someone who didn't want to be found. If he was back in Nova Scotia at all. Still, if David was working somewhere in Halifax, Joel would hear about it. Or Truro, or the Valley, or anywhere else. Word would get around. David would have to have a job in order to live. Maybe he'd want to be homeless like that crew in front of the library in Boston. If you were going to be homeless in Nova Scotia, Halifax would be the place. In this weather, in this cold, his brother would never live in a cardboard box. No, he liked the finer things, and he minded the cold too much. He could always go to a homeless shelter, Joel thought. No, that wouldn't happen either. David liked his independence too much. He would never abide by a lights-out policy. He liked to be able to come and go as he pleased, and to be able to cook his own food. He liked the great outdoors, sure, but only when he could sit in front of a warm fire. When he could prepare a meal on a big stove and eat it in peace. And besides, David liked his parties. He'd want to party with his buddies and be around crowds of people from time to time. Unless he wanted to hide, of course. Unless he was afraid to face reality like a hermit in a cabin in the woods.

Of course! The cabin at Loon Lake. Joel checked his rearview mirror and did a quick U-turn. He stepped on the gas and headed for Mountain Road. The sun was low on the horizon; maybe an hour or so of daylight left. He figured he had enough gas, and he cranked the radio up loud. Once he turned off the main road, he'd have to go about a mile down a dirt road to get to the clearing where they launched the boats. From there, the remainder of the way to the camp they went to so often as kids was on foot.

Of course that's where David would go. He could live there and not have to account for his whereabouts. He could go ice-fishing, and there was enough canned goods to last months. He could even walk or hitchhike into Oxford for groceries if the situation warranted.

Joel was surprised he hadn't thought of it before. It was safe, isolated and free, and it was the only place his brother could be. Joel headed south to Loon Lake. Fifteen minutes later he turned off the highway and followed Old Halifax Road. He always used to joke with his father that Old Halifax Road went nowhere near Halifax. He turned onto Loon Lake road. The snow had accumulated, and the road was unploughed. If he could make it to the boat launch, he could walk across the lake. It would be frozen solid. Joel knew he would see his brother in a few minutes, and this time he knew what he was going to say to him.

The more Joel thought about it, the more certain he was that David was at the cabin. Joel remembered the time his father took off by himself. His mother had been worried. When he returned two days later, he said the cabin was the only place in the world he wanted to be. And that's where David would be.

With the sun sinking in the western sky, Joel knew he needed to move quickly to get to the cabin before dark. He and David could have a good chat about everything that had transpired. They would eat some beans with bacon, and stoke the fire in the woodstove. Enjoy the roaring fire and some laughs. They could cry together about their father, and their mother too. Joel would assure him that nothing was his fault. Things just happened. He would tell him that his mother asked for him every time he saw her. They would talk about Jennifer—that there were options, and that they needed to face things and come up with solutions together. They could stay the night. Then, Joel thought, at first light tomorrow morning, they would head back to Amherst together and go see their mother in the hospital. Then they would deal with the strangeness that was now their life.

Fed by the Black River that flows down from Westchester Mountain, Loon Lake was a rich source of trout and a favourite spot in the spring. And this time of year it was one of the few lakes open for fishing. Joel scanned the frozen lake. It had to be solid this time of year. Yes, it would hold him. The ice on the lake meant that Joel could cross directly. He wouldn't have to wind his way along the trail through the woods. He'd be there in five minutes, instead of two hours or more.

He saw a handful of ice-fishing shacks on the lake, but he couldn't tell if there was anybody inside. There was an old minivan parked at the boat launch with footprints beside it where two people had put on their snowshoes and headed out for a trek. Joel wrapped the scarf around his neck, and touched his mother's cross beneath. He buttoned up his father's parka, and pulled out his woolen mittens. He closed his hand on his father's medal and squeezed it. In the other pocket he felt the cold, hard plastic case that held his hockey card. His fingers brushed the broken arms of his mother's Jesus statue. He put the mittens on. He knew the wind would be brisk in the middle of the lake, and it would be cold.

He walked down the path, taking care not to slip. He knew, if he fell on a rock or struck his head on a branch, that it would be hours, if not days, before anybody would come to his aid.

Joel reached the shore where a clear sheet of ice encrusted the rocks. Following the tracks of the ice-fishermen, he stepped out onto the ice, taking one small step, then another. As he drew his foot into the air, the pressure of the other drew cracks around his boot, and water bubbled up through. He scrambled further from shore, out towards the thicker, sturdier ice. There he tested the ice again, then stepped out further, stretching his hands out wide for balance, making his way across the frozen lake towards their father's camp. Joel didn't see any woodsmoke, but was certain he could smell it. David had to be there. There was no other place he'd be. Joel continued across the ice.

Out here, the quiet of the lake was palpable. Though the wind was rough, and the cold was raw, Joel felt warm and happy. His father's parka was thick and cozy. Overhead the sky was darkening, and the sun had reached the edge of the horizon. Joel didn't hear the first crack in the ice. It didn't register because at first it sounded like a regular step. The second crack was louder. Joel felt movement under his foot. He was in the middle of the lake now. He stood still, unsure which direction to move. Or even how to move. But he knew he needed to distribute his weight across the ice. Then he'd be able to shimmy and wriggle over to where it thickened. He crouched down low. The ice cracked again. Cold water percolated up through the crack. He stopped moving and waited for the ice to settle.

Joel spread his feet farther apart. The next step would be risky; he'd have to surrender himself to the will of the lake. He stretched out his hands, almost in prayer, then leaned forward and towards the ice. He placed his right knee down, spread his arms farther, and touched his other knee to the ice. He took a breath. He started to relax, but then another crack appeared in the ice. Water rose to the surface, leaking out across the ice. It was bitterly cold, and it soaked his knees. The crack became a chasm. Thick ice bowed and ballooned down into a hole. The water pulled him in, and he plunged down. As the lake swallowed him, he drew in a final gulping breath. Panic washed over him and he flailed his arms. He could feel the water rushing into his parka, into his pants, and he could feel himself growing heavier. The sound underwater was muffled, but he could hear himself splashing. He flailed his arms and kicked his legs. He knew he was in trouble.

Joel felt his boots touch down, sinking into muck. He swept his arms against the water but could not raise himself up. He knew he only had a few seconds, but his boot was mired in the muck. He strained and pulled and his one foot popped free. Then he freed the other.

Bursting to the surface, he gulped in a breath before sinking down again. He shook his hands, trying to free them from his mittens. He got one halfway off, and tore at it with his teeth. Then he ripped off the other. His heart was pounding. He couldn't breathe. His lungs were going to explode. He knew he had to get the parka off if he was going to live. It was weighing him down, and he'd sink to the bottom again if he couldn't free himself of it.

Joel strained at the buttons, but his hands were frozen. He couldn't feel his fingers. He grabbed at the next button and it finally popped. He pulled frantically at the zipper. Finally he wriggled loose from the parka and yanked off the scarf. It was heavy, and it snagged on his mother's crucifix. Joel saw the scarf and the dangling cross drift away from his grasp. His lungs ached. He had to breathe. The parka sank under its own weight. In a wave of panic, Joel reached for the parka. He wanted the medal and the hockey card in its pocket. But the parka sank out of reach. Joel knew he had seconds left. He propelled himself upward, pushing as hard as he could, using every bit of strength he had left. He needed air. His head pounded. Everything was silent. He felt himself blacking out. He knew now that this was the end, as his world grew still and quiet. With one last feeble stroke of his arms, he tried to rise to the surface.

Joel poked his head through the hole in the ice. He exhaled into the cold night air. He drew in a deep breath. He panted. He treaded water. The air shocked his lungs, but it was air. He took another deep breath as his mind travelled out over the ice. In the distance, he could hear a murder of crows as it settled into a pine tree for the night.

He took another deep breath. He couldn't tread water forever. He knew he had to get out of the water and then off the ice or else he'd die of hypothermia.

He took another breath and formulated a plan to get himself up onto the ice. Once there, he could crawl to the shore, then to the cabin, where he would sit in front of the fire and dry off. He'd be warm and David would help him. They'd play the battery-powered radio and the music would help. They'd talk and laugh and they'd listen to the music. But first he had to get himself out of the water and onto the ice.

Treading water, he took in a couple more breaths before forcing himself to float on his front. Slowly, his legs and buttocks rose to the surface, floating there parallel to the ice. Clawing at the whiteness, he pulled himself out of the water and onto the surface. Another crack, and the ice he'd managed to get his leg on crumbled under the weight. He didn't hear it so much as feel it. He could hear nothing, not even his own next breath. *And what will robin do then, poor thing.*

His heart pounded. His teeth chattered. He could no longer feel his hands or his feet. But he knew in the distance David would be waiting. The fire at the cabin would be warm and comforting and that's what drove him. They'd play the radio and they'd listen to the music. *And what will robin do then, poor thing.*

He sank beneath the surface, and the water shocked him back to a semi-alertness. He pushed himself back up and took a deep breath, flattening himself atop the water. He swung his right arm up and onto the ice and waited a moment before moving. This time the ice held. He stretched his arm out. He moved his arm up. And still the ice managed to hold. He kept his face out of the water, resting a second and breathing a few times, his cheek brushing the edge of the ice. Next he shimmied his right leg up onto the ice, moved it over, then brought his left leg up. The ice felt solid. He felt a rush of relief. He remained there a second and tried to slow his breathing. He wanted to make sure he did this right. If he went back in the water, he knew he would not get another chance.

Joel drew a measured breath. Rolling his hips with the last of his energy, he flipped over atop the ice. He was free. He was out. He was out of the water. He lay there atop the ice. His breathing heaved, and with one more burst of strength he rolled over two more times. He was back on thick and solid ice.

He lay there. His shivering had slowed. He was drifting away into another time and place. A place in his mind where the ice had melted away and the sun was out, and the weather was warm and inviting. As Joel slipped in and out of consciousness, the shivering stopped completely. He couldn't feel his hands or his feet. Then his body convulsed once, twice, and not from the cold this time, but from a grand mal seizure that had risen up itself out of the lake. Joel could feel its sinking darkness wash over him as he convulsed there atop the ice.

Joel's mind turned again to thoughts of warmth. He pictured himself sitting beside the fire. He was warm. He was sweating. He thought he should take off his clothes. His feet no longer felt wet, and he found himself radiating warmth. If he could have moved his hands, he would have taken off his socks. His feet were comfortable now, almost too hot from the fire.

Eventually, mercifully, the seizure ended. He tucked his head under his arm. *To keep himself warm, poor thing.* He tried to move his other hand. He was stuck to the ice, the wetness of his clothes freezing him in place. His whole body was numb. He felt his mind drift away. In the distance, he was sure, he could hear his father's voice. Or maybe it was David's.

Hey! Jo-Jo. Jo-ooo Jo-ooo.

If Joel could have answered, he would have. His lips were frozen, and he couldn't talk. He knew what he wanted to say.

It's me. It's all right. I've come to take you home.

Joel closed his eyes as a dark stillness settled over the frozen lake.

Chapter 45

Joel could hear *whump-whump-whump*. Was he dreaming? He opened his eyes. Through his frost-coated eyelashes, he could make out the big medivac helicopter thundering above him. The rotors whacking the air. Joel could see the red lights of fire trucks flashing near the boat launch. The helicopter swooped in and landed on the road alongside. The air was rich with the smell of jet fuel.

Joel was aware of something approaching him. He felt himself slipping in and out of consciousness. He couldn't move his arms. His fingers were hot and itchy but felt like they were detached from his hands.

He could hear the crackle of radios.

Command, rescue one.

Rescue one, command. Go ahead.

Contact made. One male patient, approximate age twenty-one, stand by for vitals.

Copy.

Joel opened his eyes. Two firefighters were at his side dressed in red and black flotation suits. They were pulling a rope. The ice groaned under their weight.

"We've got you, okay. We're going to move you now," one of the firefighters said. "Did you hit your head? Any head or neck pain?"

Joel tried to shake his head but couldn't move.

"Any back pain?"

They pulled on the rope. Joel could make out a big wire basket, big enough to hold a person, sliding up beside him. The man grabbed Joel under the shoulders. "We're going to slide you up and into this stretcher. You stay as still as you can. Let us do all the work, okay? You're safe now." He took hold of Joel's knees.

"One, two, three," said the other firefighter, and together they lifted Joel up onto the stretcher. "Very good. I want to do a quick check on you here." He ran his hands down Joel's neck, shoulders, chest, pelvis and legs.

The other firefighter checked Joel's wrist for his pulse. "Heart rate forty and thready."

"What's your name?"

Joel tried to speak but couldn't. He closed his eyes.

"Do you know where you are?"

Joel tried to lift his hand to point to the cabin.

"Okay, roll him," the firefighter said to his partner. He scanned Joel's back and nodded to his partner. "Okay, we're going to strap you in." He cinched a strap across Joel's chest. The other tightened a strap across his knees and hips.

"Okay, we're going to take you back across the ice. The helicopter's waiting for you. Let us do all the work."

"Command, rescue one."

"Rescue one, command. Go ahead."

"Patient responsive to voice, heart rate forty and thready. Respirations eight, shallow. No obvious trauma. Ready for you to bring us in."

"Affirmative. We'll reel you in now."

They started back toward shore, pulling Joel across the ice with the help of some colleagues onshore. Joel opened his eyes. He saw two snowshoers standing near a car. A woman was talking on her cell phone. She must have been the one who called 9-1-1. Joel wanted to yell 'thank you' to them but couldn't move his lips. He closed his eyes.

They reached the shore, lifted the stretcher and carried it up to the air ambulance. Joel could hear the firefighter talking to the paramedic in a flight suit. "Looks like he went through the ice, no trauma, no fractures, alert to voice. He wasn't talking when we first made contact. Pupils PERL, heart rate forty. Don't know his history. No witnesses."

The flight medic leaned in close to Joel. "What's your name?"

Joel tried to raise his hand but couldn't. It was numb and under the strap. "David?"

"David?"

"David?" Joel whispered again.

"Okay, David, we're going to take care of you. What happened?"

"David." Joel's lips were blue.

"Do you remember what happened?"

"Ice."

"Okay. We're going to get you warmed up. I'm Adam and I'm going to help you. I'm a flight medic."

"Dad? Roger?"

"Yes, roger," the flight medic nodded. "Roger that. That's affirmative. We're going to take care of you."

"Roger?"

"Yes, roger that, David." Adam smiled and patted him on the shoulder. "You're safe now." They loaded him up and into the air ambulance. "We got you."

"Get these clothes off him," Adam said to the flight nurse as he reached for an IV set. "I'll start a line. We'll give him a bolus of warmed saline."

Joel couldn't feel the flight nurse cutting his clothes off with trauma shears, the same kind his father had taken to work every day. He didn't even care about being naked. He couldn't feel the blanket when they draped it over him.

"This is a warm blanket, David."

Adam was prepping his right arm for the intravenous line. "You're going to feel a poke. I'm giving you an IV." He angled the catheter needle toward his arm. "Here we go. Little poke."

Joel felt nothing.

"Okay, I've got access." He prepped a bag of warmed saline. "David, I'm giving you some warm fluids. It will help bring your core temperature up. You're hypothermic."

Joel could hear the radio crackle.

"David, we're going to take off now. It's going to get loud. You'll feel vibrations. It's normal. We're taking you to the QEII Hospital in Halifax, okay? Here we go."

Joel could feel the big rotors of the helicopter cutting through the air. The aircraft shook and he felt them lift off the ground.

"We're wheels up," someone said.

"Okay, David, we're airborne. We'll be at the hospital in about twelve minutes. "

Joel felt the helicopter pick up speed. The thudding of the rotors became regular and powerful. It felt like his seizures when he was looking down over his body. He offered up a silent prayer.

"What happened?" The medic pointed a laser thermometer in his ear.

"Cabin."

"How old are you." The medic strapped on a blood pressure cuff.

"David."

"Are you on any medication?" The medic squeezed the bulb on the blood pressure cuff.

"David. Cabin?"

"David, do you have any medical conditions?" the medic asked. "Diabetes? Heart problems? Breathing problems? Seizures?"

The rotors thudded. The flight nurse covered him with another blanket, but Joel couldn't feel it touch his skin. He felt himself fading out, drifting away. He closed his eyes.

"Hey David, I need you to stay with me." The medic leaned in close to Joel's face. "Stay awake."

Joel sensed the helicopter had stopped moving forward. It hovered, and then descended.

"We're here, David. We're taking you out of the helicopter. We're moving you into the hospital." The medic unfastened the straps holding the stretcher in place. "How are you making out?"

Joel opened his eyes. "I'm cold," he said.

CHAPTER 46

"You had us all so scared," Maria said, hugging Joel as he entered the bookstore. "I was so worried."

"I'm fine." He held up a bandaged hand. "Even this is no big deal."

Pritchard came up to the front cash. "Well, Mr. Carruthers, glad to see you're back in the saddle." He added some five- and ten-dollar bills to the float. "Now let's get busy and sell some books."

Joel nodded. "And catch up on each other's news as we do."

Shortly before lunch, his neighbour Pierre bounded into the bookstore. "Hey, Joel," he said, "I heard you had some excitement in your life." He cocked his head toward Maria and winked at Joel. "Maybe not the kind of excitement you want, though."

Pierre passed him a stack of envelopes. "I've got some mail for you." He held up a large FedEx envelope with a big orange FRAGILE sticker on the front. "I signed for this one, too."

Joel flipped through the mail. "I appreciate you bringing these." One letter, addressed to his mother, was from the ambulance service. It looked like a cheque.

"They looked important," Pierre said as he headed for the door, "so I thought I'd bring them down to you. Take care, Joel."

"Thanks, Pierre."

Joel saw the San Francisco return address on the FedEx package. It was from Aunt Penny. He was surprised she'd courier it to him. He ripped it open and pulled out his tattered copy of *A Coney Island of the Mind*. He flipped it open to the title page. There, scrawled in blue ink, was one word: 'Ferlinghetti.' Joel smiled. He pulled out the rest of the contents of the envelope, including a folded piece of paper and the album *Poetry Readings in the Cellar*. In neat handwriting across the front of the album were the words: 'To Joel: May you always have jazz, even when you're in the cellar! All the best, Ferlinghetti.'

Joel smiled again and unfolded the note.

Hi Jo-Jo,
Things are heating up in San Fran, or as they say here, "The City." I can't make it for Easter, so you'll have to find all the eggs yourself. Frederick took me to City Lights bookstore. I even rocked in the Poet's Chair! Frederick said I'm finally getting some culture. I told him I have wisdom now!! Mr. Ferlinghetti's a doll. I love him. He signed your book for you. When I told him what you've been going through, he asked that I send along this record. Give your mom and David a big hug for me. See you at the fireworks in July!! Love ya!

The rest of the afternoon flew by. Joel was relieved when closing time arrived. He pulled on his toque and stepped out into the crispness of the cool evening air, starting in the direction of Palmer Court. Then he turned and headed toward Regent Street instead.

Someone called out to him from across the street. "Going my way?" It was Jennifer.

"Hey," he waved and smiled. "How are you?" He crossed the street and gave her a hug. "I actually am going your way. I'm living on Regent Street now." They walked on. "How are you, really?" he asked.

She shrugged. "I told my folks. It wasn't as bad as I thought. My father screamed, my mother cried. That was pretty much it."

Joel shook his head. "I'm sorry you had to go through that alone."

"Bah," she shrugged again. "It's not the worst thing."

"I tried to find him. But he doesn't want to be found right now."

"But he does know, right?" Jennifer asked as they turned onto Church Street.

"I'm like ninety-nine point nine per cent sure he does."

She nodded. "My parents didn't kick me out. But they did call your brother some pretty choice names."

"So did I," Joel laughed as they arrived at Jennifer's street.

"This is my stop," she said.

Joel reached in his pocket, took out a scrap of paper, and scribbled on it. "This is my new address and the phone number. Keep in touch."

Jennifer reached up and hugged him.

"I'm going to be an uncle," Joel smiled. "And I'm going to spoil that kid like mad."

Chapter 47

Joel walked into his mother's hospital room and found her sitting in the armchair, a table tray drawn close. She was doing a puzzle. "Hey, Mom," he said, and leaned over to kiss her.

Her eyes lit up. "Jo-Jo," she smiled.

"How are you doing? How are you feeling?"

"Good."

"I was talking to the nurse on my way in, and she said they're shipping you off to Halifax for a while."

"Yep."

"They're going to get you walking again."

"That's the plan."

Joel watched as his mother picked up a puzzle piece and studied it. He sat down on the bed across from her.

"Your hand?" She pointed to his bandaged hand. "I worry about you."

"It's okay." He folded his hands in his lap, covering up the bandage. "The government said I couldn't stay by myself, so they forced me to move in with the Wilsons."

"Oh, Jo-Jo."

"It's okay. They're nice. It feels weird though."

"No word from David?"

"No. He'll be back when he's ready. He knows everything."

She nodded. "He'll come back."

"Pierre dropped off some mail at the store. There was a cheque from the insurance company. The social worker lady put it in the bank."

"That's good."

"There was a package from Aunt Penny too. She got that book autographed for me. Pierre is looking after things with the house. The pipes froze. The place is a real mess."

"A mess?"

Joel turned on the television above the bed. He flipped through the channels. "Anything good on?"

He turned the volume down low and settled on a variety show with Kathy Lee Gifford called *I'll Be Home for Christmas*. Joel sat there with his mother, lost in the music as she worked on the puzzle. It was a picture of a red-breasted robin sitting on the roof of a barn surrounded by rich green pastures. Cows grazed in the background.

"Dad would have hated this show."

"Too mushy," his mother laughed.

They listened to the music from the television show till it went to a commercial break.

"I'll go get us something to drink," Joel said.

He took the elevator downstairs. The emergency waiting room was crowded. An old lady hunched over in a wheelchair. A young man slouched nearby. He looked pale, wrapped in a flannel blanket, next to a young mother rocking a baby back and forth. Joel could see three ambulances lined up outside the big double doors.

Joel plugged some quarters into the pop machine. A man in a paramedic uniform came up behind him.

"Hello, Joel," he said. "I thought that was you."

"Hey, Mr. Jenkins."

"How's your mom doing?"

"They're sending her to Halifax, to the rehabilitation centre there. They're going to teach her to walk without a cane."

Mr. Jenkins nodded. "That's promising. They do good work there."

"She's excited. She wants to get moving on her own again. She's talking a lot better, too."

"How's your hand? I heard that call on the radio. Of course I didn't know it was you at the time."

Joel looked down at his bandaged hand. "They said I should keep the rest of my fingers, but because of the frostbite they had to amputate the tip of my baby one. I'll still be able to play guitar."

"Quite an ordeal."

"Big time."

"I wanted to show you this." Jenkins held out a sheet of paper. "We're putting it in our next paramedic newsletter."

Joel took the paper from Jenkins. He saw his father's picture. The caption read 'Roger Carruthers, friend and healer.'

"There's going to be a piece in there about your father and his career. There'll be a list of resources for people suffering from post-traumatic stress. You know, for anyone having a hard time dealing with critical incidents."

"Well, that's at least something positive."

"The ambulance service is going to start a new process for debriefing bad calls. It'll help medics and firefighters cope."

"That's good there's help."

"That's the way I look at it too. You can keep that copy if you want."

"I'll show my mother." Joel held the sheaf of paper with his bandaged hand while cradling the two bottles of pop in his arm. "Thanks."

"You still have my phone number?"

"Yes, I do."

"Give me a shout if you need to. I went around to your house. It was empty."

"Yeah, I'm staying in a foster home till Mom gets better."

"Probably for the best." Jenkin's pager toned. He looked down at it, frowned, and headed for the exit. "Take care, man."

"Thanks, you too." Joel returned to his mother's room. She was focused on the puzzle.

"Oh look at you." Joel put the pop down on the bedside table. "You've got all the corner and edge pieces put together."

"The middle stuff's the hardest."

"Yep," Joel laughed. He put a straw in a bottle and offered it to his mother. She took a sip.

"Thank you."

Joel took a drink of his pop. "There's something else you should know, Mom."

"Something happy, I hope."

"Yes, I suppose it is happy." He took another sip of pop. His mother looked up from her puzzle.

"We need something happy."

Joel smiled. "You're going to be a grandmother."

"What?" She pointed at Joel. "What?"

"No, not me. David." He laughed. "Jennifer's having a baby."

"Jennifer?"

"Yes."

"I knew it."

"You knew?"

"Not for sure. Thought she might be." Her eyes watered.

Joel passed her a tissue. "She's due in July. She'll be able to finish school before the baby comes."

"Mercy." She dabbed at her eyes. "David knows?"

"I think so. I think that's part of it. Part of why he's gone."

"He'll be home."

"Or not."

"He will. I know he will. A baby," she smiled, and reached out her hand to Joel.

Chapter 48

Mrs. Wilson tapped on Joel's bedroom door and pushed it open. She placed a pile of neatly folded laundry on the desk.

Joel looked up from his bed where he was reading a book. "Thank you," he said.

He had unpacked some of his things. The Blue Mountain pottery eagle and the Jesus figurine with the broken arms were on his dresser. His guitar and his father's saxophone stood in the corner. The plastic milk crate full of his father's records was there too. His books and the photographs he had taken from his house were still packed up in the suitcase. His whole life was in this room.

"Joel, I know this holiday will be hard for you." Mrs. Wilson put her hand on the eagle. "But if there's anything I can do, any special traditions you and your family have that you'd like us to try here, we will. We'll do whatever we can."

"Thanks, Mrs. Wilson."

"Please. Donna."

"Thank you, Donna."

"Do you want a drive to work? The store will be super busy today."

"No thanks, I'll walk. It's a lot closer from here than my house."

"Wear these then." She passed him a pair of mittens. "These'll keep your hands warm. They'll fit over that bandage."

Ten minutes later, Joel made his way to the bookstore. It was a short walk from Regent to downtown. He walked past Siegfried collecting bottles in his rusted old shopping cart. Joel waved to him.

"Hello! Nice mitts!" Siegfried waved back.

Joel walked over. He took off the mittens and passed them to Siegfried.

"Huh?"

"Have them. They'll keep your hands warm."

Maria was already at the bookstore when he arrived. "Hey, you."

"Hey."

"How's your hand?"

Joel looked at his hand where a rusty red speck of blood had soaked through the gauze. It throbbed where the tip of his finger used to be. Phantom pain, he thought. Phantom pain, real injury. He understood that now.

Pritchard came up to the counter. "Joel, I need you to deliver these books to Mrs. Payne. It's going to be busy today, so hurry back."

Joel walked down Victoria Street towards Mrs. Payne's, but not before stopping at a bank machine. The bags of books were heavy. His fingers throbbed in pain.

He rang the bell at Payne's house.

"Good day, Mr. Carruthers."

"Hello, Parker. Sorry about the car."

"Mrs. Payne will be delighted to see you."

The house was warm, and the smell of pine filled the room. The fireplace crackled, and the flames danced in vivid orange and cherry red. Mrs. Payne was playing her violin. She was playing along to Joni Mitchell's "River," wishing for a river to skate away on.

Joel waited till the song finished before setting the two bags of books on the floor. "The rest of your order came in. I'm so glad I got the chance to come by."

"I'm delighted to see you. You know you're welcome here anytime. On business, or for a plain old visit."

He reached in his pocket and took out a wad of bills. "Here's the money I owe you. I want to thank you so much. Without your help I wouldn't have been able to look for my brother."

"It was my pleasure. Will you have a cup of tea?"

"I'd love to, but I can't. I have to get back to the store. I promised Mr. Pritchard."

"I'm so sorry things didn't work out for you. And your hand! When the police called me about the car and told me about you going through that ice, my heart stopped. I was relieved to hear you're okay. How is your hand?"

"It's fine. Your car was okay?"

"Yes, Parker got a lift there and drove it back. Your hand, though. I've heard you had some trouble with your fingers."

"I'll live. And the doctor tells me I'll still be able play guitar."

"And saxophone?"

"Yes, ma'am."

"That's a relief."

"Thanks for everything Mrs. Payne. I'm sorry about abandoning your car in the middle of nowhere."

"You're very welcome, Joel. I'm so glad you're okay."

On the record player, Joni Mitchell was lamenting about drinking a case of wine like you. She'd still be on her feet. "Thanks again Mrs. Payne. You'll never know how much all this meant to me."

Joel walked out into the bright sunlight. The air was cold, and his breath hung in the air. In the distance a siren wailed, heading out toward the highway. It's lonely, cold sound echoed across the flats toward Tantramar Marsh. He needed to get back to the bookstore. Things would be busy now with people running their last-minute errands. Books make wonderful gifts.

Joel thought about how Mrs. Payne created such a beautiful countermelody with her violin. Skating away would have been easy.

He walked down the walkway and swung open the gate. In Mrs. Payne's spruce tree he saw a northern cardinal, its feathers red and vibrant against the white crusted snow. He stopped and watched the bird. He wondered why it didn't fly south for winter. Why it never skated away. He watched the cardinal peck at the string of popcorn wrapped tightly around the tree.

Acknowledgments

Thanks to Chris Needham at Now Or Never Publishing for everything, including making this story better.

I live, work and have set this story in Mi'kma'ki, the traditional home of the Mi'kmaq people. I am honoured to settle here and abide by treaties of peace and friendship.

Thanks to: Carol Bruneau for her guidance and patience in teaching the craft, especially setting, specificity and balance. Writer's Federation of Nova Scotia and the Alistair MacLeod Mentorship Program. Donna Morrissey who taught me to find my authentic voice and to make up real stories. Brock Clarke for encouraging me to continue in the first place and to torture my characters. Joshua Bodwell for your open-armed welcome, steadfast belief, and support in ways big and small. Wesley McNair for dinner and challenging me to write the book. Simon Van Booy for teaching me to serve the story and convincing me it would be easy. Frank O. Smith for cheerleading and teaching me to pivot, in every scene and chapter. Everyone I have met through the Maine Writers and Publishers Alliance and at Black Fly. Sherry Cobb, my most patient reader and supporter extraordinaire. Richard Ford for welcoming me to the boathouse writing space. Richard Russo for the conversation while walking up the hill with me. Michael Ondaatje for laughing with me as we broke the three-book rule. Rick Alexander, Theresa Babb, Nicola Davison, and Jen Powley for your attention, suggestions, and confidence.

Special thanks to Charlie "Bird" Parker, Lawrence Ferlinghetti, and Joni Mitchell. To Paramedic C.T., rest easy, we have the watch from here.

Most and always thanks to my family and friends for the support and encouragement, especially Lisa, Amy, Luke, Alistair, and Jean. To you, reader, thank you, I am grateful.